Emily Rotondi lives in New Hampshire. *The Wedding Toaster* is her first novel.

For the PALS

Emily Rotondi

THE WEDDING TOASTER

AUSTIN MACAULEY PUBLISHERS™

LONDON * CAMBRIDGE * NEW YORK * SHARJAH

Ordering Information
Quantity sales: Special discounts are available on quantity purchases by corporations, associations, and others. For details, contact the publisher at the address below.

Publisher's Cataloging-in-Publication data
Rotondi, Emily
The Wedding Toaster

ISBN 9781647505936 (Paperback)
ISBN 9781647505943 (ePub e-book)

Library of Congress Control Number: 2021912003

www.austinmacauley.com/us

First Published (2021)
Austin Macauley Publishers LLC
40 Wall Street, 33rd Floor, Suite 3302
New York, NY 10005
USA

mail-usa@austinmacauley.com
+1 (646) 5125767

This book has been a labor of love. There are many people on my journey who have helped make this possible. I would like to thank everyone at Austin Macauley for taking a chance on an unknown, unpublished author and helping me make my dream come true. I want to thank all of my students who ever sat in my classroom and listened intently and enthusiastically as I shared bits and pieces of my story with them. They have always been my biggest cheerleaders. My dear friends, Kristin and P.J. McGrail. It was the toast I gave at their wedding almost fifteen years ago that served as the inspiration for this story. And lastly, I want to thank my family. Mum, Dad, Rick and Maria, I could not have done it without your support.

Prologue

I am standing in front of the mirror, gazing intently at the girl who is staring back at me, as if I don't recognize my own reflection. "I can't do it," I simply say, and in that moment, I knew I couldn't.

"But the cake was twelve hundred dollars," Kate says matter-of-factly. "Perishable goods aren't returnable."

"Never mind the cake! What about the dress!" Carrie practically screams.

"She got it at Filene's Basement. Clearance," Kate replies coolly. "And it's a good thing, too."

I vaguely look around at the scene unfolding in front of me. Me, standing in a wedding dress and my two best friends, adorned in their bridesmaid dresses, arguing over perishable goods and discount bridal gowns. *How did I get here?* I think to myself. And then it hits me. Everything hits me.

I am not getting married today.

I turn from the mirror and stand facing Carrie and Kate. "I knew I shouldn't spend a lot on a dress I would never end up wearing," I say with resolve. "It's a sign."

A heavy silence fills the room as the weight of what I've just said lingers over our heads.

Carrie responds first. She grabs my arm and pulls me in close. "Maggie, listen to me. It's just cold feet, that's all," she laughs lightly. Awkwardly. As if to convince me of a magic trick I don't believe in anymore. "Every bride goes through this." She winks, willing me to take back the heaviness that has overtaken our space in the room. I smile at the sincerity in her voice. She wants to believe it. I want to believe it. Kate breaks me from my reverie.

"Yeah, but it's usually at her bachelorette party with a few shots of Tequila in her and a random stranger's tongue jammed down her throat."

Carrie glares at Kate. "You're not helping!" she says through clenched teeth.

But my mind is made up. In an instant, I know. I throw off my veil and it falls to the ground. "There's a 50 percent divorce rate in this country," I say in order to offer up some defense for my imposing actions, but really even I know there is no defense for what I'm about to do. "I don't want to be another statistic."

"You're not going to be." Carrie looks at me and for a second, my pulse slows and my breathing steadies. For a second, I believe her.

"Jack's a good guy, Maggie," Carrie says. "He's not going to leave you."

I look at her and smile, and I even allow Kate to place the veil back on my head. After all, I do know Carrie's right. I know Jack won't leave me. This I can guarantee because I am going to beat him to the punch. I've had a front row view of what heartache can do to you. I do not want to be another statistic. And, as my two best friends straighten my veil and blot my lip-gloss, and tell me everything is going to be okay, my mind is racing. I am going to leave Jack. And somehow, I know this will be the biggest regret of my life.

But I do it anyway.

Chapter One

The last wedding, I was supposed to be at was my own, but here I am sitting at my best friend's wedding, sucking down the blasts of air my inhaler offers me, and praying in vain that I will make it through the day. My mother recognizes my utter discomfort. She leans over and whispers in my ear, "Relax, Maggie. It's not your wedding this time."

I envy her ability to remain subtly detached from the ceremony unfolding in front of us. Ben is placing the wedding band on Carrie's finger and it awes me how sensual the gesture is. My uncle Hor on the other hand (Hor is short for Horatio and not indicative of a certain character trait), well, he sits on the other side of me, bawling like a baby and dabbing his eyes with a tissue.

Three years ago, that was almost me. On the morning of my wedding, I stood in front of the full-length mirror in my bedroom, wearing my strapless silk wedding dress, and realized I didn't recognize the girl staring back at me. I left a message on my mirror written in lipstick. *I'm sorry.* I threw some clothes into my overnight duffle and climbed out the window and down the trellis, leaving my wedding dress lying on the floor.

I took a cab to the airport and bought a ticket to Australia where I stayed for two months. I didn't realize until I went into the restroom after too many glasses of wine, six hours into a thirteen-hour flight, that I was still wearing my veil. Well, that and the fact that the middle-aged Aussie gentlemen sitting next to me kept casting suspicious looks in my direction.

"Are you visiting Australia for business or pleasure?" he had asked me after I returned from the restroom, my veil now tucked haphazardly into the back of my jeans. I honestly don't think he knew what to say. It was one of those situations where you can pretend not to see the weirdness unraveling around you and ignore it, which makes it even more weird, or you can address it tactfully, hoping that in the end it will just all go away.

"I just walked out on my own wedding," I said to him, not knowing until that moment that I would admit the unforgivable. "So, I guess that pretty much creates a whole new category for travel."

"Ahh. So you're running away."

"As far away as possible."

He turned to me. "Let me give you a piece of advice, love. Your problems will still be your problems. Even in the Southern Hemisphere."

Carrie and Kate saw the dress lying in a heap on the floor and knew what had happened before they even saw the lipstick message. It was only 35 minutes until the ceremony and they hadn't been able to reach Jack in time so that he could be spared the worst humiliation of his life and for that, I am still sorry. I still don't regret what I did, but I feel guilty every day that Jack had to face that humiliation in public. He had been standing at the altar, waiting to become a married man, when Carrie walked down the aisle, instead of me, and handed him a note. *She's not coming.* The organist had already started playing the Wedding March.

Carrie told me months later that Jack had crumpled the note in his fist, turned to face the guests with all the courage and grace he could muster and apologized. "Sorry that you all had to come out here for nothing, but there is not going to be any wedding today." He then walked down the aisle, slow and calm amid a dead silence, let himself into the pastor's waiting room and broke down like a baby.

I find myself thinking of that moment now. As I look at Carrie and Ben, slipping rings onto each other's fingers and smiling bashfully at one another, I wonder what the outcome would've been for Jack and me, up on that altar, had I gone through with it. I wonder if he would have looked at me the same way Ben was looking at Carrie, like a little boy opening up his presents on Christmas morning. I know he would've. More importantly, I wonder if I would have looked at him the same way. I wonder if we would have had a happily ever after.

I had a lot to answer for when I got home from Down Under. I guess I really didn't get it. I had this idea in my head that everything would be normal. I would go back to work at the paper and see Jack there and we would laugh about all of this over a latte at Starbucks. That's how Jack and me met. We both worked at *The Hub*. Jack wrote a home improvement column that ran every Saturday and I wrote a pet advice column that ran every Wednesday. Shows you the propaganda that's at work in today's media. I never owned a pet in my life, except for goldfish that never lasted more than a week because I would forget to feed them; but because my dad invented the Fetch It, an aerodynamic contraption made entirely out of plastic and painted various psychedelic colors that allows you to throw a tennis ball for a dog with a longer range than humanly possible, the powers that be decided that that made me an expert on the best dog food to buy or how to get your parrot to stop swearing. (I mean, it's not rocket science people, just stop saying 'fuck' or 'shit' in front of your bird!) Boy, was I wrong. About Jack and a normal life, I mean, not about the bird.

I never saw Jack again. I walked back into work to find his cubicle empty and myself the object of judgmental stares and whispered murmurs behind my back. Even my boss was less than sympathetic.

"What makes you still think you work here?" he said when he saw me. I didn't know how to answer.

"You leave for two months, Maggie, leave us all stranded here, destroy one of our best columnists in your fiery wake and you come strolling in here, proud as a peacock, and expect everything to be the same?"

That started to put it into perspective for me. "I sent an email," I offered feebly.

Ed snorted. "You lost the column."

"But I had a byline!" I protested.

Ed snorted again. "Had a hell of a time replacing you, but now that we have, I'm not about to let all that hassle and headache be for nothing." Ed took out a white handkerchief from his pocket and mopped his brow. He does that when it's close to deadline and he has to send the paper to the presses and he still doesn't have the layout he wants or the column he wants or a reporter gets sloppy with his facts and there's no time to change it. He does this when he's upset. I had worked poor Ed up.

I just stood there; mouth open. I hadn't expected this but I was in no position to argue.

"Obits. Take it or leave it."

I took it. It's what I still do today. I write obituaries for people I have never met. I make observations about their lives from the bits of information I glean from their loved ones and then try to weave their life story together for the ones left behind. I guess you could say that I have the last word.

Even Carrie and Kate gave me sort of a hard time when I got back. "Maggie, what the hell happened?" Kate had said to me. "We're not in high school anymore. It's not like standing Joey Mitchell up for the junior prom (which I did). There are other people's lives involved! Grow up, for Christ's sakes!"

Carrie was a little more sympathetic but I could tell she was still disappointed in me. I had let her down. The only thing she had said to me about it, which stung like hell, was, "Maggie, you need to stop using the fact that your dad died as an excuse to act any way you want. It doesn't give you license to treat people poorly."

I looked at her, both hurt and confused. "Carrie, I don't do that—"

"You do, Maggie. You've done it your whole life. I don't even think you realize you're doing it, but you do." Then Carrie hugged me and Kate hugged me and we never talked about it again. That's what friends do. You accept each other, unconditionally. And you forgive.

Even Uncle Hor had something to say about it, although it was in his own kind way. He's lived with my mom and me in the house in Beaumont ever since my dad died. I was only five when my dad died so in a lot of ways Uncle Hor has been like a dad to me, except he never busted me when I missed curfew as a teenager (which happened quite frequently). In fact, he'd leave the porch window open for me so I could sneak past my mom without receiving her wrath. Anyway, Uncle Hor rocks, but even he couldn't understand my motives for bailing on my own wedding.

"Jack MacDougal is a good man, Maggie Mae (Mae is my middle name). I don't want to see you miss out on something wonderful," he took my face in his hands. "You know, love is a wonderful thing. Not everyone is given it. It's a gift. And I think even your mother would attest to that."

To tell you the truth, I was a little surprised by Uncle Hor's reaction. Uncle Hor had had a serious lady friend for quite a few decades, but when Dolly got the chance to go to Nashville and record a country album, she took it, and that was that. That was in 1991. Uncle Hor stayed behind because he didn't want to leave Mom and me alone. I still wonder sometimes if he's ever regretted that decision but selfishly, I'm glad he stayed because I couldn't picture my life without Uncle Hor in it on a daily basis. Uncle Hor is a good man and his loyalty absolutely humbles me. And I was perfectly happy to hear that Dolly's album had flopped miserably.

14

There were days that I wished I had never come back from Australia. But my mom understood. She understood me. When I would be sitting on my bed, feeling lost and defeated and like no one got me, my mom would come in and put her arms around me and tell me just what I needed to hear to keep me going. "We only have one life to live," she would say to me. "You have to live it the way you want. No one else has the right to tell you how to live it or what you should have done. No one else has the right to make judgments about you until they have walked in your shoes."

And just like that, my mom would let me off the hook. She got me. She got me because, in effect, she was me. I am my mother's daughter. I have her same blue eyes and long, dark hair but even more than that, I have come to adopt her same tainted view of love. I realized then the depth of heartache my mom must have felt when she lost my dad. She had loved once and she had lost.

I still thought about him at times. When I went to Starbucks and ordered a latte and could call up exactly how Jack ordered his, or when I saw someone in a restaurant with the same smile as him, or when someone at the paper made some off-color remark and I could imagine exactly how Jack would respond. I wondered where he was and how he was doing and sincerely hoped that he was doing well, but I always thought about him in a detached sort of way. It was as if I was outside of myself, remembering things that belonged to someone else.

There was never anyone else. Jack was my first serious relationship. There was a boy in college, Sean Reilly, who I would have sex with when I got too drunk or too horny or too stressed about midterms and needed a pleasant distraction, but it was nothing. He was just a stupid frat boy. Other than Sean, Jack was the only man that I ever slept with. It's not that I'm a lesbian, not that there's anything wrong with that, I just never felt like I needed the company of a man. I'm used to being on my own and I like my independence. I don't want to have to answer to anyone. I don't want to have to account for where my money goes or balance a checkbook or do someone else's laundry. I don't want to have to worry about anyone's needs except my own. And it's not like I don't have biological needs, but like my mom says, "We don't need men, dear, we have vibrators."

I use mine quite frequently.

I enter the main ballroom of the Boston Harbor Hotel. I survived the actual wedding ceremony and hoped to God that I can pull off a repeat performance during the reception. My inhaler is running low. Thank God Carrie didn't ask me to be a bridesmaid, which I really appreciate. Not because I'm morally opposed to it, just because no one likes being a bridesmaid. The dresses are always hideous.

I spot my mother and Uncle Hor across the room, snacking on shrimp cocktail. Even though I haven't checked the seating cards, I know I'll be seated with them. I approach the table slowly and nonchalantly, as if being present at a wedding is second nature to me. As if the activity going on around me does not give me pause.

I catch the end of their whispered conversation as I approach. "This should be Maggie's wedding," Uncle Hor says. I wonder if he knows I am standing two feet behind him.

"Oh, Hor, stop."

"Maggie gave up her chance for love. She may never get another one."

"Just eat your shrimp cocktail."

Just hearing the words makes me wince. My mouth goes dry and my head starts to swim…and I haven't even started drinking yet. I turn and head for the bathroom.

And that singular decision changes *everything*.

Chapter Two

I enter the ladies' room and quickly retrieve my inhaler from my bag. I suck in deeply, drinking air in like water. I look up and see Carrie looking in the mirror, adjusting her veil. She looks beautiful and I can't help but feel a stab of envy. I can't help but think back, trying to picture, how I looked in my veil. She looks at me in the mirror and smiles. "I was wondering when you'd get here," she says.

I walk over to her, looking at both of our reflections in the mirror and fluff out her veil, making sure it is securely set. "You look beautiful," I tell her and I throw my arms around her. I let the moment linger, believing that Carrie is a better person than I am.

A god-awful sound brings us back. I realize it is the sound of someone groaning from one of the stalls. It sounds like trajectory slapping the water in the commode. "Uhh! God help me!" the voice from the stall moans. I recognize it immediately as Kate's. Something is definitely up.

"Is Kate okay?" I immediately ask.

"Uh…she'll be fine," Carrie answers tentatively. "But I just wanted to let you know that you're giving the toast."

My body stiffens. My blood turns to ice. I wonder if I heard Carrie correctly. I check to see if I have cotton swabs stuck in my ears, which might impair my hearing. But then I remember that I'm out of cotton swabs…they are on the top of my shopping list written on a post-it and stuck into my wallet. "*What!*" I spit out at the top of my lungs.

"Kate doesn't like to speak in front of large crowds," Carrie says to me earnestly. There is a pleading in her eyes, and I wonder if I'll be able to come through for her. "That's why she's in there puking her brains out."

Still, my mind is racing. I am searching my brain for a plausible solution. "She's a lawyer!" I finally come up with in defense. "Isn't she used to speaking in front of a court room full of people?"

17

Kate emerges from the stall and goes to the sink where she splashes water on her face and rinses her mouth out. "Shit! Anyone have a breath mint?"

I look at her, unbelievably. "Kate!"

She turns and looks at me. "Oh, Come on, Maggie! No one actually listens to me in the courtroom for Christ's sakes!"

Carrie looks at me with that same pleading look in her eyes and it almost breaks my heart. "You write for a living," she says to me. "You can spin some words together."

Still, I will not go down without a fight. "Carrie," I say fervently, "I write about dead people! And besides, given my own personal history, I don't think you'd want me blessing you with words of wisdom on how to maintain a successful marriage! God, it's almost morbid!"

Kate interjects, "I think it's friggin' hilarious."

"Kate!" Carrie and I say at the same time.

Kate turns towards the mirror and reapplies her lip-gloss. "Oh, Come on. We've been best friends since seventh grade. One day you'll look back on this moment and laugh at the irony of it," she pauses to smack her lips together, blotting the pink stain on her mouth. "And besides, Maggie," she adds, "you do get out of wearing *this*." She makes a sweeping gesture with her hands and points to the bridesmaid's dress she has been coerced to wear.

"You told me you liked it in the store!" Carrie replies emphatically but Kate ignores her and looks straight at me. "It's time you pulled your weight today."

"But I'm not even a bridesmaid!" I retort. "You can't ignore proper wedding protocol!" Carrie whips around to face me. Her cheeks are red and her eyes are bulging. There has only been one other time in my life when I've seen Carrie so upset and that was when The Backstreet Boys broke up.

"Bullshit, I can't ignore wedding protocol! It's my goddamn wedding!" Did I mention that that was also the only time I have ever heard Carrie curse? And now she's done it twice in one sentence. Yup, Carrie was definitely upset. "Listen, Maggie," she continues, although her voice does seem to have gone down an octave and her eyes are no longer bulging, "I'm sick and tired of making excuses for you. Kate's right. I need you."

I look helplessly at my two best friends, trying to plead silently with my eyes. Both Carrie and Kate stand in front of the door, arms crossed, blocking any escape I might be planning. I'm not getting out of this one. "Kate," I sigh, "just give me what you have. Do you have note cards or something?"

Kate smiles sheepishly and nods towards the trash receptacle. "I did but, uh, I needed something to wipe my mouth with in a hurry."

"Are you kidding me!" I scream.

"Not really. But it's probably a good thing. It was the same toast I was going to say at your wedding." Carrie and I look at her, mortified, but Kate just shrugs her shoulders.

"Great," I mutter. "What the hell else could go wrong?"

Chapter Three

I know most of you here know Carrie and Ben in one capacity or another. So, you know, unequivocally, what great people they both are. I am truly honored to be standing up here today, able to share with you a more private perspective.

As Carrie's roommate for the past two years, I've been lucky enough to spend a lot of time with Carrie and Ben as a couple. And what I've noticed about Carrie and Ben, in the times I am with them, whether it's sitting on the couch watching TV or eating dinner together on some random Tuesday night, is how much they appreciate each other. Whether it's Ben letting Carrie pick what show to watch or getting up to do the dishes after dinner or Carrie keeping the fridge stocked with cookie dough because she knows how much Ben likes to eat it raw, or taking Ben's car to fill it up with gas because she knows he's tired and doesn't want him to run back out again, in the rain, when he gets home from work. Or on Sunday mornings, when they are both camped out on the couch, drinking coffee and reading the paper and they don't even realize that their pinky fingers are wrapped around one another. And what I always think to myself, when I catch them unaware in moments like this, is this is the real thing. What I think about love is, it doesn't matter so much how you treat each other when you're out and about with other people, trying to meet expectations and preoccupied with making a good impression, but what matters is how you treat each other in these seemingly insignificant moments, when it's just the two of you. When your lover is sick or your lover is tired or when they have a bad day at work. And it has been such a gift for me to be able to catch these most private glimpses of Carrie and Ben because they have truly taught me what love is, or at least what it should be. Love is comfort. Love is compromise. And love is respect. And Carrie and Ben have that in spades.

So, if you'll please join me in raising your glasses. to Carrie and Ben, may your lives together be filled with laughter, and happiness. Congratulations!

—Carrie and Ben

August 2

I sit at the table, wringing a napkin in my hand and tapping my feet while my mother and uncle and the rest of the guests are eating shrimp cocktail. Soft orchestra music is playing in the background but I can barely hear it over my rapid heartbeat and the quickness of my breath. I reach into my bag to grab my inhaler. My mother stops her fork halfway to her mouth and looks at me. "Maggie, what on earth are you all in a dither about? You're shaking the entire table!"

"Oh. Sorry," I mutter, and I stop tapping my feet.

"Really, Maggie. You've taken more hits from your inhaler today than Bob Marley probably ever took from his bong. What are you so nervous about?"

The music stops and the bandleader approaches the mic. "You'll find out soon enough," I say and I shut my eyes, bracing myself for the words that are coming.

"Ladies, and gentlemen, Maggie McDonald, friend of the bride, would now like to say a few words."

"I wouldn't quite put it that way," I mutter to myself as I get up from the table. My mom and Uncle Hor just look at me, their mouths hanging open. I walk across the dance floor, trying very hard to ignore the searing quiet and awaiting stares all around me. I smile nervously and wonder to myself what the hell I'm doing.

I'm just about to reach the mic when I hear a crack and I stumble, plummeting forward, like I'm the goddamn tackle on the high school football team. I look down and notice the heel of my left shoe has broken and is now hanging by a thread, dragging behind. It makes me sad. They are Jimmy Choos. There is a collective "ooh" from the room and I'm pretty sure, at this point, there is simply nothing else I can do. At this moment, I just surrender.

"Oh, screw it," I mutter to myself. I take a deep breath, smooth my dress, walk calmly to the mike and take it in my hand. *It doesn't matter now;* I think to myself. I've just embarrassed myself as much as humanly possible for one night. I clear my throat and nonchalantly kick off my shoes.

"Hi everyone," I begin. "Carrie asked me to say a few words...like literally a few minutes ago...in the bathroom."

The room waits, wondering if they heard me right. I can see it on their nameless faces. I don't know what they expect. They don't know my story (well, actually, most of them probably do. Carrie and I have most of the same friends). I don't think it's a half-bad opening, given the circumstances of this whole debacle. I laugh nervously and go on. "I told her she was crazy. I mean, I write obituaries and given my cynical nature and the fact that I walked out on my own wedding, I don't exactly think I'm the most qualified for the task at hand."

I hear the words coming out of my mouth as I'm saying them. Hell, I even know it's a train wreck but the thing is, I can't stop. It's like word vomit spilling out of my mouth; it just keeps coming.

"I mean, personally, I don't think marriage is anything more than a business arrangement. You know, agree to do my laundry every day for the rest of my life and in return, I'll take over sole responsibility of your money and spending power but I'll pay your taxes. Please...as if that's really an appealing prospect."

I pause, wishing I had my inhaler with me. There is a deadpan silence settling over the room. I see my mother looking around nervously, with an awkward smile on her face, probably hoping that as few people as possible realize that I am her daughter. Uncle Hor looks down and appears to be muttering something under his breath. Probably a colorful array of newly invented and highly imaginable curses.

But then, I focus in on Carrie, and it physically makes me hurt. She is bending over, her face buried in her hands, and I wonder how I can hurt her so much. Carrie, who brought me chocolate chip cookies, that she baked herself, every day when I had mono in seventh grade and let me copy her math homework, every day, in eighth grade, so I wouldn't fail (I fell sorta behind due to the mono). Carrie, who in high school moved the bottle in a flash (I saw her), so I could have Tom Simmons in the closet during a breathless session of Seven Minutes in Heaven, even though I knew she secretly lusted for him. Carrie, who didn't judge me for what I did to Jack, but just hugged me and told me it was okay and loved me unconditionally. I couldn't do this to Carrie. The sight of her made my eyes brim. I quickly tried to right my wrongs. I am a woman of words, after all. I believe in the dignity of words and there is nothing more I want to do in this moment than to send my friend a lifeline.

"But one thing I'm sure of," I utter, "is that life won't work that way for Carrie and Ben."

Carrie looks up at me. I can see her holding her breath, not quite sure of what might come out of my mouth next and not quite sure she wants to hear it. I have no idea of what I'm about to say, but I know I want it to be for Carrie. I may have made a mockery out of my own wedding, but I won't make one out of my best friend's. Hell, even I have standards, as hard as that is for some people to believe.

I close my eyes and suddenly I am flooded with visions of Carrie and Ben. I see them sitting on the couch on a Sunday morning, drinking coffee and reading the newspaper together, comfortable in their silence. It startles me really. I had no idea I had been such a keen observer of Carrie and Ben's relationship. I had no idea that these images took residence in my memory.

Suddenly, I know just what to say...

Chapter Four

The toast was a total hit. Guests came up to me all night, both friends and strangers alike, congratulating me on a job well done. Uncle Hor couldn't stop crying as he hugged me and whispered in my ear, "There's hope for you after all, Maggie Mae." But really Uncle Hor's reaction didn't surprise me at all…he had been blubbering all day.

Even my mother seemed taken aback by the speech. "Nice job, dear," she said to me as she patted my arm, but she hesitated for a moment, as if she wanted to say something but wasn't quite sure what. But it was really Carrie's reaction I cared most about. I didn't give the toast for anyone except her.

"Maggie, that was beautiful," she says as she wipes the tears from her eyes and throws her arms around me.

I smile as I hug her back. "Words are my business. Besides, I had great inspiration. I meant every word of it."

"Yeah," Kate says. "If I knew you were that good, I would've had you say mine when Bernie and I got married."

"You eloped," I retort.

"We could have skyped," Kate replies. I roll my eyes.

"Oh," Carrie adds, before she is whisked off to make the rounds, "nice touch about the pinkies."

"What?" I ask, surprised.

"You know…the pinkies. How you said we would entwine our pinkies while we would read the paper on the couch."

"What do you mean?" I ask, confused.

Carrie looks at me. Now she is a little confused. "Ben and I have never done that."

"Oh," I say. I remember now. That was something I did with Jack.

I stand outside on the deck, admiring the view of the Boston skyline from the harbor. *It sure is a pretty city*, I think to myself. The last of the guests are doing the Electric Slide on the dance floor but I need some air. It has not been an easy day for me. In the end, it had all worked out for Carrie and I was glad for that, but I was feeling a little unanchored. It felt like I was spinning around without the pull of gravity to hold me down. I gulped down the last of my wine and quickly decided that I could use another.

I sit down at the bar, glad to not have any company. I want to sit and wallow in my self-pity without being bothered. I mean, is that too much for a girl to ask?

"Another pinot?" the bartender asks me and I nod my head. "Here you go, love," he says as he hands me the glass. Something in his voice makes me look up. There is no denying that Australian accent. The bartender pauses and studies my face for a moment. "Well now!" he laughs heartily. "The runaway bride, if I recall correctly. Last I saw you; you were in quite a state."

"Heh," I say feebly. "I remember." I take a gulp of my wine. Really, it was something I would much prefer to forget. It wasn't my finest hour. But clearly the bartender did not pick up on the degree of my awkwardness.

"So," he says as he takes a dishcloth out of his back pocket and starts wiping down the counter, "did you find what you were looking for Down Under?"

"I wasn't looking for anything," I say somewhat defensively. "Just a vacation and a suntan." I swirl the wine in my glass around and take another gulp.

"Well, love, sometimes it's hard to know what you're looking for until you find it."

"What about you?" I ask. I'm tired of being the one on the hot seat. "Given your accent, you're clearly not a Boston native. Do you make the twenty-hour flight between here and there as a hobby?"

He shrugs his shoulders. "I'm here on business. Just so happens I'm staying at this hotel and they needed extra help with the event." He stops wiping the counter and winks at me. "You know, us Aussies know our way around a bar." I laugh despite myself. Aussies really are very affable people. And if you've never been to the Land of Oz, I highly recommend it as a destination.

"So, how is it you ended up at a wedding anyway?" he asks as he refills my glass. "Thought you had somewhat of an allergy to weddings, now didn't I?"

"The bride is my best friend. There was no avoiding this one."

"Well, it's a good thing you didn't or we all would have been deprived of that beautiful toast," an unfamiliar voice remarks. I turn to look for the source and notice a hunched-over figure sitting at the end of the bar. A little, old man jumps off of his stool and makes his way to the empty stool next to me. "May I?" he asks.

"Be my guest," I say. He sits down next to me and extends his hand.

"Morty Finklestein. It is a pleasure to meet you."

I take his hand and am taken aback by how strong his grip is. He must be close to eighty. "Maggie McDonald. Nice to meet you."

"So, Maggie, that was quite some toast you gave. Spoken from the heart, to the heart."

"Wait a minute!" the bartender interrupts. "*You* gave the toast?" he laughs. "Well! Will wonders never cease!"

"What's that supposed to mean?" I'm beginning to get my druthers up.

"Well, love, you must admit the irony of the situation! Hahaha!" I was about to give some witty, clever response, but Morty interjects.

"Is this something you do often, Maggie?"

I hold up my wine glass. "You mean drink? As often as possible…especially under the current circumstances."

"I mean give the toast. At weddings."

I shake my head. "Oh, no. This was definitely a one-time gig. It was sort of an emergency situation."

"Well," Morty says, holding up his glass to toast, "thank goodness for emergencies." I smile and let my glass clink against Morty's. It finally occurs to me that I don't know this funny little man at all.

"Are you related to Ben's grandpa Howard?" I ask. Certainly, the geriatrics are all related.

"Oh, no! I just happen to be up here on business. Elks Convention," he reaches into his pocket and retrieves a membership card. "Just so happens I was walking by the ballroom when I heard your toast. May I ask, Maggie, what it is you do for work?"

I pause before I give my answer. The irony of what I do for a living is not lost on me. "I write obituaries, actually. For *The Boston Hub*."

"Aah! So, you do this for work. You toast the dead!"

I thought about what this eccentric old man had just said. "Yeah, I guess I do." I mean, I try to garner a piece of family history, some interesting tidbit or fact that would make the dearly departed stand out, but mostly it comes down to when they died and who they left behind. It's sad, really. No human being should leave the world without being properly toasted.

It suddenly occurs to me that I don't even know how my dad's obituary reads. I hate to admit it, but my memories of him are beginning to fade. I remember him carrying me on my shoulders, telling me I could pick a star for him out of the sky. And I remember he and my mom dancing in the living room. Just dancing and twirling, like there was no tomorrow. Yes, I would like to think that my dad was properly toasted when he left this Earth.

Morty's voice breaks me from my reverie.

"I'm getting married myself; Labor Day weekend."

"Congratulations!" I say and clink his glass again.

"Yup. I lost my Evie fifteen years ago; God rest her soul. After 48 years of marriage," Morty stops to bless himself. "Anyway, I moved down to Clearwater retirement home seven years ago, down in Sarasota, couldn't take the New England winters anymore, and that's where I met Addy. We had been playing Scrabble together every afternoon for the last seven years and finally I said to her last spring, 'let's get hitched,' and she said, 'let's go for it.' No one likes to be lonely, now do they, even at our age."

"Scrabble!" I tease. "So, you're a man of words as well!"

"I am, I am!"

"I hate to bust up the party, mates," the bartender interrupts, "but it's closing time. And this bloke is wankered."

I close my tab (I also pay for Morty Finklestein's Bloody Mary...I don't know why...I guess you could say I can be quite gratuitous at times...and I do like Bloody Marys). The bartender gives me a wink, as if he knows where my life is headed and what lies in store for me.

"Thanks, love," he replies and walks off into the night. I swear I can hear the faintest laughter as I watch his shadow disappear.

Morty clears his voice and I turn my attention back to him. "I have a proposition for you, Miss McDonald," Morty says to me, and my eyes practically bug out of my head. I mean, really. An old man propositioning me at a five-star hotel…what am I supposed to think?

It doesn't get any better when he says, "Now, I'm willing to pay handsomely." At this point I am about to throw my glass of pinot in his face (and it's an *expensive* pinot…and believe me…I take my wine *very* seriously). But then Carrie and Kate come out on the deck looking for me and I know I must act like a lady, at least for a minute.

I make the introductions, not able to look Morty in the eye while doing so. Of course, Carrie and Kate think Morty's story is adorable. I still think he's a creepy gigolo, but then I hear something that changes my mind.

"Addy and I don't need much," Morty says. "We live in a nice place, all our needs are taken care of, but I would like to give her a gift. And so, I was inspired, you see. I'd like you to give a toast at our wedding, Maggie."

So, gentlemen still live in the world. I was a little ashamed of myself that I thought the worst of poor Morty Finklestein. His definition and my definition of "proposition" seem to differ greatly. As much as his definition pleases me, I don't think I'm the best person to fulfill his request.

"Oh, Mr. Finklestein, thank you, that's very nice, but today was just a one-time thing. It's not something I do on a regular basis."

"Please, Maggie," there was a pleading and a slight sadness in his voice now. "When you get to be our age, you don't know how much time you got left. What is left, I want to be special. You can make it special, for Addy and me."

"She'll do it for a thousand," Carrie says all of a sudden. I shoot her a wild look of disbelief and she shoots me her look that says, 'Don't you dare open your mouth.'

"And expenses," Kate chimes in. I can't believe what is happening. I shoot her the same look and she gives me back the same look as Carrie.

"Done!" Morty Finklestein excitedly opens up his wallet. "Here's my business card. Call me on Monday and we'll discuss the details. Labor Day weekend, don't forget! September 5th is the wedding but I'd like you to come for the whole weekend as my guest, or even the whole week, if you want. Sarasota is a beautiful place, you know. Lot's to do. I'll send you a plane ticket."

"A weekend will be fine," I say quickly. I can hardly believe the words that come out of my mouth. I can't believe that I am actually agreeing to do this.

"Maggie McDonald, you have just made an old man very happy," Morty says, and I smile in spite of myself. He turns and waves his cane. "Call me Monday, don't forget!" And he disappears into the hotel, whistling a happy tune. And I am left with my two best friends, the night wrapped around us, with a prospect I never would have imagined.

Chapter Five

I extend my legs out and recline my seat as far back as it can go, like a cat stretching in the sun. I had called Morty back on that Monday, against my better judgment. Carrie and Kate thought it would make for a good story. "What the hell?" Kate had said.

Uncle Hor thought that, somehow, it would lead me on a quest for love. "Who knows, Maggie Mae," he said to me with a twinkle in his eye, "who knows what you'll find down there in Sarasota." I think he was hoping for a husband. I just wanted a suntan.

But it was my mother who offered the best scenario, which is why I agreed to this gig. "Florida. That's nice, dear. You could use a nice vacation." Love and a good story I can do without, but I am in dire need of a vacation.

So here I am, twenty minutes into a three-hour flight, to my vacation at a retirement community. Also, against my better judgment, (I make a lot of bad decisions, in case you couldn't tell), I conceded to come for a week instead of sticking to my original weekend plan. It had been my idea too, if you can believe that. Morty had given me all the details over the phone; how they met (Scrabble), where they went on their first "off-site" date (Daddy-O's Beef Burger Palace), what their preferred late afternoon cocktail was (a gin and tonic for Morty, a glass of Pinot for Addy), and what their favorite movie was (*Casablanca* for both of them. Morty said it was serendipitous that of over thousands of movies ever made, they had the same favorite, and a black and white one, at that).

I went over my notes, my collected bits of information, just like I do when I sit down to write an obit, and I realized it wasn't nearly enough. When you toast the dead, scattered facts are all you have to go on but when you toast the relationship between two living people, you need to see them interact. You need to observe whether they hold hands under the table or smile secretly at each other, even if they don't realize they are, or if they eat

30

food off of each other's plates at a restaurant, because that stuff speaks volumes. I take the business of words very seriously.

I called Morty back before he had a chance to buy my plane ticket and extended my three-day, two-night stay at Clearwater Retirement Community to a seven-day, six-night stay. Morty was more than happy to accommodate me but there was one stipulation to this plan.

"The thing is Maggie, I want this to be a surprise, you see. I don't want Addy to know why you're here until the wedding, so I'm going to have to insist that you pretend to be my niece, well, grandniece anyway."

I think Morty took into account the large age gap at that point. So now, not only do I have to keep my track of my tidbits of info on Morty and Addy, but I also have to basically remember a whole family tree (and not my own, which I can hardly do) so I won't blow my cover. It occurred to me then that I should have charged more.

I sigh heavily and take out my laptop. I click open the "family tree" file to bone up on where exactly I fit into the Finklestein family so I wouldn't answer a question incorrectly at the Sunday afternoon pot roast. Apparently, I am the daughter of Morty's nephew, Justin. "Don't worry, no family is coming except my son and my grandson," Morty told me. "Everyone else is either dead or divorced."

Apparently, my "father" is on the dead side (Jesus, even undercover I can't have a father who's alive). He had died in a dog sled accident in the Yukon. "Really?" I asked, intrigued.

"No!" Morty replied. "He fell from a ladder installing a window but this sounds more exciting!" I think Morty was getting a little over excited about the undercover work.

"You want a piece of advice for free, Morty?"

"What's that?"

"Don't start a marriage with lying."

And so, it was decided. I was Morty's grandniece, daughter of Justin and Kathy, visiting from Portland where, evidently, I run a dog grooming business. Justin had died in a tragic window-installing related accident ten years ago and Kathy was a permanent resident of the Betty Ford clinic.

"Do I have to change my name?" I asked sarcastically.

Morty thought about it for a minute. "Umm…no. That would get too confusing. At my age I'm not apt to remember which name to call you."

Morty was quiet for another second. "Maggie McDonald sure as hell doesn't sound Jewish, though."

I laughed. It really didn't.

"Well, we'll settle on Maggie Finklestein then." And then I laughed again at how ridiculous that sounded.

"Well, welcome to the family, Maggie Finklestein. Welcome to the family." I think Morty liked the way it sounded.

A sea of nameless strangers greeted me as I walk through the gate and look for the funny, little man I had met just a month earlier at the Boston Harbor Hotel. Morty was coming solo to get me so we could go over the specifics of our plan one more time. I was undercover after all.

"Maggie!" I hear my name right away but it takes me a second to find Morty (he's kinda short). But then there's no mistaking Morty. He emerges from the crowd, wearing a Hawaiian shirt, khaki Bermuda shorts and blue knee socks with white, orthopedic shoes, his toothless gums flapping away. "Here we go," I mutter to myself. I realize how much I am dreading this "vacation."

"Hi, Morty!" I say with all the false enthusiasm I can muster and resign myself to the fact that I will be spending the next week with a toothless, old man at a retirement home. It's all I can do not to cry.

It's about a twenty-minute drive from the airport to Clearwater. We drive along a flat, Florida highway in Morty's white Cadillac. He has to sit on a plump, fluffed up pillow in order to see out the windshield. I stealthily reach for my seat belt and Morty preps me on the upcoming week.

"So today, we'll just relax. We'll show you around the place, maybe relax by the pool (I did perk up at the mention of a pool). Addy's very excited to meet you." He leans across the row seat (the car swerved) and squeezes my hand. "She's cooking a special dinner tonight to celebrate your arrival."

"That sounds delicious." I was just hoping it wasn't pot roast.

"So, you're clear on the family history, Maggie?"

"Yup. Daughter of Justin and Kathy. And Justin did *not* die in a dog sledding accident."

Morty concedes. "Okay, okay. We'll just stick to the facts. More confusing otherwise."

We pull into a gated community with palm trees lining each side of the drive. I look at my surroundings through the window with pleasant surprise. A whole, little community is perched among the palms. Well-manicured grounds host fountains and botanical gardens and along the perimeter stucco, pink townhouses form a ribbon hugging the coastline. Morty is smiling at me. He had gauged my reaction and is happy with the outcome.

"I didn't know you were right on the beach," I say surprised.

"Wanted to surprise you." Things are definitely beginning to look up.

We pulled into Morty's driveway and a tall, slender woman with a silvery white bob and a welcoming smile stands waiting at the door. She waves as the car pulls in and walks over to meet us.

"Is that the housekeeper?" I ask Morty. I thought that this welcoming was perhaps a paid service.

"No! That's Addy."

I gasp out loud. I can't help it. I had somehow pictured Addy quite differently. I had envisioned a plump, jolly little woman with short, thinning white hair from too many bad perms and the same toothless grin. But this woman, to put it quite frankly, is foxy (at least for the over 65 crew). What particularly strikes me is the height difference between them. Addy must have at least 4 inches on Morty.

"Hey, babe," Morty says as he climbs out of the car (it requires a little bit of a jump).

Addy turns to me and gives me a warm, all-encompassing hug. "It's so nice to meet you, Maggie! We're so happy to have you stay with us!"

"Thanks," I say, as I pull away quickly (I'm not big on close physical contact when I first meet someone. A handshake would do). "It's nice of you to have me."

"Well, you're family." Addy smiles and takes my bag. Morty grabs my other one from the trunk and we go inside. I feel a little guilty about letting two elderly people carry my luggage but I don't want to be rude.

We sit on the patio, overlooking the golf course, and eat tiny chicken salad tea sandwiches and drink lemon aide. Morty had wanted to start with the alcohol right away but Addy would have none of it. "Morty, it's only 1:00. You can have a cocktail later." I could've gone for a cold one myself.

"So, Maggie," Addy starts, "tell me about your business."

"Huh?" I'm feeling discombobulated. She catches me off-guard, and it takes me a second to recall the intricate details of our covert operation.

"I love dogs," Addy says as she reaches for another sandwich. Her arm is long and lean and tan, absent of the normal arm flab you would expect to find on someone her age. They're athletic arms, or the arms of a dancer. I feel bad thinking it, but I can't quite see what Addy is doing with Morty. Anyway, back to the dogs.

"Tell me, which breed is the hardest to groom?"

"Boxer," I blurt out nervously.

"But don't they have a short coat?"

"Well, yes," I say hesitantly, "but that's why they're hard to groom. You run the risk of tearing the skin if you brush too hard." I'm impressed with myself. It's not a bad response under pressure.

"Huh. I would've thought a breed like a Bichon Frise or a Pomeranian would be the hardest because of all that hair. Which are the hypoallergenic breeds again?"

"Uh…" now I am panicking. Hypoallergenic? The only hypoallergenic things I know about are earrings and moisturizer.

"Addy, let's take Maggie down by the pool. The gang's all dying to meet her. Shuffleboard should be going on now…" Morty stands up quickly and reaches for Addy's hand. He shoots me an apologetic look; which I think I'm entitled to. This undercover stuff is getting a little out of hand.

I sit on my bed before I turn in for the night and go over the events of the day. I have my notebook out to record any observations or thoughts of inspiration. It had been an okay day. Not what I would have picked for a vacation but not the worst thing in the world either. I guess you could say I had been pleasantly surprised. My first impression of Clearwater was quite different than I had imagined. I had never really thought about the difference between a retirement home and a nursing home. I had imagined a gray, bleak building filled with old people in wheel chairs and drooling, with moth-eaten Afghans draped over their shoulders and staff in white coats running around trying to feed them Jell-O. But Clearwater isn't like that. It's clean and there's a pool and a beach and valet parking. The people are, you know, old, but it doesn't turn out to be such a bad spot. I had met Fern, Boris, Stella, Ida, Eugene, Clarence and Alma, or otherwise known as "the gang," and we had basically spent the day drinking cocktails either by the pool or on the patio. It

34

wasn't unlike a spring break for the over 65 crew. Actually, it was kind of fun. But I still don't know what to write. I mean, you can't very well toast a senior couple at their wedding and tell them how fun it was getting drunk with them. I need a distraction. I throw my notebook down and pick up my cell phone.

"Hi, Mom."

"Maggie! So, how was the first day?"

"Well, you know, not the vacation I had in mind but not so bad, I guess. Although, the nightlife scene is totally dead. It's only 9:10 and I'm already in my pajamas. I don't think I've done that since I was twelve."

My mother laughs. "Just think of the money, dear. That's really why you're there."

"How's Uncle Hor?"

"Oh, he's fine. He's playing tonight with Arnie and Joe." Uncle Hor thinks he plays in a band, but he really doesn't. He plays Harmonica with two other gents who are just as eccentric as he is. They take turns playing in each other's garages. That's about the extent of it. I smile at the thought anyway.

"He's still convinced you're going to meet someone at this wedding," my mother said indifferently. "He's been saying the rosary every night."

"Well, tell him not to get his hopes up. He'd have a better chance of meeting someone down here than me. Doesn't he know I'm at a retirement home?"

I say goodbye and turn back to my notebook. I start writing down bland, ordinary facts that I already know so that at least the pages aren't blank. Blank pages bother me. I jot down in list form; *Casablanca, Daddy-O's, Scrabble, gin and tonic…*but it's not eliciting any strong reaction in me. These words don't convey to me the essence of Morty and Addy's relationship. They're just words. I need more. I need to observe them more closely.

I sigh with frustration. I'm having a hard time seeing what drew Addy to Morty. I don't mean it the way it sounds. I mean, Morty's great. He's the liveliest eighty-two-year-old I know. He's got a great zest for life and a magnetic personality (really, he does) and you can't help but like him. He actually reminds me of Uncle Hor in a lot of ways, except Uncle Hor is only sixty-seven. But Morty is, well, funny looking. And old. Not that Addy is young, but she's younger than Morty, and looks younger than she actually is.

And Morty is loaded. He has to be, to afford a place like this. I can't help but wonder if Addy has ulterior motives. Don't get me wrong, Addy's been great. She's been a gracious hostess, a good cook, an active conversationalist (which is a good thing, except when the topic of conversation turns to dogs), but it almost seems as if she is too perfect, like she's trying too hard. And they sleep in two, twin beds instead of a King or a Queen, which I think is a little strange (I took the liberty of peeking in earlier). This is the cynic in me coming out. It's my mom in me coming out. I wonder what my dad would have thought if he saw Addy and Morty together. My dad was a romantic. I think he would've seen the sweetness of it.

"It's only the first day," I say out loud. I have five more days to discover what makes Morty and Addy tick before the wedding and I know what I need to do. I need to spend some one-on-one time with Addy. I need to find out, woman to woman, what attracts her to this funny, little man.

I put my notebook away and trudge down the hall to brush my teeth. I can't believe I'm going to bed at 9:30. I pass Morty and Addy's room, and hear the sound of soft laughter, just barely audible, float out from under the half-closed door and into the hallway. I sidle up next to the wall and carefully crane my neck to take a peek in.

Addy and Morty are in their respective beds, holding hands and reading to each other. I can't hear what they're reading; their voices are soft and low and the words sound like nothing but murmurs, but their eyes are smiling behind their glasses and a subtle glow has crept into their cheeks. I know it's a private moment, but I can't help myself. This is the stuff that my toasts are about. This is the stuff that I celebrate. It is in these seemingly insignificant moments that we find moments of truth.

I think back to Carrie and Ben's toast and I smile. *What matters is not so much how you treat your lover in the company of others; what matters is how you treat each other when it's just the two of you.* And just like that, I have found what I was looking for. I had been wrong about Addy, and I am glad. It seems like love might live here after all.

We walk along the beach, collecting beach glass and conch shells. It is the morning after my epiphany, and I can't help but feel a little guilty. I had eavesdropped on something precious last night, something tender, but I also know it was what I needed in order to compose a kickass speech. But it also isn't enough. I still need Addy's story. This early morning stroll serves this purpose quite well.

It had been Addy's idea. She is already sitting on the patio, reading the paper and drinking orange juice when I come down for my requisite cup of coffee. It's only 7:30 am but when you're in bed at 9:30 pm, you don't feel the need to sleep in.

"Would you like to take a walk on the beach with me, Maggie?" Addy asks as she pours me a cup of coffee. "I find that there's nothing like an early morning walk on the beach to start your day." I couldn't refuse.

"Do you walk the beach every morning?" I ask as we walk barefoot in the sand.

"Absolutely." Addy draws in a deep breath. "There's nothing like the feel of the sand between your toes and the salty air on your face. I grew up in Ohio, you know. Columbus. After being land-locked for so long, I find I can't bear to be away from the water." We pause for a second, looking out towards the horizon. "The openness of it, the expansiveness of it," Addy says almost to herself, "it's like a whole world of possibility out there, reminding you to grab hold of it."

"Does Morty ever join you?" I ask.

"Oh, sure. But most mornings he does a Tae Kwon Do class at the Rec. center."

"Really?" I have to bite my lip to keep from laughing out loud at the thought of Morty in one of those black karate outfits, doing Kung Fu moves in slow motion.

Addy looks at me. "Sure. Every morning. Monday through Friday. That's where he is now. It's important at our age to keep active. Morty golfs, too. And I play tennis."

"That's great," I say. I'm surprised to hear how active they are. Well, maybe not Addy because she looks so great, but definitely Morty. I just figured that when you got old, you sat around watching TV or playing board games (Scrabble didn't surprise me) or taking naps. I never considered the possibility that you could be active. Athletic, even.

"Can I ask you something, Addy?" I ask, tentatively.

"Of course, Maggie. You can ask me anything."

"What drew you to Morty? I mean I know you met playing Scrabble, but what drew you to him? How did you guys end up in love?"

37

Addy smiles, and not a sly, little smile, either. It's a big, wide, laugh-out-loud smile. It's the type of smile you can't hide when the thought of something unspoken makes you happy.

"He makes me laugh," she says honestly. "He makes me smile. I remember once when we were playing Scrabble, we made the rule that you could use foreign words, just to make it more interesting. Well, Morty meant to spell *gracias* but he spelled it *grassy ass*! He was truly convinced that that's how you spell it!"

I laugh too. It's not too hard to imagine. I can easily imagine Morty using profanity. I picture him yelling out all sorts of naughty things on the golf course and causing a ruckus.

Addy turns quiet. I think we're having a bonding moment. "I know it sounds funny, Maggie, but this is my second chance. This is my chance, at sixty-nine, for true love." I wait for her to go on. This is a critical moment and I don't want to press her. We start walking again, slowly.

"I was married once," she says flatly, as if she is talking about someone else in another life. "For forty years, I played the part. The perfect wife, the perfect mother..." her voice trails off, remembering painful things. "But I wasn't happy. Don't misunderstand, I love my sons," and her voice cracks, "but I gave forty years of my life to a monster of a man." Addy stops walking and gingerly pushes her hair back from her cheek to expose an inch-long scar in the shape of a crescent moon. She touches it gingerly and looks out to the water.

"Oh, Addy..." I say.

"My first husband was a fierce alcoholic. This is what happened to me when I left the roast beef in the oven too long on Christmas. Smashed the beer bottle he had been drinking from, without a moment's hesitation, and came at me with a fury. All because I burned the damn meat!" She is crying hard now, and I put my arms around her. I am crying a little, too. It's the most awful thing I have ever heard.

We stand there for a moment, not saying anything, and then Addy composes herself. She wipes her eyes and stands up straight. "I'm sorry, Maggie," she says with her familiar, warm smile, "that was ages ago. Another lifetime ago. This is a happy time for me. I didn't mean to bring my skeletons out. I guess I just want you to understand, truly, what Morty means to me. How much I love him."

We start walking again, arm in arm. "Your uncle is the most wonderful man I have ever met."

"Huh?" Instinctively, I think of Uncle Hor. It takes me a second to remember that Addy is, in fact, talking about Morty. This undercover crap is beginning to drive me crazy. I'm just waiting to put my foot in my mouth.

Addy looks at me. "Well, I know he's eccentric, but he's tender and he's sweet and he appreciates me. He holds the door open for me, he doesn't say anything when I cheat at Scrabble and when I'm napping, he covers me with a blanket. They're little things, Maggie, but no man has ever done them for me before."

She stops and turns to me, "In my sixty-nine years on this Earth, this is the first time that someone has appreciated me." She is crying again, but it is a cry of gratitude. "Love is a gift, Maggie. Always remember that. I've had to wait a long time, but I've finally received it, and I couldn't be happier."

"My uncle used to say that," I was talking about Uncle Hor again but it didn't matter. Something told me that Morty believed that, too. Besides, he could have said it, at one point in his life.

"Well, he's a special man," Addy says and she squeezes my arm.

"Yes," I respond. "Yes, he is." This time I was talking about Morty, although it could apply to Uncle Hor too.

"And what about you, Maggie? Have you ever been in love?"

I ponder how to answer. My history is way too complicated and I don't want to go into it. I haven't talked about Jack in a long time, and part of me, in this moment, wonders why it's still so painful to.

"No," I say, although not too convincingly.

"You don't sound so convinced." (I told you it wasn't convincing).

"I thought I was once, but I wasn't."

"Did you get your heart broken?" Addy asks sympathetically.

"No. Actually, I think I broke someone else's."

Addy loops her arm through mine again. "Well, you're young, Maggie. You have all the time in the world. But just remember what I said. It would be a shame to live a life without love."

We walk back to the condo and find Morty, in his black karate suit (I had pictured it exactly in my mind), reading the paper on the patio. Addy bends down to kiss him on the cheek and he grabs her face and plants a big wet one right on her lips. Addy laughs, giddy as a schoolgirl and Morty winks at me. I smile, the words to my toast already taking shape in my head.

I sit on my bed, reviewing my toast. The wedding is tomorrow and I am satisfied with the final product. All in all, my vacation at Clearwater has been a pleasant surprise. I can't say it's been a bad vacation after all. In fact, I would consider coming back. Morty and Addy have already invited me to come down in the winter. "I remember those New England winters, Maggie, and I don't miss 'em," Morty said. "Come down in the winter, when a little sunshine will do you some good." Maybe I would.

The week went by quickly. We had dinner at Daddy-O's one night, the site of the famous "first date" and Morty and Addy ate off of each other's plates. We watched *Casablanca* one night and Morty and Addy held hands on the couch. During the days, we sat by the pool (I was a big hit in my bikini with the elderly gents. I must say, I do have a nice figure) with Fern, Boris, Stella, Ida, Eugene and Clarence, drinking lemon-aide (spiked, of course) and playing Scrabble (I won one game with *zit* on a triple word score. Morty was disqualified for *asshole*. We had made the "No Profanity" rule before we started. Morty doesn't listen very well. Maybe he's hard of hearing). Eugene and Clarence even taught me how to play Shuffleboard, which turns out I'm pretty good at. We would always end the day with a late afternoon cocktail (or two or three) on the patio. And I walked the beach with Addy every morning at 7:30. I found myself really looking forward to this time. I know what Addy means about being near the ocean, especially at this time of day. Everything is quiet except for the roll of the surf and the sky still has a subtle hint of pink in it. I enjoyed my time with her. Addy looked at the world differently. Her eyes would shine with the wonder of finding something undiscovered when she picked up a sand dollar or a seashell, and she would laugh like a little girl when the water would seep between her toes and erase her freshly made footprint. Addy found joy in simple things. She had the curiosity and vivacity of a child and I found myself marveling at what a beautiful thing it was. Jack had had that same quality too. I remembered how Jack used to exhibit that same innocent enthusiasm when the Sox beat the Yankees or when we would take his black Lab to the beach and Jack would laugh like a little kid when Max dove into the surf after a runaway tennis ball. Surprisingly, I realized that I missed it.

I tuck my toast safely away and take out a plain note card and envelop. I have one more thing I need to do. I know Addy has two sons. Michael was married and Addy even has two grandsons, but she hasn't seen them since they were babies. I don't know why but I didn't ask. Some things you just don't push.

I had asked Morty about it one afternoon during a shuffleboard match. Morty's expression had changed when I had brought it up. His face grew dark and there was a pained look in his eyes. "They won't be coming," he said in a flat voice. "They don't talk to her since the divorce. Their father is worse than ever, dying of kidney failure from too many years of hard drinking and somehow, it's Addy's fault. They blame her for their father's mistakes. Won't even let her see the grandkids and that kills Addy most of all. I called and left a message but I never heard anything back." Morty was quiet for a few minutes. "It's the one thing I wish I could fix for Addy and I can't," he said and he began to cry softly.

I reached over and squeezed his hand. "I'm glad you're here, Maggie," he said. "It's not even really a lie anymore. I do feel like you're family."

Then I started to cry. I felt that way, too.

When we get home, I open my laptop and google Brian and Michael Morris of Columbus, Ohio. After sifting through countless, irrelevant articles about other Michael and Brian Morris's, I find what I'm looking for. An address for Michael Morris. I couldn't find one for Brian but I figure he can pass on the news to his brother. Brothers are supposed to share.

I take out a pen out and write a brief message.

Your mother is getting married tomorrow, September 5, in Sarasota, Florida. I just thought you should know that. I am giving this toast at the wedding tomorrow and I wanted you to have a copy of it. Your mother is an amazing lady and it has been my pleasure getting to know her. You should call her sometime. Please pass this news on to your brother.

Sincerely,
Maggie McDonald

I put the note in the envelope with the toast, seal it, and go to bed, hoping I am doing the right thing.

It's only 10:00 am and the wedding isn't until 1:00. but I am going over to the Rec. Center early to help set up. I grab my purse, my toast securely inside, and walk down the hall and out the door. I have to make a quick stop at the mailbox first at the end of the street. I have to let Addy's sons know that their mother is getting married. I think of Jack, a quick flash that floods my mind. I wonder if he woke up that morning and had any inclination that he, in fact, would not be married at the end of the day. I shake the thought off but that familiar, sour taste of regret still lingers.

Morty and Addy both show up, which is a good start. Hell, it's further than I got on my big day. Anyway, they both look gorgeous, like two-teenagers on prom night, and finally it's time for my toast. I stand up and approach the mic, unsure of how I'd be received. But I know my talent. I know words like the back of my hand and I find myself oddly at ease. I open my mouth and let her roll.

Morty asked me to say a few words today in honor of this very special occasion, but before I do, I have a confession to make. I am not Morty's niece. My name is Maggie McDonald, and Morty and I met about a month ago under serendipitous circumstances (or at least that's the way Morty describes it!). Morty and I ended up at the same wedding in Boston. I was supposed to be there, giving a toast at my best friend's wedding, and Morty was not. He stumbled in, quite by accident, and heard my toast. He introduced himself to me afterward and told me he had never heard such beautiful words spoken (I don't know about that but I think we can all agree that Morty certainly knows how to charm!). Morty asked if I would consider coming down here because he wanted to give a gift, the gift of words, to Addy (It's not hard to believe considering they met playing Scrabble!). So, our plan was born. I came down here, as a business proposition, posing as Morty's niece, in order to surprise you today, Addy, and give you the gift of these words.

So down I came, one week ago today, in order to observe Morty and Addy, to observe their relationship, to observe what makes them tick and to celebrate this day with words. And what I've observed in the week I've been here with Morty and Addy is nothing short of awesome. And I don't mean that in the colloquial sense, how we all use that word up in Boston, throwing it around like it has no meaning, but I mean AWESOME. I once read a quote somewhere, I don't even know who wrote it, but I never forgot it. "True love is a friendship set on fire." Now, I don't know whom it was written about originally, but as far as I'm concerned, it was written about Morty and Addy. During my week with Morty and Addy, I have not only seen a deep love, but a beautiful friendship. And the secret is as simple as this; Morty and Addy enjoy their time together. They enjoy playing Scrabble together, they enjoy watching Casablanca together, they enjoy sitting on the patio in the late afternoon sun, having a cocktail (or two) together. They enjoy simple pleasures together, like walking on the beach or reading to each other in bed, before they go to sleep. Morty and Addy enjoy each other. They have fun with each other and they have taught me, in the time that I've been here with them, that's what life is really all about. It's spending time, quality time, with the people you love most, doing the things you love most.

Morty and Addy, these words are for you. They are my gift to you, but the really ironic part is that I am the one who feels like I've been given a gift. In one week, you have taught me that love is light-hearted, that love is fun, that love is patient and that love is kind. I've seen it every day, in the way you hold hands on the couch, in the way you laugh at each other's jokes like no one else is in the room, in the way you each light up and your skin glows and your eyes smile when the other one walks into the room. I've seen it in the way you let each other cheat in Scrabble. I've seen it in the both of you. And even though I'm not technically family, I feel like I'm family. You've opened your home and your hearts to me and I thank you, from the bottom of my heart. But I thank you even more for showing me what love is, and what love can be.

So, if you'll please join me in raising your glasses. to Morty and Addy, may your lives together be full of fun, laughter and love.

Chapter Six

I sit down at the end of the day, take off my strappy, black stilettos and take in the scene around me. Alma is still walking unsteadily and keeps yelling, "Mazel Tov!" even though we told her it was a non-denominational wedding and Fern is still spinning records like she is Fat Boy Slim. Eugene is currently leading Boris, Ida and Clarence in the Electric Slide and Morty and Addy are off in a corner, dancing slowly, cheek to cheek, despite the faster tempo.

The toast had been a big hit, and the uncovering of our undercover reuse had been received with a mixture of disbelief and amusement. Personally, I had been all too glad to let the cat out of the bag; all that undercover business was getting a bit tricky at the end. I had to keep remembering who I was related to, where I went to school and what I did for a living and which breed of dog was hardest to groom (I had never heard such words, either. If someone had asked me before this trip what a Pomeranian was, I would've said it was an exotic type of Oriental rug).

I reach in to my purse to get my lipstick when a tall, distinguished looking gentleman with gray hair and a mustache and wearing a beige, hounds tooth suit, takes the seat next to me. I can't remember who he is, although I had met him briefly earlier, but I had noticed him looking at me at random times throughout the day, like he wanted to talk to me but didn't quite have the courage to do it yet. At any rate, I brace myself. I have a feeling I know what's coming.

"Hello, again, Ma'am," he says in a thick, southern accent as he stretches his long legs out and reaches into his pocket for a pack of cigarettes. "Do you mind?" He asks as he holds the pack up, asking for permission. I do mind, but I don't protest. He lights up and inhales deeply. "Quite a day wasn't it?" A stream of smoke blows sideways from his mouth. I nod my head and smile.

"And your speech, little lady, that was just about the most beautiful damn thing I ever heard."

"Thanks," I say. "I had great inspiration."

We both look at Morty and Addy. They had just joined in with the rest of the gang for a round of the Hokey Pokey. They were currently shaking their left elbow all about.

"Cruise Cartwright," he says as he extends his hand. "I know we met briefly earlier but a southern gent like me always introduces himself twice to a pretty lady."

I take his hand carefully. I knew my hand would smell like smoke afterward and I hate that, but I didn't want to be rude. "Maggie McDonald."

"I knew that," he said as he exhales again, blowing the smoke over his shoulder. "I remember from your toast. And is that something you do often? Make beautiful toasts at random strangers' weddings?"

Yup, I was right. I know what's coming. "Oh, no. This was just a one-time thing. Sort of a serendipitous event, actually."

"Well, how about making it a two-time thing?"

Bingo. I sort of smile and half-laugh, which I guess Mr. Cartwright took as an invitation to enlighten me when what I really meant for him to do was to stop talking and leave abruptly.

"You ever hear of the Cartwrights from Charleston, Ms. McDonald?" he asks as he lights his third cigarette, in just as many minutes.

"Uh, no, can't say that I have."

"Doesn't surprise me. You're a Yankee." He takes out his box of cigarettes and slides it towards me.

"No, thanks, I don't smoke." I really didn't care for Cruise Cartwright.

He laughs. "No, I didn't suppose that you did. Which is too bad because I would be a richer man, but I want to show you the fine print on that box there." He points to the bottom, where tiny words that looked like you would need a magnifying glass to read, were printed, gesturing me to read it out loud.

I look at the green and white package of *Southern Grass Cigarettes* and, squinting madly, read, *Product of Cartwright Plantation, Charleston, South Carolina.*

"That's me," Cruise Cartwright says, pointing to himself, proud as a peacock. "The family business. My great granddaddy started it in the

45

antebellum times. Had slaves back then. But now we got some fancy machines to do the work and we're politically correct as well." I think he was trying to be funny but it came off as arrogantly obnoxious. And I still didn't know what any of this has to do with me.

"What does any of this have to do with me?" I don't mean to sound rude but I am getting impatient.

A shadow falls across Cruise Cartwright's face. It changes his whole demeanor in a flash and an expression of regret settles into his brow.

"My son," he says dejectedly. "Sam. My only son. Doesn't want to follow in the family business. Is morally opposed to these." He holds up a cigarette and tries, without success, to muster a smile at his attempt at a joke. "Wants to change the world and he wants to start by cleaning up the rivers." He stifles back a laugh. "A multi-million-dollar business at his fingertips and he wants to save the trout. What does that say about my son, Sam, Ms. McDonald?"

"That he's a good man." Usually I'd criticize anyone who would give up the bucks, but I admire Sam's conviction and besides, I am morally opposed to smoking. Not so much for the health reasons, but for the aesthetic reasons. Cigarette smoke smells terrible and makes everything else in its vicinity smell terrible.

Cruise Cartwright smiles a sad, knowing smile. "Yes, that he's a good man. I know that, and I wish that he knew that I know that. But you can imagine how these things go, Ms. McDonald. Rifts in the family, stubborn pride at stake, family politics and before you know it, everything has gone to hell in a hand basket."

I just nod my head. Really, I have no idea how such things go but I pretend I do anyway.

"He up and left two years ago. Took off for Tennessee. Helping to clean the river and save the trout or bass or whatever fish they got up there. Says the world is in trouble and the only way to solve the problem is with clean water, or some mumbo jumbo like that."

He pauses to light up, yet again, and then continues, "My sources tell me that he got himself a girl there. A pretty blonde with a sweet smile. They tell me a wedding is imminent."

"Sources?" I ask. The whole thing sounds a little mafia-esque.

Cruise Cartwright flashes me that deep southern smile. "Ms. McDonald, when you own a tobacco plantation, you can afford to have sources."

Enough said.

"So, I come to you with a business proposition, Ms. McDonald. Would you be interested in performing another toast, for my son Sam?" His expression changes again and I wait for him to go on. "The damage has been done, and I know that. I have to make peace with that. But he's my son."

Something resembling hope and renewal shine in his eyes. "I want to give him somethin' and your words seem like the perfect thing to me."

I sigh. I can feel myself already getting sucked in. I'm getting soft, and I feel a secret twinge of resentment towards Morty and Addy for making me this way. They had turned me into a damn marshmallow.

"Do you have a card?" I ask, resignedly.

Cruise Cartwright excitedly pulls one from his pocket. "I can pay handsomely." *Good,* I thought to myself, *because my rate just went way up.*

I stand at the terminal, suitcase(s) in hand, and ready myself to say goodbye to Morty and Addy. There is the slightest catch in my throat as I hug them both and wish them well. I would miss them.

"You come down anytime you want," Addy said as she hugs me. "You're family."

Morty hugs me and then hands me a white envelope. "Here, Maggie. Your paycheck for a job very well done, plus tip for great service." He gives me a wink and I think I see him blink a tear away.

"Thanks, Morty. Anytime," I say, and then I blink away a tear. I feel a little guilty about taking the money. It really hadn't felt like work at all.

I settle into the flight and stretch out my legs (in business class. Morty had me upgraded as a surprise!). My eyelids grow heavy as the plane careens down the runway and lifts into the air but thoughts and memories of the last week swirl in my head just the same. I think of Morty and Addy, holding hands and feeding each other spaghetti at Daddy-O's and I hope that my mom would get to do that with someone special one day. I think of Boris and Clarence and Stella and Ida and Alma, drinking champagne and doing the Electric Slide and I think that Uncle Hor would've love to have been at that wedding. He would fit right in. I think of my toast, the words I had used to describe the essence of Morty and Addy, and I think that my dad would be proud.

We are cruising now, at standard elevation, and I let my eyes close and dip into sleep. I close my hand instinctively and feel the smooth, cool sides of a 2-by-3 business card dig into my palm. I drift off, dreaming of Charleston and trout and dancing cigarettes, anticipating what is to come next.

Chapter Seven

Believe it or not, my life returned to normal when I got back to Boston. I resumed my role in the world as a young, professional, somewhat self-centered young woman who didn't have room in her life for romantic notions and fairytale stories. I mean people didn't stop dying just because I had taken a brief hiatus to a retirement home and they didn't stop dying when I got back. Deadlines loomed over me like a perpetual black cloud and I busied myself with giving my clients' their last words instead of toasting eccentric strangers at weddings.

But there were times when I found myself wondering what temperature it was in Sarasota (I even googled it once and then had it posted daily on my homepage) or whether there was any place to play Shuffleboard in the greater Boston area or whether Morty and Addy were playing Scrabble and what unutterable word, either foreign or otherwise, Morty had used on a triple letter score. These thoughts didn't consume me, but I had them from time to time, and when I did, I would feel a subtle flicker inside of me, like there was a part of me coming alive.

Uncle Hor loved to hear my stories. I told him about the retirement home that looked and felt more like a four-star resort, my walks on the beach with Addy, Morty's dangerous driving habits and all the endearing idiosyncrasies of "the gang," otherwise known as Fern, Boris, Stella, Ida, Eugene, Clarence and Alma. His eyes would light up as he imagined a place in the world where everyone was just as quirky as he was. It made me a little sad to see Uncle Hor in those moments. It reminded me how much he had given up for Mom and me.

Carrie and Kate thought it was an adorable story, the stuff that Hallmark movies are made of. Kate had even suggested that I should write a screenplay about it. I had actually entertained the notion for about a day and got lost in the fantasy of which Hollywood star would, of course, play me. I had George

Burns picked out for Morty but then I remembered that George Burns is dead and that bummed me out a little bit. He would have been perfect as Morty. Anyway, it wasn't out of the realm of possibility. All the big Hollywood stars have at least one, cheesy Hallmark movie under their belt. Anyway, I decided I just didn't have the time or the inclination, and I busied myself with writing my obituaries.

I hadn't expected to hear from Cruise Cartwright, so you can imagine my utter surprise when I heard from him on a random Tuesday afternoon in early October.

"Ms. McDonald, it's Cruise Cartwright. How are you this fine day?" Fine day? It was forty degrees and raining cats and dogs in Boston but I held my tongue. When you're dealing with a southerner, you have to remember to be polite, just so they don't constantly refer to you as a damn Yankee.

"Uh, fine," I say instead, "and, how are you?"

"Well, love is in the air, Ms. McDonald, love is in the air."

"Oh?"

"My son, Sam. My sources tell me he popped the question to his gal and the wedding is set for the sixth of November."

"Well, isn't that nice," I reply meekly. My inkling of where this is going has now turned into an absolute certainty, and I haven't made up my mind about how I feel about it. In my mind, "sources" translates directly to "muscle men," which translates directly into some faction of organized crime. I'm not sure I want to get mixed up in such a scene (although, I must admit, a little part of me found it to be quite alluring). I decide to feel the situation out.

"So, I'm calling you here now, Ms. McDonald, to request your services. To request your services for my son, Sam, and his bride-to-be, Ella. I know I explained the circumstances to you in Florida. It's imperative it be kept top secret. They can't know it's from me."

So much for feeling the situation out. Cruise Cartwright is talking as though I have already accepted the job. Not only is he talking like I have already accepted it, he is talking as though rejecting it is not even an option, and given his somewhat questionable yet sketchy ties to mafia-like activity, I decide I better accept it, but I will milk it for all it's worth.

"My fee is five thousand dollars," I find myself saying. I can hardly believe it. My rate for Morty and Addy was only a thousand, but they had surprised me by giving me three. "For superior services rendered," Morty had written in his note with, a smiley face.

I feel I can up the ante now, especially since I am getting involved under questionable circumstances. "And expenses," I add.

"Done," Cartwright answered. "And there is another matter that needs attention."

"You mean my cover?" I ask outright. There is no sense in beating around the bush. I have already agreed to do it.

Cruise Cartwright laughs a deep, throaty laugh, reflecting both his southern roots and his two pack a day *Southern Grass* habit. "You're a sharp one, Ms. McDonald, you're a sharp one; despite bein' a northerner. I have, as a matter of fact, worked out a plan."

I can't wait to hear this one. And evidently, Cruise Cartwright can't wait to share it with me because he hardly pauses to inhale before he is enlightening me with the specifics of his plan.

"You'll go as the photographer who was hired by *The Tennessee Tribune* to document the upcoming nuptials and the preparation of it."

"Huh?" I'm stunned. Posing as Morty Finkelstein's niece for a week was one thing, but posing as a photographer was something else entirely. I don't know anything about photography. The only camera I own is a 35-millimeter point and shoot I had bought when Jack and I went to Aruba on vacation. I haven't even upgraded to digital yet. My stomach begins to make funny sounds (or maybe it was my throat). Something tells me this is a bad idea.

I decide to try a different tactic first instead of owning up to the fact that I know nothing about taking pictures.

"Uh, Mr. Cartwright, I don't mean to sound rude but why would *The Tennessee Tribune* be interested in Sam's upcoming nuptials?"

I think it's a fair question. I work for a news publication after all, and I know a thing or two about what constitutes a newsworthy event. No matter how small the community or the story, there has to be a hook. There has to be something that makes it, well, interesting. I don't know what's so interesting about some tree-hugger in a trailer park marrying some chick…unless the connection to Big Daddy smoking his Southern Grass is uncovered and Sam is discovered to be heir to a multi-million-dollar fortune, which of course he would use to save all the fish and trees in the lower Tennessee Valley, unless the muscle men had something to say about it…oh, God, I'm really getting carried away (I tend to do that). It would make a good story though, sort of like my half-conceived screenplay. I make a mental note to file the idea away for later.

At any rate, Cartwright shakes me from my reverie. "Oh, that don't matter, Ms. McDonald! These are simple folk. They're as dumb as doornails! Grew up in rural Tennessee with nothing but the good sense to wear shoes outside once it snowed. And Sam! He's so smitten; he won't stop to think about the 'why.' Take it from me, Ms. McDonald, the cover's as good as gold."

We work out the logistics and comb through the details of our grand design. I would arrive on November 1st (I'll be picked up at the airport by a limo!) and be taken to Sam and Ella's, er, trailer. They were expecting me. Well, not me exactly, but they were expecting a photographer from *The Tribune*. Turns out they were tickled pink to think that the good folk of Tennessee had such an interest in their wedding. Sam was hopeful about the publicity it would bring to their cause.

Staying in a trailer for a week doesn't excite me too much, in fact, I am downright dreading it. But, as always, the integrity of words wins out over my own level of personal comfort, and I decide I could deal. There is just one more minor detail I need to attend to before we hang up.

"Uh, Mr. Cartwright, there's just one more thing."

"Yes?"

"I'm going to have to insist on first-class."

Ed gives me a hell of a time, taking another week off. "For Christ's sakes, Maggie! You just took a week off six weeks ago!"

"That was my vacation time!"

"Well, now you're out!"

Oops. A new tactic is called for. I lower my voice, smile, and subtly flip my hair. "C'mon, Ed. It's not like people are going to stop dying just because I go to Tennessee for a week. This is the 21st century. I'll bring my laptop and work on the job. I'll email my obits to the office and give you a progress report every day." I give my hair another subtle flip. The hair flip always works.

Ed sighs. "Fine, Maggie, fine. But if your work doesn't get done, you don't get paid."

"It will, Ed. Cross my heart."

52

Ed snorts. "Like I haven't heard that one from you before."

"What's that supposed to mean?"

"Nothing, Maggie. Nothing. Just make sure you meet your deadlines, huh? And don't try to use technical difficulties as an excuse, either. Last I heard Tennessee had wireless, just like everywhere else."

I smile. "Not to worry, Ed. Not to worry. You can count on me."

Ed doesn't look any more assured. "That's what I'm afraid of."

Chapter Eight

I sit in my big, comfy, roomy seat in first-class, wondering what the hell I'm doing. Mr. Cartwright has sent me a top-of-the-line, professional model digital camera. Turns out I not only have to pose as a photographer but also have to, in fact, actually take pictures while I'm there. It's part of the arrangement. Problem is, I don't know the first thing about how to use the damn thing.

I have never been a big tech person. It has always been easier to let someone else deal with gadgets and widgets. I have a laptop that I used for work, and I know how to email, and text on my cell phone, (and operate my vibrator. It's a deluxe model, with various speeds and tactile experiences) but that's about the extent of it. I don't even know how to download music onto my iPod. Jack had bought me one for Christmas one year, complete with his entire CD collection downloaded onto it (he had a kickass one. Everything from the Dooby Brothers to Van Halen. Really…you'd be impressed). I haven't downloaded a single song onto it since. Not for any sentimental reason, but just because I don't know how.

A hard pit begins to form in my stomach and I feel like I am in quite over my head. The camera hadn't arrived until yesterday, and now it is tucked away in the baggage compartment. I do have the user's manual with me and I am skimming it profusely, trying to learn the meanings of such terms as pixel and SLR and LCD monitor. Really, between learning all the dog breed names at Addy and Morty's and learning all this new-fangled technical jargon, I feel like I should consider myself well versed in a foreign language. This was getting out of hand.

"Shit!" I say, out of pure frustration. "Shit, shit, shit!" An attractive but snooty looking middle-aged woman, wearing a cashmere patina and drinking a vodka and tonic, sitting across the aisle, shoots me the dagger stare.

"Sorry," I say out loud, but I'm really not. She can take her daggers and choke on them. She has no idea what I'm about to get myself into.

I think of Mr. Cartwright's "sources;" Hal and Sal. They even have names now. They'll be 'keeping an eye on things,' Mr. Cartwright told me, while I'm there. He told me not to be alarmed if I see someone lurking in the bushes or hiding behind a tree, and I wonder if I should have asked for a 'no assassination or bodily harm' clause in the contract. And there is a contract this time. A real contract. Drawn up in pen and signed by a witness. Mr. Cartwright had sent it to me by certified mail to sign. This job is all very official. I have to live up to my end of the deal. And that means learning how to use this goddamn camera.

I get into Knoxville and, as promised, Sal and Hal pick me up in a black stretch limo with tinted windows. They nod to me when I arrive, hiding behind big shaded sunglasses, and take my bags for me and escort me to the car, but they don't say one word. They grunt and nod and point, but I never hear either one of them utter one syllable. For someone who loves words as much as me, it's a hard adjustment. Anyway, we found some way of communicating because operation pickup goes off without a hitch, which makes me feel astronomically better about the state of things. At least I am off to a decent start.

We drive for about a half hour when the car comes to an abrupt stop outside of a gas station on a road entitled Main Street that seemed to only include a post office, a general store, a volunteer fire department and said gas station. I look around and wait, and wonder if the tank needs to be filled or if Sal or Hal need a slurpy or something from the food mart. No one seems to be doing anything. We are at a virtual standstill until Sal (or it could be Hal. I can't really tell them apart with their sunglasses on) finally utters his first words in an hour.

"We're to leave you here. Their trailer park is about a mile straight up the road. You can't miss it."

"What!" I say, somewhat panicking. "I'm supposed to walk a mile, carrying my luggage? I have high heels on!"

Both men start laughing, which both pisses me off and makes me feel better. At least I know they are human now. And that they can speak.

"This aint New York, little lady," the other one says (I don't know if it's Sal or Hal). "This is Tennessee backcountry. It aint our fault you don't have the sense to dress appropriately."

"I'm from Boston," I say, as I fling open the door and grab my bags, before swiftly shutting it in their faces. It's my only defense.

The men pull a U-ey and drive away down the road. I have a sneaky suspicion that the next time I see them, it will be under even more unconventional circumstances than this. At any rate, I don't seem to have any other options available to me. I am, as either Sal or Hal had eloquently pointed out, in Tennessee backcountry. It's not like I can jump on the T or hail a cab. I throw one bag over my shoulder and pull my suitcase along behind me (at least it had wheels) and wobble down Main Street (which really wasn't a main street at all).

I walk into Shady Creek Trailer Park with blisters on my feet, a crick in my neck and about as much patience as a sophomore on prom night. And my outlook on the state of things is not improving. Logically, I know Sam and Ella live in a trailer, but I guess I didn't know what that truly meant until I got here. I had envisioned cozy, little log cabins, with smoke rising out of the chimney and a farmer's porch with Adirondack chairs perched on it. I guess I must have been remembering the little resort cottages that me and my mom used to go to every summer in New Hampshire. They had been small, but quaint, and they had a certain charm about them. But *this*…this is not quaint. It's downright rudimentary.

I have been camping exactly once in my life, in college, and I had hated every second of it. And Shady Creek seemed to be nothing more than a campground with trailers instead of tents. They weren't even the luxury model RV complete with a gourmet kitchen, master suite, and private bathroom and Jacuzzi that I had seen on a Behind the Music documentary on VH1 on Brittany Spears. She had one of those RVs as a tour bus. But these, these were just trailers. Doors were hanging off hinges, loud music vibrates from one of the trailers and a foul order emanates from another. Stray, barking dogs roam around freely and a group of toothless, shoeless residents open their doors and gawk at me like I'm some sort of circus show attraction as I make my way down each row, looking for the *welcome* sign with a fish on it (Sal or Hal had told me I could find Sam and Ella's place by that sign). It suddenly occurs to me where the term 'trailer park trash' actually came from (not that it's any stretch of the imagination). "What did I sign up for," I mutter to myself. This is definitely not what I had in mind.

A big bear of a man with a gray, bushy beard and wearing overalls rounds the corner. "Can I help you, Miss?" He has a deep, gruff voice marked with a southern twang that I, oddly enough, am getting used to at this point; but his voice also has kindness in it, and that makes me feel decidedly better.

"I'm looking for Sam and Ella's trailer." I get the feeling that everyone around here knows each other, if they aren't already related. Last names are an extraneous nomenclature.

His eyes twinkle and he lets out a big, hearty laugh. He reminds me of a hillbilly Santa Clause. "You must be the photog from the paper."

Turns out I was right. Everyone did know each other, as well as everyone else's business.

"Uh, yes," I say. "Maggie McDonald." I extend my hand (at least this time I can use my own name).

He almost crushes my fingers in a firm and vigorous handshake. "Name's Earl, Earl Calhoun. Ella's my daughter."

Turns out I was right again. Everyone did seem to be related.

"It's nice to meet you," I say.

"Well, we're just thrilled you're here. Ella's tickled pink that she's going to be in the papers. And Sam's just hopin' it will bring some publicity to all the work he's doin' to clean up the river. Says it might bring in some government funds or somethin' like that." Earl reaches to take my bag from me, for which I am monumentally grateful. The crick in my neck is getting worse. "Sam's real smart, you know. Ella's real lucky to have him." He slings my bag over his shoulder and motions for me to follow. He keeps talking, but that doesn't bother me. It means that I don't have to talk.

"Not that he's not lucky to have Ella," he goes on. "My Ella's a great girl. They're a good match." I just smile politely and nod my head. Not having yet met Ella or Sam, I am in no position to comment. "Here it is." We approach a trailer that looks like every other one in the park. Except this one has the fish. It is bright blue, with what seems to be a psychotic smile on its face. It looks like a smurf-fish.

Earl opens the door wide, without knocking, and walks right in, as if it were his trailer. "Hellooo," he calls out. The trailer can't be more than 100 square feet. There is a general room, used for sitting and cooking, and a small, little bedroom and even smaller bathroom. I think the entire space is smaller than my walk-in closet. It's official. I am staying in a shoebox.

"They must be out by the river," Earl says. "That's their favorite place to be."

I hear a low whistle outside and a rugged, attractive, guy, who I take to be Sam Cartwright, walks into the trailer, making it all but impossible for three people to be sharing the same space. I'm not complaining though. He is *really* good looking.

"Hey, Papa Earl. What brings you by?"

"This is that photog from *The Tribune*."

"Howdy," Sam says to me as he takes my hand. He has a strong face and liquid brown eyes and dimples that remind me of Jack.

"Hey," I say as I take his hand. Well, this is a pleasant surprise in an otherwise bleak, and foreboding day. I hadn't been expecting this at all.

"Sam Cartwright. Nice to meet you." His smile could light up the Eiffel Tower.

"Maggie McDonald," I reply. "Likewise."

It doesn't seem like it will be a bad week after all. Things are shaping up very nicely. Sam, although, granted, he is young, is very nice to look at. I know that he is only twenty-two, but he exudes such a confidence and maturity about him that that fact is easily forgotten. Not so much forgotten, however, is the fact that he is engaged to another girl. I allow myself a full minute of impure thoughts and X-rated fantasies involving Sam, myself, some sexy lingerie and exotic pieces of fruit.

Get a hold of yourself, I tell myself after the two minutes has passed (okay, okay…it was two minutes. It's been a long time since I've had sex…). I am back in business mode. I have a job to do.

"Where's Ella?" Earl asks, bringing both me, and my libido, back to Earth.

"Back at the river. She took Mutt for a swim. You know how he loves to chase them balls in the water."

Hmm, a dog that chases tennis balls. I wonder if they have the Fetch It.

"Well, Sam, why don't we show Ms. McDonald around the park? Ella shouldn't be too long."

I emerge from the trailer wearing jeans and sneakers; much more appropriate attire for a trailer park in Tennessee than high heels and cashmere. It had been somewhat of an awkward predicament. I realized that Sam, Earl and myself were standing in what would be, for the next week at least, my bedroom. No other room was big enough for me to lug my suitcases into, dig through them and change. That task would require some sort of acrobatic skill or a super flexi superpower, of which, I possess neither. Instead I just say, "Uhh…" Sam gets the message.

"We'll wait for you outside," he says, his cheeks turning red.

We continue down the row of trailers but stop in front of the trailer two doors down from Sam and Ella's. "Hey, Beau," Earl yells. "You in there?"

A big, brawly man wearing overalls and a flannel shirt opens the door holding a shotgun. "What's up, Daddy?"

I gasp out loud when I see the gun. I can't help it. It is just not a scene I am used to seeing. In more civilized places in the world, people simply did not tote around shotguns (they didn't live in trailer parks, either).

Sam just shoots me a side-glance. He is beginning to understand. "You're not from these parts, are you?" he asks me. I'm relieved. Having to play the part of a southerner would be out of my realm. I simply cannot relate to this way of life.

"No," I say. "I'm from Boston."

Sam smiles. "You can tell."

"Maggie, this is Beau, my oldest son," Earl says.

"Nice to meet you, ma'am. You're gonna find that this park here is filled with Calhouns."

Just like I said. Everyone is related at Shady Creek.

We spend the afternoon exploring Shady Creek…not that there is that much to explore. It is row upon row of RV's—there must be fifty in all—that serve as the primary residences for the Calhouns and the rest of the inhabitants of Shady Creek. I feel like I am in an alternate universe and I can't understand, for the life of me, why Sam Cartwright, who could stand to inherit millions of dollars, if he so chose, who was probably used to a life of luxury back in Charleston, would willingly give all that up for this.

Besides Beau, and his wife Carleen and little Beau Jr., I also met Brady and Cooper; Ella's other two brothers, and their wives, Ellen and Jo-Ann. They all live just a few doors down from each other. In fact, at the end of their row is a hand-carved wooden sign nailed to a tree that reads, "Calhoun Street." Earl and Etta, or otherwise known as Ma and Pa Calhoun, live in the middle of the row with their off-spring scattered around them in both directions. It's a tight, little family nucleus.

Sam also points out to me the various trailers of friends and extended family, all of whom I will meet at some point during my stay at Shady Creek. There is Irma and Carl Calhoun, Earl's first cousins, and who boast the largest large-mouth bass ever caught in the state. They had their prize possession stuffed and it hangs over their door. Huey and Doris Calhoun are Earl's aunt and uncle and the hottest tickets I've ever met (besides Morty and Uncle Hor). Huey grows "organic medicinal plants" in a little garden behind his trailer and both of them wander around smoking pipes which give off a sweet clover scent and wear *Grateful Dead* T-shirts they bought at Fanny's Traveling Flea Market (Fanny set up shop in Shady Creek one Sunday a month. Evidently, it's the social occasion of the, well, month).

Sam and I enter a green clearing surrounded by a canopy of trees and with a large fire pit in the middle. There are a few picnic tables scattered here and there and we sit down at one. The timing is perfect. I decide it is time to conduct a fishing expedition of my own.

"This is where the wedding will be," Sam says, waving his hand to introduce the scene before me. "We call it the campground."

"Well, it's not exactly Charleston, is it?"

Sam smiles. "Alright, Maggie, alright. Seems to me you know my past." He stretches out his legs and settles in for what is to follow. "You must have about a million questions right now, about why I would throw it all away for life in a trailer park. Although, last I heard, you were the photographer, not a journalist." Sam shoots me a sideways glance. "Where's your camera, anyway? Shouldn't you be taking pictures?"

Oops. Busted.

"Oh, it's back at the trailer," I say nonchalantly. "I'm just getting the lay of the land. All photographers need to do their homework first. You know, discover where the best angles are." I add a feeble laugh here. Really, I have no idea what I am talking about. I don't even know how to use the damn camera yet. But Sam seems to buy it (I am getting good at this undercover stuff). "So, you were saying?" I try prompting him back onto the subject of his past. I want to hear Sam's story. I am curious.

"Not much to tell. I came to Tennessee about a little over a year ago. The summer between my junior and senior year at Chapel Hill. I was a Biology major, although my dad thought I was business," Sam pauses for a second and a smirk settles on his face. "Gettin' groomed for the so-called family business."

He picks up a pebble and skips it across the grass. "Anyway, I came to Knoxville to volunteer on The River Project."

"The River Project?" I ask.

"The initiative to clean up the Tennessee River. Get pollutant levels down, stop decomposition of the watershed. I mostly took water samples and got scuba certified to pick up trash on the riverbed. It's a damn shame how people treat their rivers. Did you know the bass population is down 30 percent in the Tennessee alone?"

"I didn't know that," I say. Really, why would I know that?

"The Earth is three-fourths water," Sam goes on. "People need to start treating it with the respect it deserves." He is getting fired up now. I am discovering that Sam is a very passionate person. Passionate about the river, passionate about fish and, I suspect, passionate about Ella. I can see why he decided to stay here, why he turned his back on millions. It's in his blood. Sam would never be happy unless he was doing what he loved with the person he loved. It isn't my place to pass judgment on someone else's choices, even if there is a million plus dollars at stake.

"Anyway," Sam goes on. "I didn't go back to school. Came to Shady Creek to find temporary housing. Was all I could afford since my dad cut me off when he found out I quit school. I met Ella here and the rest is history."

"And you're happy, Sam?" I don't mean for it to come out the way it does, like I am questioning his decisions. It's just personally I don't think I could have walked away from a million bucks. "No regrets?" I ask more gently.

"Hell, no. I mean, look around you, Maggie. I love this land. This is some of the most beautiful scenery you'll see in the whole country. Did you know there are 178 tree species in Tennessee alone? Hickories, yellow poplar, gums and ashes..."

As a matter of fact, I didn't. I do look around me but I don't think I see the same picture that Sam does. All I see are a few picnic tables and row upon row of trailers. Granted, the grass was really green and the trees are pretty, but it's not like I had never seen a tree before. They do have trees in Boston after all (although I couldn't say with 100 percent certainty whether they were hickories or yellow poplars or gums and ashes). Green grass too, although not at this time of year. In Boston it was more dead and brown in November.

"And Ella?" I ask. I know I'm pressing my luck. Even I recognize that our conversation is sounding more like an interrogation, and that isn't my role here. I am supposed to be the photographer (one who actually totes a camera and knows how to use it), but I need this information in order to make my toast. It is a crucial conversation, actually. Sam just doesn't know my motives.

Sam just smiles the biggest smile I have ever seen. "She's the whole reason I stayed." He picks up another stone and skips it across the walkway, like a child dancing with glee. "The river led me to Ella. Now, if that's not fate, I don't know what is."

I think of Morty when Sam says this. He would've said it was 'serendipitous,' and I smile.

"What about your dad? Do you still talk to him?" I already know the answer, but I want to hear Sam's take.

"Nope," he says shortly. "Once I made my decision to stay in Tennessee and volunteer with The River Project, my daddy told me I just made the decision to not be a part of the great Cartwright legacy," Sam snorts. "Like I would want any part of a business that knowingly breathes toxins into the environment. Anyway, It's not about the money, Maggie. I don't need my daddy's corrupt money or his gold platinum credit card. I got everything I need right here."

I have to admit that I admire Sam's passion and his commitment, although personally, I could do some serious damage with a gold platinum credit card, and I'd sure as hell pick the credit card over saving a bunch of fish. But still, there is something so undeniably sexy about a man who stands up for his convictions. Jack had been like that. It was one of the things that had attracted me the most to him (besides his dimples and his smile) and I find myself overcome with a wave of nostalgia.

"Well, speaking of both Ella and the river," I add lightly, "I'm beginning to question whether they really exist. I haven't met either of them yet."

Sam laughs. "Ella should be here soon. She just took the dog for a swim. She has afternoon pickup so she won't be too much longer."

"Afternoon pickup?"

"She drives the school bus for Shady Creek Unified School District. Well, she and Etta share it. Etta does morning drop-offs and Ella does afternoon pickups." This is getting stranger and stranger. I am beginning to feel like this is all straight out of an episode of *The Waltons*.

There is a rustle in the trees and I find myself wishing I had Beau's shotgun with me. I have no idea what kind of wildlife they have in Tennessee. I breathe a sigh of relief when a sandy-colored dog with black markings comes bounding out of the trees and is running full speed straight for Sam, tail wagging and jowls drooling. "Maggie, this is Mutt," Sam tells me as he scratches Mutt's ears. He is definitely aptly named. And at least his name will be easy to remember. I won't have to worry about foreign sounding names like Pomeranian or Bichon Frise this time. Mutt jumps up on me, demanding to be pet, scratched, and/or fed.

"Mutt, show some manners," a female southern drawl says behind me. I turn around and see one of the prettiest girls I have ever seen. It surprises me actually, and I feel guilty that it does. I had been expecting missing teeth and greasy hair and bare feet, but this girl appeared to have none of those things (although she is wearing flip-flops, which is almost like bare feet). She has long, blonde hair that is caught back in a loose ponytail, and big green eyes, that remind me of a cat. In short, she is a hottie. I really have to learn to stop making pre-visual judgments of people, but then again, it's not really my fault. We are in a trailer park.

"You must be Ella." I stand and try to push Mutt off of me while I extend my hand. "I'm Maggie. It's nice to meet you."

"It's so nice to meet you, Maggie! Really, Sam and I are so excited to have you here with us! Sam's excited about the publicity it will get for the river, but I'm just so excited to be in the papers! I feel like I'm famous!"

And I am reminded that I am in a trailer park. Ella is a pretty little dish, but not so much goin' on in the upstairs department. I can see why Sam is attracted to her, but Ella certainly doesn't seem to be his intellectual match. Sam doesn't seem to mind though. He has his arm draped around her, like a protective blanket, and is nonchalantly rubbing her shoulder with his hand. I'm a little jealous, actually.

"I'm really looking forward to my time here," I lie. I'm not looking forward to it at all.

We start walking while Mutt trails behind, stopping to sniff every scent that he picks up. Some of them I can even smell, and I shudder to think what could possibly give off such a stench. Ella loops her arm through mine, like we are off to a square dance.

"Have you met the family?" Ella asks. Sam continues to rub her back. He really can't seem to keep his hands off of her.

"Yes," I say. "Now, let me see if I get it all right." I am happy for a mental task to keep me distracted from Sam's hands. I rattle off the entire Calhoun family tree with only one mistake.

"Oh, so close," Sam teases.

"You did really good, Maggie! There are a lot of us to keep track of. She's really smart, Sam!"

"Ella, darlin'! Ella!" A cheery, heavy-set woman with long, gray braids and wearing overalls (really, what is with the overalls?) is walking towards us down the row. I figure it must be Etta. She's the only one of this cast of characters I haven't met yet.

"Ella, darlin', here are the keys. You better hurry up now. School's lettin' out soon." Etta approaches us and holds out a big silver ring key to Ella.

"I'm comin', Mama. Mama, this is Maggie, the photographer from *The Tribune*."

"Nice to meet you, darlin'!" Etta says as she practically suffocates me in a big bear hug. "We're so glad you're here! You gonna make my little girl famous!"

Really, what kind of warped sense of celebrity do these people have? "I don't know about that, but I'm sure gonna get some nice pictures." Was it me or was I beginning to detect the subtle hint of a drawl in my voice?

I sit on my bed, which is really a not-pull-out couch in the little cramped room that also contains a stovetop, a mini fridge (there isn't room for a standard size one), a kitchen table and other random appliances and furnishings, trying to figure out the damn camera. I had given up on my laptop hours ago. I don't know why I brought it in the first place, I mean, I should have figured there wouldn't be wireless in a trailer park. These people didn't even have TVs, never mind Internet access. They probably don't even know what the Internet is. Needless to say, I won't be able to do any work while on this trip. I didn't so much care about that but I will definitely be in hot water with Ed. I'll have to do a lot of hair flips when I get back in order to get out of this one.

I have to call Carrie and ask her to email Ed for me and explain the situation. At least I have cell service (not that anyone here has cell phones, or regular phones for that matter. They just yell to each other from their doors when they need something).

"How's it going down there?" she asks me.

"I'm in hell. Truly."

Carrie laughs. "It's an experience, Maggie. You'll be able to write a book about it when you're done. Suck it up."

Carrie is the optimistic one. I should've called Kate. She would have commiserated with me.

I don't even get any sympathy from my mother. "It sounds quaint, dear," is all she says after I lament about my accommodations and the downright dismalness of my surroundings. I guess I can't blame her. I did call during *Desperate Housewives*. She probably wasn't listening to me. I told her to record it for me. I don't even answer the phone during *Desperate Housewives*.

I do make some progress with the camera. I take a few pictures of Mutt, who is lying loyally by my feet, but when I look at them on the LCD monitor, all they look like are blurry blobs of fur. "Shit!" I mutter to myself. Oh well. At least I know where the on/off button is and the picture-taking button (I don't know the technical name but it's the button that takes pictures so I figure picture-taking button is an acceptable label). Like everything else in my life, I figure it out while I go along.

Sam and Ella take me down to the river the next day, and of course Mutt comes too. It's only 7:00 am and I am still half asleep but between the lumpy couch that had given me a major crick in my back, Mutt jumping up and licking my face at the crack of dawn and Sam and Ella wanting to get an early start so I could see the "early morning mist" on the river (a great photo opportunity, Sam had told me), I had no hope of sleeping in. At least I have my camera with me this time.

We walk through the campground and down a hidden path through the trees. I hadn't realized the river was so close. We walk less than a half mile along a dirt path through a thicket and come to a clearing. And there is the mighty Tennessee. It looks like nothing more than a mountain stream trickle.

"Huh?" I say, bewildered.

Ella and Sam laugh. "This is just a tributary," Sam says. "The Shady Creek Tributary. It feeds into the Tennessee. The main part of the river is a half mile down."

"But look, Maggie," Ella says to me as she comes up behind me and guides my vision with her finger, pointing eastward through the trees, "isn't it pretty?"

I follow her finger with my eyes and gasp in spite of myself. The sun is just beginning to peek through the branches, casting a soft, misty glow on the leaves and the water and all around, an early dew mist rises from the ground like magic dust. I instinctively reach for the camera and start shooting automatically. A moment like this is meant to be captured. Sam looks at me with satisfaction. He knows I am getting it.

I get up every morning at 7:00 am for the rest of the week, and me and Mutt head out to the river on our own. I want to see that scene as often as possible and perfect my shots. My first shots of it aren't bad for an amateur but I want to reflect its true beauty, which I haven't seemed able to do yet. I want to enhance the color, find the perfect angle, zero in on a focal point and blur out the background. I gradually take the camera off of automatic settings and try playing around with manual ones; changing the shutter speed and ISO with the flip of a switch to manipulate the shot I want. I am turning into a bona fide photographer.

Photography was turning into an obsession for me. I couldn't help but snap a shot of every scene or interaction that was happening around me. I snapped pictures of Mutt, chasing balls and sniffing trees and sleeping at my feet (I was getting quite accustomed to having a dog around). I shot pictures of Beau and Brady Jr., walking down the row with fishing poles in hand and a look of young determination on their faces. I captured the look of pride on Earl's face as he showed his two grandsons how to catch and release on a fly-fishing rod on the banks of the river, and the look of admiration on Etta's face as she watched her husband in a moment of tenderness.

And I shot pictures of Sam and Ella. I took snapshots of them on the river's edge, wading through the water and holding hands. I took pictures of them whispering into each other's ear and laughing at some secret joke that only the two of them knew. Through the lens, I caught the honesty and tenderness of their relationship. You only had to look at the shots to know their feelings for each other were real. People don't know how not to be honest when they don't know people are observing them. Sam and Ella were so caught up in each other that half the time I think they forgot that I was even around, which was fine by me because it would allow me to make my toast more authentic.

Still, I often wonder what the constant attraction between them is. Sure, they are both genetically pleasing to look at; I can understand the physical attraction between them, but at the end of the day, Sam and Ella are just so different. If I hadn't seen what I had seen through the camera, I wouldn't think that they're a good match. Sometimes I still wonder. I mean, looks only last for so long.

Mutt jumps up on the couch, demanding his nightly ear scratch. Mutt and I have become pretty tight. I mentally file away a note to send him the Fetch It when I get home.

"Not now, Mutt," I say as I scratch his ears anyway. I am scrolling through the camera, deleting the bad shots and admiring the good ones. The memory card is almost full and Mr. Cartwright hadn't given me an extra. It isn't even the wedding day yet. I silently gulp and pray that there won't be some sort of penalty in the form of a missing finger or broken limb for failure to calculate adequate memory space for wedding day pictures.

Mutt's ears prick at the sound of something that evidently only he can hear. "What is it, boy?" I hear it now, too. It's a quiet clack that seems to bounce off the window. One sound and then a few seconds later another follows. It doesn't take me long to figure out that someone is throwing pebbles at the window in order to get my attention. I briefly wonder if it is one of Shady Creek's finest residents calling for a booty call. I didn't pack my vibrator and I miss it terribly. Hell, depending on who it is, I would consider accepting it. My dreams are dashed however when I see Hal's (or Sal's) face peep through the window.

Mutt lets out a guttural growl when he realizes the presence of something sketchy lurking outside and I have to cover my mouth so I won't scream when I first see a pale face staring back at me through the window. I really don't think I have to be concerned about Sam and Ella hearing though. There is a rapid, consistent thump coming from the bedroom and at random intervals I am sure I hear the high, pleasure-filled moans of sexual ecstasy (damn, I'm jealous). I quickly give Mutt his chew bone to keep him occupied and quietly slip outside.

"What the hell are you doing here?" I ask Sal/Hal in an angry whisper. "You scared me half to death! Sam and Ella are right inside!"

"Status check, Ma'am," Sal/Hal says. "Mr. Cartwright wants me to report on the state of things."

This is just not a normal way of conducting a status check. I mean, really. A quick email would suffice. I have to mentally remind myself that I am, in fact, in a trailer park in backcountry Tennessee, and that they do not, in fact, have email. Logistics always seem to get in the way.

I bite my tongue and force myself to calm down. "Fine," I say between clenched teeth. "Everything is going according to plan."

"And the pictures? Mr. Cartwright has requested a preview of the pictures you've shot so far."

I look at him in disbelief. "It's digital!" I practically scream. "The trailer isn't exactly equipped with wireless, in case you haven't noticed!"

Sal/Hal just looks at me. Apparently, he has no idea what I am talking about. I am getting nowhere. "The pictures, ma'am," he says.

"I can't give them to you!" I scream. I don't even bother to whisper this time. There was enough racket going on in the trailers around us to cover my voice.

Sal/Hal slowly moves his hand to his coat pocket. I am convinced he is about to pull out a gun and I silently curse myself for not insisting on a "no bodily harm" clause in the contract. I don't know whether to laugh or cry when I see him take out a cell phone.

"Mr. Cartwright aint gonna be happy about this." Sal/Hal just continues to grunt into the phone. It makes me feel better, really. I have never heard him talk as much using real words, as much as he has tonight. Hearing him grunt again is familiar. It makes me feel like I know what to expect.

"I'll tell her, sir," Sal/Hal says and then clicks off the phone. I close my eyes and cross my fingers behind my back. I'm afraid to hear what it is he said he would tell me.

"Mr. Cartwright seems to have forgotten about the technological disadvantages here. He said that you could just email him everything you got when you get back to Boston. And he's sorry for the misunderstanding."

I open my eyes and blink a few times in order to convince myself that this moment is real. Then I just stare at Sal/Hal for a few seconds in utter disbelief. It's not a big deal? Mr. Cartwright was sorry for the misunderstanding? I had been convinced that Mutt would find me face down on the river bottom the next day. It takes a minute to adjust to the fact that this scenario is playing out drastically different from what I had expected, although it is an undoubtedly better outcome, at least for me. It looks like I had pegged old Cruise Cartwright wrong. Hell, I pegged Sal and Hal wrong. I was getting an education down here in Tennessee. You never know when someone will surprise you. I must admit though, it was a little bit of a let-down to realize that Mr. Cartwright was not part of a southern mafia crime family, threatening to commit some unfortunate act if I did not meet my end of the deal. I had secretly found the whole thing to be quite exciting.

Anyway, I am thankful for how the whole thing turns out. I count my lucky stars and head back in the trailer to scratch Mutt's ears.

I go down to the river with Sam, Ella and Mutt the next morning. Sam needs to take some water samples to test for Nitrate levels in the water before the whirlwind of getting ready for the wedding begins. They both seem to have the glow of after-sex on their skin and their eyes seem to smile at each other, containing some well-hidden secret. It is all I need to know to safely conclude that they have no idea of what went down outside the trailer last night. I feel immensely better about that detail but there is still the matter of preparing my toast. The wedding is tomorrow night and I still don't have the faintest idea of what I am going to say. Pictures I have plenty of, but words seem to be escaping me at the moment, and that I am not accustomed to.

Sam unpacks the test tubes from the testing kit and hands a few to Ella and me. He must read the look on my face because he laughs his cocky laugh and says, "might as well work while you're here."

I open my mouth in protest but Sam answers before I can say anything. "Now, C'mon Maggie. Don't tell me you can't handle filling little tubes with water." He looks at me with a smug look on his face. He knows that I am the type of woman who never backs down from a challenge. I close my mouth in a slight pout and take the test tubes from him. It doesn't really bother me though. Sam and I have a sort of competition going. During my week here, we have constantly tried to out-challenge each other. This is just another example of one of our playful flirtations. If I didn't know better, I would say that Sam Cartwright was definitely flirting with me. I have to admit that I have developed a little crush on Sam since being here, and if Ella weren't in the picture, I even think that it might be reciprocated, but I know better. I am an intellectual equal to Sam. He is able to relate to me on a different level, a level not present in the inhabitants of Shady Creek. As much as Sam loves Ella and the rest of the crazy Calhoun clan (and I had no doubt that he did), he is different from them, and it is that fact that I keep coming back to. Would life at Shady Creek really be enough for Sam?

Ella takes the test tubes eagerly, and even lets out a little giggle when they clink together in her hands. Sam looks at her adoringly. Her reaction makes him happy. Ella is as giddy as a schoolgirl, just happy to be included in a part of Sam's world. She wants to contribute, to give something of herself to Sam's great cause, and in that instance, I get it. I understand the essence of Sam and Ella's relationship. It is a living example of perfect symbiosis. They appreciate each other. Ella appreciates that Sam includes her in his work and Sam appreciates that Ella wants to please him. They make each other feel important, and that's enough. It's so simple, really.

The simplicity and sweetness of it unexpectedly makes my eyes well up and, in this moment, for reasons I can't explain, I think of Jack. Jack had always made me feel appreciated, something my already expanding ego probably didn't need. He opened doors for me, always letting me enter a room first, he brought me chicken soup and fashion magazines when I was sick (going to the store himself and deliberating over whether he should buy me Vogue, Cosmo or Elle. Inevitably, he would always buy me all three) and he would smile at me like I was the only person who mattered. I was beginning to realize that it was the little things that mattered and I realize that although Jack had appreciated me, I had never appreciated him, and for the first time in a long time, the taste of regret begins to fill me.

We make our way to the campground at dusk. It's a pre-wedding celebration, although I am beginning to realize that you don't specifically need an occasion to celebrate at Shady Creek. These people like to party, and the Calhouns are no exception. Out of my five nights spent at Shady Creek, we had spent three at the campground. Beau, Brady and Cooper would bring their guitars and harmonicas and jam some Blue Grass while the wives would shriek and clap their hands and contort their bodies into ungodly shapes. Etta and Irma and Doris, because of bad knees and/or bad backs, would just whoop and clap their hands.

"Sing with us, Maggie," they would say to me as they clapped their hands and stomped their feet, but mostly I just looked on in horror. Besides, I was never a fan of Blue Grass.

I sit on the picnic table, a blanket wrapped around me and drinking my fourth Bud Light. I intend on going back to the trailer soon to write my toast. I am pretty sure of what I am going to say but I want to survey the scene one more time, just in case I glean any more helpful observances. I learned a long time ago that writers are observers. It's probably the most requisite quality to being a writer, and I know I've said it before, but I like to be thorough.

Ella comes over to join me after a few minutes. I realize I haven't had any one-on-one time with Ella and I am glad for it now. I want to get Ella's feelings, in her words, before I write my toast.

"Hey, Maggie," she says in her sweet, cheery voice. "Havin' a good time?"

"Great. Just feeling a little tired. I might turn in soon."

"Alright, just make sure you have your wits about you for tomorrow. No turning in early on the day of the wedding!"

I smile. Ella is sort of a dimwit but I love her enthusiasm. "Can I ask you a question, Ella?"

"Shoot, Maggie."

"What do you love the most about Sam?"

Ella smiles and her whole face lights up as she thinks of all the little things she loves that add up to one great big love. It's really a beautiful thing.

"There are so many things, Maggie. I mean I love the way he cooks his eggs, all runny with a squirt of Tabasco, and the way he mushes around his toast in it. I love the way he sings in the shower, or to me at night in bed, even though he can't carry a tune to save his life. I love his strong hands and the dimple in his chin."

I smile. I had noticed Sam's dimple (his hands, too). Jack had one too. There is no doubt about it; girls are suckers for dimples.

"I love the way he loves the river," Ella goes on. "How he puts his heart and soul into somethin' because he believes in it and wants to share that knowledge with whoever will listen." Ella is quiet for a minute, digesting all the things there were to love about Sam. "I love that he loves this land. I think that's really what we have in common. This land is my home and I know it may just seem like some old trailer park out in the middle of nowhere to most people, Maggie, but I love it. I love walkin' bare foot through the cool stream and feelin' the stones in between my toes. I love walkin' through the woods and seein' an old Horn owl peekin' back at me. I love the early mornin' when the mist is risin' up from the river and the mountaintops are comin' through it like some magical thing. I love this land."

I am both surprised and moved by the depth with which Ella spoke. She isn't just some pretty dimwit blonde who thinks Sam is a good catch. Ella loves him. She loves who he is and what he stands for. Ella listens to Sam. She makes him feel appreciated. And I know what she means about the land. I love those early misty mornings too, and I had about fifty pictures to prove it.

"Sam's a good man," Ella goes on. "I don't know why his daddy don't see it that way. That's my one regret. I regret that he won't be at our weddin' tomorrow."

I want to say something to comfort Ella. I want to tell her why I am really here and that Sam's father at least did care a little, but I know I can't say anything. I had given Cruise Cartwright my word. For whatever reason, he did not want Sam and Ella to know of his intentions. It's a shame, really. I wish both Sam and his dad knew how much I would give to have my dad back. These damn southern men and their southern pride! As far as I'm concerned, they both need a kick in the ass. I think of Addy and the letter I had written to her sons. I wonder if they had reconciled or if her sons were just as pigheaded as Sam and Cruise Cartwright. I hadn't heard anything since my visit. I'm reminded in this moment of why I've chosen to be single (or at least one of the reasons); men suck.

No, that was wrong. Some men sucked, not all. Jack didn't suck. He didn't suck at all. Sam didn't suck. He had given up a lot to be with Ella and he did it happily. And even Cruise Cartwright didn't suck because, despite it all, he loves his son. Paying me five thousand dollars to be here proves it. Addy's sons still suck though, at least until I hear otherwise.

"Well, I'll let you go, Maggie. I don't mean to be yammerin' on an on when you're tired."

"No, I'm glad you did," I tell her. And I am.

Ella smiles and gives me a hug. "You go get your beauty sleep now, 'cause there will be no turnin' in early tomorrow, you hear?"

I hug her back. "Captain's promise," I say and I head for the trailer, with Mutt at my heels, to prepare my toast.

The wedding is a smash hit. We had been at the campground most of the day decorating and, I have to admit, the place cleaned up pretty nicely. Irma, Doris and Etta had been in charge of table couture. They had covered the picnic tables with white plastic tablecloths that they had picked up for a steal at Fanny's Traveling Flea Market the last time it had come through town. Etta had picked pebbles and stones from the stream bed and put them in old milk bottles (yup, still have milkmen in these parts. That is, if you don't actually milk your own cow) filled with water from the river and white, floating votive candles that they used for centerpieces.

I spent most of the day hanging white lights from the hickory and maple branches with Ellen and Jo-Ann. It was much more complicated than it looked and I managed to, on more than one occasion, tangle the lights around myself instead of the tree branches. In the end though, it all came together. Cooper had also made a bride and groom scarecrow in the likeness of Sam and Ella as a surprise. It was very cool. And now it was time for my toast. I stand up, confident in what I have to say, and go to work.

I hope y'all don't mind but I wanted to say a few words in honor of Ella and Sam today. I know that technically I'm just the photographer, but since my stay here at Shady Creek, I feel like I've become a friend. Ella and Sam have graciously opened up their homes and their lives to me and what I've come to realize, in the week that I have spent with them is how important the little things are in life, and in love.

Through the camera lens, I've captured the little things, the small gestures that Sam and Ella do for each other every day. Whether it's Sam rubbing Ella's shoulder nonchalantly after she throws the ball to Mutt or picking up a stone from the river that he knows she'll love because it's perfectly smooth and round and will fit into her palm perfectly, like a secret. Or whether it's Ella, bringing Sam a cup of coffee every morning before he heads to the river or waking up herself at 6:00 a.m. to go to the river with Sam to help him collect water samples, and doing it with a smile, every time, even though she has every reason in the world to sleep in. Or whether they're holding hands while they walk along the river's edge, or laughing at some secret joke that only the two of them know. I have learned something through watching Sam and Ella through the lens. I have learned that actions speak louder than words. Looking through the camera, what matters is what I see, what I capture, and not what I hear. And what I've seen is the simplicity and sweetness of Sam and Ella's love. I have seen the pureness of their actions towards each other, the honesty and tenderness of their actions, and I have it on film to prove it. It is through the small things that we show how much we truly love each other, and that's why I know Sam and Ella's life together will be long and happy. Through small gestures, they make each other feel important. And so, I feel truly humbled to have learned a little something about love from observing Sam and Ella. Always treat each other with appreciation. Do it through the little things, but do it every day. Continue to learn from each other and continue to grow, both as a couple, but also as people. Sam and Ella, I know only good and happy things will greet you as couple, because you do these things so beautifully. You are truly an example to all of us.

So, if you'll please join me in raising your glasses; to Sam and Ella. I know your lives together will be filled with happiness, laughter and love.

Chapter Nine

It's a hit. Multitudes of people come up to me afterward, congratulating me and telling me what a great job I did. Etta embraces me in one of her great, big, bear hugs and lifts me off the ground and keeps me there for about thirty seconds but I don't mind. I hug her back just as hard. Ella comes up and hugs me. She is crying but it is a happy cry and I know I have done my job. Sam looks at me and smiles, nodding his head in approval in a slightly arrogant way, but I know he's kidding. I point at him and wink and am silently grateful that he will make Ella happy, but a little sad also that my time with him is coming to a close. But it is Earl who surprises me the most.

"Maggie, I want to thank you for everything," he says as he shakes my hand warmly. "You don't know what it means to me to have you say those words about my little girl." His voice cracks and a few tears stream down his face. "I know this is the right thing for her because someone as smart as you sees it. I mean, the rest of us see it, me and Etta and the boys, but we're simple folk. We know a simple way of life," Earl pauses for a second to blow his nose. "I only want the best for my little girl and now I know this is it, thanks to you."

Now I start crying. I don't say anything but lean up and give Earl a big hug instead. Actions do speak louder than words sometimes. I had given the words that mattered in my toast; there was no need for any more.

I sit back, take another swig of my Bud and soak it all in. It had been a beautiful event really. It wasn't fancy. It wasn't something that you'd see in bridal magazines or even something that I'd probably ever see again. I try to put my finger on what about this wedding truly touches me and I realize it is the community and simplicity of it. A close-knit group of people coming together and trying to make this day beautiful for people they love. They had managed to make a trailer park beautiful with ordinary things; water, stones, white lights. The locale didn't hurt either. Yes, we are in a trailer park in the backwoods of Tennessee, but the weather is pleasant (I'm beginning to see the draw of the South for this fact alone) and Sam and Ella were able to be married outside at sunset in the middle of November. Morty and Addy's wedding had been the same way. Granted, theirs had been a little fancier, but the essence of it had been the same. A community of people coming together to celebrate love.

I am suddenly hit with a sharp pain of loneliness. I don't have this in my life. Even my almost wedding had been filled with Jack's family and friends. The only people I had had there were Mom, Uncle Hor, and Kate and Carrie. Even Bernie and Ben hadn't been in the picture then. I wonder how I had been able to get along in life with so few people in it, and I feel a deep ache for my dad. He would've liked this. He would've liked to be here, and I take comfort in knowing that he would've been proud of me. I'm beginning to see the beauty in unexpected places. I am my father's daughter.

I scroll through the camera; perusing the shots I had taken during my time here, reliving my stay. I surprise myself at what a good photographer I've become. I had really taken some beautiful shots. I make a mental note to ask Sal/Hal tomorrow to have Mr. Cartwright email me the pictures. I assume I would have to turn the camera over to Sal/Hal tomorrow before I leave. I'm a little bummed out at this thought. I really wish I could keep it.

I feel the presence of someone standing next to me but I am so engrossed in reviewing my shots that I don't look up until I feel a hand on my shoulder.

"Maggie?"

I almost fall off the table when I see who it is. It's her hair that gives her away. Her face has aged some; there are more lines around her eyes, but her hair is still as red as a hot, spicy pepper (although I would bet that it's a dye job now, but a damn good one). It has been close to twenty years since I last saw her but somehow it feels like just yesterday. Still, I can't keep the surprise out of my voice.

"Dolly?"

She envelopes me in a warm hug and it's like no time has passed at all. "It's good to see you, darlin'."

We look at each other for a minute, letting the time that separated us seep away and getting used to the women we have become in its absence. "What are you doing here?" I finally ask.

"I drove down from Nashville. I sang and wrote the jingle that goes with Sam's public service announcement." Dolly, all of a sudden, brakes into song.

Save the river! (uh-huh!)
Save the river! (uh-huh!)
The fish are dyin'
And the kids are cryin'
And you know what you have to do…
Save the river! Save the river!
It's up to me and you!

She finishes with a two-step and a twirl and I just stand there with my mouth open. Evidently, Dolly hasn't had any more hits since her one-hit wonder in 1987, which is why she moved to Nashville in the first place. I have to admit though; it is a catchy little tune.

"Got to be on TV and everything. My friend Randy choreographed it and I sang. We had our own little music video playing on WKR TV. It ran most of last year. You can still catch it weeknights at 10:30, right after the nightly news."

"Wow," I say. It's all I can really say. "I didn't know Sam had done a public service announcement." But then again, they didn't have any TVs that I knew of at Shady Creek.

"I heard about your toast," Dolly goes on. "I'm sorry I didn't hear it, darlin'. Didn't arrive 'til just a little while ago. Got stuck in one heck of a traffic jam comin' down from Nashville, but your toast was all anyone was talkin' about when I got here. I really wish I got to see it, Maggie. I was so surprised when I saw that it was really you. I thought for sure there must be another Maggie McDonald in the world."

Dolly pauses for a second, as if she is putting two and two together. "How is it that you know Sam and Ella?"

It's really too long of a story to even explain. And I can't reveal that I've been hired by Sam's dad. I hesitate for a second, trying to find the right words to say and I think of Morty. "Through serendipitous circumstances," I tell her. After all, it's true. Dolly seems satisfied with my answer. Our courteous exchanges are out of the way and now it's time to say out loud what is on both of our minds.

"How's Hor?" Dolly asks cautiously. I'm not sure, but I think I might have heard a trace of regret in her voice.

"He's great," I say, a little too quickly. I don't want to give any secrets away. This is the woman who had broken Uncle Hor's heart. She isn't going to get away with it scot-free.

Dolly gives a little smile. "That's good. I'm glad to hear that."

I can't tell if she is really glad to hear that or if she is just saying it to be polite but there is a sadness in Dolly's eyes and a longing in her voice, as if she is sorry it had ended the way it did, and all of a sudden, I see myself in Dolly. It's as if I am looking in a mirror. I mean Dolly had just followed her own dreams. She hadn't meant to hurt Uncle Hor. Wasn't it the same thing that I did to Jack? Neither of us had wanted to hurt anyone. Both of us had just wanted to do what was best for us without the commitment of a man to hold us back.

I look at Dolly now, with new eyes. When I look at her, I see myself, and I can't blame her anymore. The truth of the matter is that sometimes love is just a big, old mess. It doesn't always turn out like it did for Sam and Ella. Sometimes it turns out like it did for Dolly and Uncle Hor. And me and Jack. In the end, it doesn't work out, but that doesn't mean you weren't in love.

A man in his late thirties, wearing a cowboy hat, approaches us. I have never seen him before and for a split second I wonder if it is one of Cruise Cartwright's men coming over to settle business matters with me. But he sidles right up to Dolly and puts his arm around her. I'm not sure of Dolly's connection to him but I wonder if she is robbing the cradle, so to speak.

"Don't mean to interrupt, Dolly, but we best be gettin' on to Nashville if I'm gonna make my flight tomorrow mornin'."

Dolly glances at her watch. "My, I didn't realize how late it is. We're gonna be drivin' all night. Ah, to hell with it! Makes me feel like a kid again!"

The cowboy extends his hand to me. "Randy Rhodes. Nice to meet you."

"Oh, where are my manners? Randy, this is an old, dear friend, Maggie McDonald. Down all the way from Boston. Last time I saw her she was only about twelve years old! What a small world!"

"Nice to meet you." I shake Randy's hand.

"Maggie gave the toast that everyone is talkin' about," Dolly says.

"Ah, the wedding toaster. I'm sorry I missed it, ma'am. Everyone's sayin' what a mighty fine job you did. Is that what you do?"

"Give toasts? Well, I guess you could say I sort of freelance."

"Randy is the one who choreographed the service announcement I was telling you about," Dolly says. "We've been dear friends ever since. He's like the son I never had."

I feel infinitely better that I now know the nature of their relationship. I don't want to have to extinguish my newfound feelings of affection for Dolly and start referring to her as an uber-cougar.

"He's come all the way from Jackson, Wyoming. And he was gentleman enough to fly into Nashville and drive with me so I wouldn't have to make the drive alone."

Randy gives a bashful smile. I can tell he doesn't like to be the center of attention. I like him immediately. He is soft-spoken and polite but there is something about him I can't put my finger on. He seems sort of sad.

"Why don't you get the car, Randy?" Dolly says. "I'll meet you out front in a few minutes."

"It was nice to meet you, Ma'am," Randy says as he tips his hat to me.

"Likewise," I answer and he heads off, shoulders slightly drooped, to fetch the car.

Dolly looks after him for a minute. "Poor Randy. He's head-over-heels in love with his dance partner back in Jackson but she won't give him the time of day, but she's got it bad for some rodeo rider who thinks of her as nothing more than a notch in his belt. I think it was hard for him to be here."

Yup, I'll say it again. Love is nothing but a big, old mess sometimes. It reminds me of why I'm still single. Life is just less complicated this way.

Dolly turns to me and hugs me. "It's good to see you, darlin'. You've turned into such a beautiful woman."

I hug her back just as tightly. "It's good to see you, too." What I'm really saying is 'I'm sorry.'

Dolly pulls away from me and looks at me with tear-filled eyes. "Maybe it's best you don't tell Hor you saw me. No need to go dredging up old skeletons."

I look at her and nod my head. I know she just wants to spare him the pain he had already gotten over. "I understand."

Dolly gives me another quick hug. "Take care, Maggie," and then she is gone.

Cruise Cartwright himself picks me up in front of the gas station on Main Street the next morning. "You surpassed even my expectations. A job well done, Ms. McDonald, a job well done."

"Thank you, Mr. Cartwright. It was a pleasure." And it was. "Wait a minute," I say, "you saw the toast?" Cruise Cartwright just smiles and I know that somehow, he had.

When we pull up to the airport, I hand him back the camera. "Keep it," he says to me. "From what I understand, you've turned into quite the photographer. Who knows, you might use it again one day."

"Thank you, Mr. Cartwright," I say, and then, quite surprisingly, I lean over and hug him. I think of how just a week earlier, I had been convinced that Cruise Cartwright was Mafioso, and I laugh out loud. He's a marshmallow. He's a father who loves his son.

I take the memory card out of the camera and hand it to him and he hands me an envelope containing a very large amount of cash. *For services rendered* is printed on the envelope. My job here is done and, oddly enough, it makes me a little sad. Don't get me wrong, I am thrilled to be going back to the comforts of my bed, running water and other technological advances that, until my stay at Shady Creek, I had taken for granted, but there are things that I will miss. I will miss Ella's laugh and Sam's smile. I will miss the early morning mist and Mutt lying at my feet. I'll miss the mild weather and I'll miss that all-encompassing community feeling. I will miss these hillbillies and all of their eccentric and quirky ways.

"You know, Mr. Cartwright," I say all of a sudden, "I know it's not my place to say, but I think you should try talking to Sam. I think he would like that."

Cruise Cartwright looks at me, and his eyes fill ever so slightly. "Maybe I will."

I smile. The possibility of it is good enough for me. "Goodbye, Maggie," Cruise says, and as a true southern gentleman, he lifts my hand and kisses it. "I hope our paths cross again one day." I go into the airport, waiting to be whisked back to reality.

Chapter Ten

Reality hits me like a wet rag when I get home. It's still raining; it hasn't stopped since I've been gone, and I find that my mood matches the dismal weather. I have a backload of obits to write since my weeklong hiatus from the paper and Ed is not happy. Needless to say, I am going to have to flip my hair a lot.

"Give me one reason why I shouldn't fire your ass right now," Ed says to me on my first day back at the office. "I've had people calling all week, wondering why their loved one's obit wasn't running. Two of them threatened to go to *The World*."

Ed mops his brow with a handkerchief at this point. Any thought of losing business to our archrival, *The World,* gets him worked up.

"They didn't have wireless down there (hell, they hardly had electricity). There was nothing I could do, Ed. I'm sorry." I add a not-so-subtle hair flip for emphasis.

"You still haven't answered my question," Ed says, although a little more gently than his previous tone conveyed. I told you the hair flip always works. "Why shouldn't I fire you?"

"Because, I'm good with words," I pause a minute for dramatic effect. "And you know it."

Ed hangs his head in concession. It's true. He can't argue this point.

So, I go back to work writing obituaries. I make up all the ones I had missed in a day and even stay late at the office to do it, which is a first for me. As a rule, I *never* stay late at the office. I'm back in the business of toasting the dead. I pay tribute to the lives they lead and the love they shared, which is not unlike my "other" job, but it's beginning to not feel right anymore, like a pair of jeans that are beginning to get a little snug around the waistline. There is a part of me inside that is beginning to change.

I can't put my finger on exactly what it is, but I am feeling restless. My life and interests just don't satisfy me anymore, but I don't know why. I do have some bright spots. I joined a greater Boston shuffleboard league that plays on Thursday nights (I am the only member under age fifty-five). Me and Mom and Uncle Hor started playing Scrabble on Sunday nights (I am undefeated so far) and I started getting into my photography. I started walking around Boston on random afternoons, snapping shots of Old North Church, The Statehouse, the swan boats and Copley Square. I would walk through the South End and take pictures of charming walk-ups and elegant brownstones. I shot the Citgo sign from Beacon Street and the entrance of Fenway Park from Yawkee Way. I found myself at all the spots that I knew my father loved and I was able to see, for the first time, the beauty he saw and I smiled at the fact that my dad would be pleased about that. I was seeing Boston as an artist's city. But most days I just felt blah. It was like the weather was a reflection of my mood. Everyone noticed it.

"Maggie, you've been moping around for days," my mother says to me on one random Saturday. "Call Carrie and Kate and go shopping or get a pedicure or something. Spend some of the big bucks you've made toasting weddings. Why have you been in such a bad mood, anyway?"

I shrug my shoulders as I pace around the kitchen. I have too much nervous energy. I don't know what to do with myself. "This crappy weather," I say finally. To tell you the truth, I don't know why I have been in such a bad mood lately but the weather seems as good a reason as any. And besides, it's true. We are having crappy weather.

"Well, get an umbrella and go out. I can't concentrate with your pacing. I need to get these papers corrected." My mother turns her attention back to the stack of papers she has in front of her and her cup of coffee and I grab my keys (and an umbrella) and go out to find something to do to occupy my time.

I end up at Kate's apartment. There is no reason that I go to Kate's instead of Carrie's except that Kate lives closer and I'm being lazy. Bernie was putting in a Saturday at the office and I'm glad that I get some rare one-on-one time with her. That's what happens when your girlfriends start getting married. I don't even want to think about what will happen when Kate and Carrie start having kids.

"So, what's up?" Kate hands me my tea and sits down on the couch next to me. It's too early for wine.

I shrug my shoulders. It seems like my blanket response for everything these days. "Do you ever feel, I don't know, just sort of, blah?"

Kate looks at me like I am speaking a foreign language. "No," she says matter-of-factly.

I realize then what a silly comment it is to say to Kate. Kate is Kate. There's only black and white with her. She's fabulous, and lives a fabulous life, and knows she's fabulous (although not in a conceited way. I guess you have to know her to know what I mean). She works hard, usually gets what she wants, and when she doesn't, she just shrugs it off and moves on to the next thing. If she has a problem, she solves it, and that's all there is to it. Kate has no use for moping. Kate and I are actually a lot alike, but the problem is that I am in the mood for moping. I am beginning to wish I had driven the extra ten minutes to go to Carrie's instead. Carrie's more sympathetic.

I quickly try to amend my response to a more acceptable one. "It's this shitty weather," I say. The weather is also my blanket excuse for my mopey mood. Sometimes I change the wording though. In front of my girlfriends, I can swear. In front of my mother, I try not to use profanity, although I've been known to slip once or twice.

"Well, get over it. You've been in a foul mood ever since you got back. Look at you. you're in sweats! And you don't even have any makeup on!"

"It's pouring out!" I say defensively.

"And that's fine, but it's not like you, Maggie. You're always dressed to the nines and you never go out without at least mascara and lip gloss on."

I can't argue this point. It's true. I am sort of a fashion plate. I love clothes. I love looking pretty, even if I have nowhere to go, but I just don't feel like putting forth the effort lately. Besides, I had gotten used to dressing down at Shady Creek. It's sort of liberating to not get so dolled up all the time (not to mention what a time-saver it is). At least I still wear shoes outside.

"I saw Dolly in Tennessee," I say all of a sudden, and I feel a huge weight lift from my shoulders.

Kate looks at me, open-mouthed and speechless. She knows Dolly. She knows the history. "What!" she finally says.

"She was at the wedding. One of those coincidences."

83

"Well, no wonder you're in a foul mood." At least she is being more sympathetic now. "What did she say?"

I shrug my shoulders. "Nothing really. She was glad to see me. She's still living in Nashville," I pause for a minute. "She asked me not to say anything to Uncle Hor. She doesn't want him to know I saw her."

Kate gets up and goes into the kitchen, retrieving two wine glasses. "I think we need some wine for this," and she uncorks the bottle. Kate proceeds to pour two very large glasses of pinot and comes back to join me on the couch.

"You haven't said anything, have you?"

"No. I said I wouldn't—"

"Well, that's good," Kate interrupts before I can finish my thought. "No point in bringing up bad memories. Best to just let it lie."

"It's amazing how much like my mother you are," I say. "She would have said the exact same thing, word for word."

"Well, I take it as a compliment. She's a smart woman."

"I meant it as one," I say, and I finish my wine.

I leave Kate's an hour and a half and two glasses of wine later. And then I drive straight to Carrie's, where I'm sure I'll indulge in two more glasses of wine. I need a different perspective on the matter at hand, and I'm pretty sure Carrie will offer me one. I mean I heard what Kate was saying. I don't want to cause Uncle Hor any undue heartache. He had been through it over a decade ago. The last thing I want to do is to dredge it up for him all over again, but still…I can't help but wonder if maybe Uncle Hor should know. I mean, maybe I ran into Dolly for a reason. Or maybe all of these weddings I've been attending have been going to my head. Let's face it; my track record isn't great. Who was I to be offering advice about love? But being at those weddings and observing the relationships between Morty and Addy and Sam and Ella make me wonder if maybe love is worth it after all. I don't mean for me, but for some people. Maybe it's worth it for Uncle Hor.

I arrive at Carrie's and find myself sitting on her couch with yet another glass of wine.

"So, what do you think?" I ask her after I have filled her in on the scoop. "Should I tell Uncle Hor?"

Carrie is pensive for a minute, swirling around her wine and mulling over the possible outcomes of telling Uncle Hor or not telling him.

"Well, you told Dolly you wouldn't tell him…" Carrie says, thinking out loud. "And I can see your hesitation in telling Hor. You don't want to rock that boat twice."

"Exactly," I say. I am beginning to wonder why I was second-guessing myself in the first place. "But the thing is," I go on despite myself, "there was something in Dolly's eyes when she asked about him. Like she missed him."

I wait for Carrie to respond, to offer me advice or agree with me; I need her input on this (she is much better at handling these things than I am), but she just looks at me with a subtle smile. "Maggie McDonald," she finally says, "I do believe you are turning into a romantic. Your dad would be proud."

"Yeah, right," I scoff, but deep down I am beginning to wonder if maybe Carrie is right. And I do hope that my dad would be proud.

"You'll know what to do," Carrie says as she refills my wine glass, "When the time is right, you'll know what to do."

Me, my mom and Uncle Hor usually go to the Duck Wok in beautiful downtown Beaumont for the brunch special on Thanksgiving. It's the finest Chinese cuisine around (or so the sign says), but it's the weekend before Thanksgiving and my mother still hasn't made the reservation. Not that any of us needed to worry. It's not like the typical American family has their Thanksgiving dinner at the Duck Wok, or any other commercial establishment for that matter. Most typical American families eat a huge feast of turkey and gravy and mashed potatoes and squash and green beans and cranberry sauce (it's very important not to forget the cranberry sauce; it adds just the right balance of sweetness…God, I'm getting hungry) at home with extended family and apple pie for dessert. But, then again, my family is not the traditional American family. I mean, not that I'm complaining. I love my mom and Uncle Hor to pieces; I wouldn't trade them for anything, but it might be nice for once to not be so *un*traditional, especially around the holidays. I think of the tight feeling of community I had felt at Shady Creek and the way there was always a Calhoun around if you needed a favor, needed some milk or just felt lonely. I think of the fun I had had with Morty and Addy and the rest of the gang and how nice it had felt to just belong in the company of others. I want to feel that again.

I bring it up during our Sunday night Scrabble game. Mom has just earned sixty points with *jackass* on a double word score. Uncle Hor is laughing hysterically. Actually, it is pretty funny, but probably one of those things you have to be there for. Anyway, I figure she's in a good mood since she's winning.

"Mom, did you make reservations at the Duck Wok yet?" I ask nonchalantly as I land *quagmire* on a triple letter (I told you I'm good with words).

"What the hell does that mean?" Uncle Hor asks.

"It's a predicament. A quandary," I say as I record my score.

"A what-ery?" Uncle Hor asks. Evidently, he doesn't know the meaning of quandary either. Maybe it has something to do with the Q's.

"It's what I'm in now since my daughter is now winning…again!" my mother adds sarcastically. "Couldn't stand to lose for even one turn, Maggie?"

Uncle Hor just shakes his head. "You two sound like you're speaking a foreign language sometimes."

"So, have you?" I ask again. We had gotten a little off-track.

"Have I what?"

"Made reservations at the Duck Wok yet."

"Damn, I forgot. I keep meaning to but I've been preoccupied with doing first quarter grades. Why do schools do that anyway? Time holidays and report cards to occur in the exact same week. Don't they know that preparing for the holidays is a very stressful thing?" I just roll my eyes. The only preparing for the holiday that occurred in our house consisted of making a phone call.

"I'll do it tomorrow," she says. "I mean I'm sure they're not booked." My mom and Uncle Hor laugh. It's an inside joke. Of course, they wouldn't be booked.

"Well, maybe we should do something different this year," I press on cautiously, although I realize now that maybe my *quagmire* move was ill-timed because my mom is no longer winning and maybe now, she's in a bad mood. But I can't help it; I like to win.

"Like what? We always go to the Duck Wok."

"I don't know. Maybe we could cook a turkey and have it here."

"Oh, and are you going to cook the turkey?" She asks sarcastically.

"I could," I say, even though my cooking capabilities don't stretch beyond making a grilled cheese sandwich.

"Maggie, it's too much work for only three people! All that skinning and peeling and roasting and mashing and baking...what has gotten into you lately? I think you turned positively daffy down there in that trailer park, that's what I think. Hell, they probably hunt and shoot their own bird down there."

I can't say anything. They probably do. But I'm still not ready to let go of my wish for a nice, traditional Thanksgiving at home.

"Well, we could invite some other people and everyone could bring a dish. What's Denise doing for Thanksgiving?"

"She's spending it in New York with Steve's family! Where is this coming from Maggie? We are going to have Thanksgiving brunch at the Duck Wok like we always do and that's the end of it!" My mom is not yelling. She definitely is not yelling, but her voice has escalated in pitch and tone. I have pressed a nerve. My mom *never* loses her cool, but she has just lost it a little. Not a lot, but definitely a little.

"I'm going to bed," she says as she gets up from the table. "Close up the house before you come up." I let out a sigh, admitting defeat, and start picking up the game board. Uncle Hor helps.

"It was his favorite holiday," he says after a few minutes.

"What?"

"Your father. Thanksgiving was his favorite holiday," he pauses for a second, caught in a memory. "He made the best turkey stuffing you ever tasted," he says with a laugh and a smile. "What I wouldn't give for a taste of that again..." and his voice trails off.

I smile. I would have loved to taste it too.

Uncle Hor turns back to picking up O's and S's and G's and puts them in the bag. "That's why we always go to the Duck Wok on Thanksgiving. Let it go, Maggie Mae. Some things are too painful to remember." He looks at me then and I could see him remembering something that had nothing to do with my mom or dad. "Let it go," he says and we go back to picking up letter pieces in silence.

The next day it's as if nothing had happened, but I still feel bad. I come home from work and find my mom in the kitchen boiling pasta and slicing tomatoes.

"How was your day?" she asks me, like she asks me every day when I get home.

"Fine," I say as I plop down at the kitchen table.

"Anyone of notoriety die lately?"

I think for a minute. I do so many obits that they all blend together, which I feel bad about because I think when someone dies, they at least deserve the respect of being remembered, even if it's only by the obit writer. The famous ones tend to stick out, but the regular Joe Schmos don't, unless it's someone who died in some tragic accident that had been on the news. It's just one of the occupational hazards of my job.

"No," I say finally, after mulling over the names of the deceased I had written obits for that day.

My mother goes back to stirring the sauce. "Dinner will be ready in about twenty minutes. Are you hungry?"

"Starved. Where's Uncle Hor?"

"Band practice. They got a gig at the Knights of Columbus this weekend, believe it or not. At a senior citizen pancake breakfast." I laugh at the image. I can just picture Uncle Hor blowing on his harmonica, his cheeks turning red and an elderly couple getting up to dance the polka after enjoying pancakes and fruit. Actually, I think maybe I'll go. I do love pancakes.

"Did you make the reservations at the Duck Wok?" It's a peace offering; my subtle apology to my mom without having to actually say 'I'm sorry.' It's not that I am opposed to saying it, I mean, I am sorry I had made my mom feel sad and I understand now why she was. Really, I got it, but actually saying those words would mean making my mother acknowledge that something *had* happened last night, and that is something my mother *never* did. My mom likes to pretend like everything is fine and dandy all the time, even if it isn't. It's her coping mechanism, and she has done it for as long as I can remember. I can't blame her; I have adopted the same survival mechanism and most of my life it's been stuck on autopilot. I don't expect my mom to change. Problem is, I think I am beginning to.

"Yup," my mother answers me. "One o'clock."

I look at my mother as she stirs the sauce and cuts up cucumbers for the salad and I wonder if this is what she would be doing at this moment if my dad were here. I wonder if my dad would be cooking dinner and singing with Sinatra as it played on the stereo. I wonder if he and my mom would tango in the living room in a whimsical moment and end up in a tangle on the couch, laughing. I have a clear memory of my mother laughing from when I was little. I don't remember where we were or what she was wearing, but I remember her laughing. It was a pretty laugh. Soft and fluid, like the song of a bird. It was probably from when my dad was alive because I haven't heard her laugh like that since. Don't get me wrong; my mom laughs. She laughs at one of Uncle Hor's corny jokes or when she is playfully ribbing me for some silly incident, like the time I wore my shirt inside out all day and hadn't even noticed it, but I haven't heard her laugh *that* laugh since that day.

I say it before I have time to stop myself. It's like word vomit; spewing from my mouth uncontrollably. I had told myself that I was not going to tell her; there was no point. But then again, on occasion, I have a tendency to put my foot in my mouth. "I saw Dolly in Tennessee," I blurt out.

My mother stops stirring and looks up, staring me straight in the eye. "You didn't tell, Hor, did you?" It's more of a warning than a question.

I shake my head. "No, of course not."

She immediately resumes her stirring. "Well, good. No need for him to know." And that's it. No question of what Dolly was doing or how she was doing or if she seemed like she missed Uncle Hor. Nothing. To ask questions would interrupt my mom's carefully created illusion. To question would require her to break down walls that have been in place for over twenty years.

Chapter Eleven

The three of us sit at a corner table at the Duck Wok. I can tell my mother is relieved with the predictability of it. It has been a somewhat unpredictable week for her and this she is not accustomed to. We munch on the breadbasket while we wait for our food and I wonder if my mom is secretly thinking about the turkey stuffing my dad used to make. The bread is kind of stale.

"So, any more weddings booked, Maggie Mae?" Uncle Hor asks me. The question sort of surprises me. I mean toasting weddings isn't my job. It's just something that sort of fell into my lap through 'serendipitous circumstances,' as Morty would say.

"No." Even as I say it, I realize how I feel. The truth is I like toasting weddings, and no prospect of one on the horizon sort of bums me out. I think it's part of the reason I have been depressed lately. That, and the crappy weather.

"Well, tell us again about the wedding in Tennessee. Tell us about the guests. What kinds of characters were at this wedding?" Uncle Hor lets out a loud, raucous laugh and I can't help but smile. But Tennessee also reminds me of Dolly. I am becoming less and less sure of how to dance around this topic. It hits me all of a sudden. I look around at where I am and what I am doing. I look at my mom and Uncle Hor, the two people I love most in the world, and I come to the conclusion that this is not the life that Uncle Hor would have chosen for himself if circumstances had been different. It makes me sad really, an elderly gent sitting in a Chinese restaurant on Thanksgiving with his niece and his great-niece. Not that Uncle Hor doesn't love us; I know that he does, but he deserves more than this.

"Well, it's funny you should ask." My mother stops chewing her egg roll and looks straight at me with a *don't you dare* look in her eye. She knows what is coming. I clear my throat, anticipating the moment that is about to change Uncle Hor's life, for better or for worse. But whatever the outcome, I have to give it to him. I have to give him this chance. I take one, last deep breath and let it out, "I saw Dolly at the wedding."

There are few things on this Earth that can make me cry. The slow, drawn-out roll of a cello. A single, lonesome strum of a guitar. A beautiful waltz. Seeing my uncle crumble like a deck of cards.

The rain continues to patter softly against the window outside but inside it feels like the world has stopped. No one says anything for what seems like years although it is really only a few seconds. Uncle Hor turns dead white and instinctively grabs the edge of the table to keep him from falling over from the shock of hearing Dolly's name. He looks so fragile in this moment, like a delicate figurine that had just been cracked, and I am reminded again of just how cruel love can be.

"She asked how you were," I add in a frenzy. I am desperate to ease the awkwardness in the room. "She wanted to know how you are..."

Uncle Hor puts his hand up and instantly I stop talking. He wants to stop the hurt. My mother is afraid to look up. She just looks down at her plate and chews slowly so she doesn't have to say anything. Everyone just wants the moment to end.

Uncle Hor gets up. He stands up slowly, takes the napkin from his lap and throws it on the table. The rain continues to pound the sidewalk outside but somehow it seems like a fitting backdrop to the drama that is unfolding inside. To Uncle Hor, I imagine, it seems like a welcome relief. He walks right out into it, and continues down the street.

The car ride home seems to take hours. My mother drives carefully and methodically, but with an aggression I am unfamiliar with. Every turn is taken with precision but also with overzealous speed. The wheels squeak at every corner and I seriously wonder if my mother is trying to kill me. Neither of us speaks, but I know what my mother is thinking. I am her daughter after all; it is only a matter of time before the words will be unfurled like fireworks.

We enter the house and my mother throws the keys down on the kitchen counter.

"What the hell were you thinking!" she spews the words at me like a rattlesnake releasing its venom. Her tone makes me wince.

"I thought he had a right to know." It is the only defense I have to offer, but I believe it. I am not sorry I had told him.

"Oh, you had to tell him! You had to tell him! Because you know what it's like to have your heart ripped from your chest, right, Maggie? You know what that feels like!"

I don't say anything. The truth is, I don't know what that feels like. I have just seen the repercussions it has caused for the people I love.

"The truth is, you've never had your heart broken, Maggie," my mother goes on. "And the truth is, I hope you never know what that feels like. I'm glad you're the one who ended it with Jack. I'm glad you're the one who broke a heart instead of having yours broken. Because you don't know what it feels like. You don't know how much it hurts."

My mother looks at me and, for a minute, I think I am looking at her past self, the self that I had been too young to remember. The self that had suffered through great heartache. I have never seen her so vulnerable. She turns and heads upstairs and I am left contemplating how things could change in an instant, and if it all was really worth it. I am left wondering, in the dark of the kitchen, if love is really worth it.

We find a note on the kitchen table the next morning.

Dear Lila and Maggie,

I have gone on a road trip of sorts...just don't quite know where I'll end up. I don't know how long I'll be...just have some things in my head that I need to sort out. I will call when I get to where I'm going but, as I said before, I'm not quite sure where that is at the moment, so don't expect to hear from me too soon. I am not taking my cell phone; I need some peace and quiet to think, besides, I still don't know how to retrieve voice messages so what's the point? Please don't worry about me. I will be in contact soon. I love you both.

Uncle Hor

My mother looks at me and, without saying a word, gathers her things and leaves for work. I become aware of unpleasant sensations shooting through my body. My mouth is dry and my throat feels like a swollen balloon. My stomach feels like it has dropped to my knees. I am not accustomed to feeling so out of sorts, and I don't like it one bit.

I reflect on the events of the previous day and decide, unequivocally, that love is definitely not worth it. It's not worth Uncle Hor leaving on some random road trip without his cell phone, it's not worth my mother not speaking to me and it's not worth having unpleasant sensations zinging all throughout my body. No, I decide, love is definitely not worth it.

Chapter Twelve

We didn't hear anything from Uncle Hor for two weeks, but I know where he is. There is no doubt in my mind that he is in Nashville. There are still questions he needs answers to. Although I have no doubt about where he is, I have no idea how things are faring for him. Either Dolly would see him, jump for joy and throw her arms around him, or she would try to let him down as gently as she could for the second time in his life. I honestly don't know which scenario would be better. I guess I am hoping for the first one, which means, I guess, I am a romantic after all.

Things at home resume to normal during this time. Well, not really, but sort of. My mother and I exchange pleasantries and make small talk. She asks me how my day was, and I say fine, and I ask her how her day was and she says fine, and that's about it. In one way, it's comforting. My mom always acts like nothing is wrong, even when things are terribly wrong, so in that sense, she is acting normal. But on the other hand, even my mother can't deny the awkwardness and the emptiness in the house. It looms over us and waits in vain to be recognized.

I find some bright spots in these tortuous weeks. My shuffleboard team has just made it to the semi-finals (I am lead scorer) and I got an email from Morty and Addy. They had just returned from a delayed honeymoon in Disneyworld, of all places, where Morty proudly reported that he had gone on Space Mountain five times in a row.

It was a record, seemingly, for senior citizens. He was awarded his own set of Mickey Mouse ears by Goofy and Donald to mark the occasion. And it had all started with a bet he had made with a ten-year-old he met in line. I smile at the thought. It was one hell of a bet, and I wasn't a bit surprised to hear of it. I expected nothing less from Morty.

Come down and visit us when you can, Maggie, Morty wrote. *The weather is beautiful down here and we miss you. A lot has happened for us since the wedding—all good things—and we can't help but think that it is all because of you. You are our own lucky charm.* I cry, despite myself, when I read that. I haven't cried in years either, but I am so grateful to hear those words. It's comforting to know that I have done some good for someone, because I seem to be making nothing but a mess for my own family.

I write a quick reply and think that maybe I will go down and see them for a long weekend. And then I check flights on the Internet to see if there is anything available for this weekend. Warm weather and friendly faces are very enticing to me at the moment, but I know that now was not the right time. I am still waiting for Uncle Hor to come home.

Hearing from Morty and Addy stirs up a lot of stuff inside me. I realize that I am just as bummed out because of not having any more wedding gigs on the horizon as I am about Uncle Hor. I had fallen in love with toasting weddings, despite myself. Even though I don't want (another) wedding of my own, I realize I enjoy watching people fall in love. Well, I guess they're already in love by the time I get to them, I mean, that is the whole point of a wedding, right? But I guess what I mean is, I like witnessing the journey of it. I like watching the chemistry between two people unfold. I love catching a moment of grace in an unanticipated moment. I love observing the moments of delicate sweetness in a relationship. And I like to think my toasts help celebrate that. I like to think that I do some good. Maybe it's the part of my dad in me that is being awakened.

But it's no use. I have not had one offer, not even a glimmer of interest, at Sam and Ella's wedding. My mind races back, trying to remember any of the eccentric guests I met who could be a prospective client. Then I remind myself to be realistic. All of the guests at the wedding had been eccentric, and most of them had been Calhouns. I had met Dolly's friend Randy, the cowboy from Wyoming, but Dolly said he had just had his heart broken, so he definitely wouldn't be in the market for a wedding toaster. It's time to accept my fate; my reuse as the wedding toaster is over. At least now I can get a new black dress. I was getting a little sick of wearing the same one all the time.

My mother comes home the next day with, of all things, a Christmas tree in tow. I haven't even realized that Christmas is only a week away. I haven't even started my shopping yet. "Is that real?" I ask, as my mother tries in vain to push and pull it through the front door.

"Yes, it's real. And you could at least help me get it in." I put down my cup of tea and pick up the head and pull as my mother pushes from the rear. This technique gets the tree in, but it also sends me, my mother and the tree sprawling onto the floor in a tangled heap.

"It's a good thing you don't teach physics, Mom." I roll the tree off of me and spit pine needles out of my mouth.

"Very funny." She rolls over and tries to find her way out from under the sprawling branches. "I'm too old for this shit," she says, out of breath.

"Why did you get a real one this year? We always opt for a fake."

"Believe me, now I wish I had gotten a fake. I just thought it would be a nice change is all. Do you have plans tonight?"

I shake my head. "Nope."

"Well, how about we put this sucker up and have an old-fashioned tree-trimming party."

"Sounds good. Just let me go change. I think I have pine needles in every open crevice in my body imaginable." With that, we both burst out laughing. The kind of belly aching laughter that makes you bend over and hold your side and no sound comes out of your mouth. It was like the ice had been broken, and I knew that things between me and my mom would be okay.

We order pizza and drink wine and trim the tree with lights and tinsel and ornaments I had made in the second grade. We get the stepladder out and my mom puts the star on top. Even though neither one of us says anything about it, I know why my mom has gotten a real tree this year. We had gotten a postcard from Uncle Hor, a week ago, from Little Rock.

Just enjoying an extended road trip. Hope to be home by Christmas. Miss you both.

I had immediately consulted a map of the US and, as my instincts had predicted, Arkansas was indeed in the neighborhood of Tennessee. I couldn't tell from the tone of the postcard how Uncle Hor was, emotionally, which is unusual because Uncle Hor wears his heart on his sleeve, but at any rate, we know he is coming home. The real tree is a way of marking the occasion. Uncle Hor will love it. Part of me is sad that he isn't here tonight to help us trim it. This type of thing is right up his alley. Uncle Hor is hokey that way.

I go out the next day to do my shopping. I need a diversion. Although things are better with my mom, I still have a lot weighing on my mind. I'm worried about Uncle Hor, I am feeling unsatisfied at work and for some reason, I have been thinking about Jack a lot, lately. I don't know why; maybe it's because it's the holidays. Anyway, I was quite proud of myself that I was getting it done so early, although by some people's standards, I'm sure it would be considered late. Carrie usually has all of hers done by Thanksgiving, and Kate has hers done by Labor Day for Christ's sakes. "You can't beat the end of summer sales," she always says proudly. "I bet I've saved over 500 bucks." But I've never been one of those people. Usually, I do it all Christmas Eve day. I mean it's not like I have tons of people to shop for. I always buy for my mom and Uncle Hor of course, and Carrie and Kate, but other than that, there is no one on my list. I've never been one of those people to buy things for my co-workers. I mean, who really wants a bar of hand soap or a box of chocolates? By not buying my co-workers chocolates, I'm helping them to stick to their New Year's resolutions, which they'll make exactly one week later, to lose that extra ten pounds. I'm giving them the gift of being free of temptation. That's the way I justify it to myself, anyway.

Of course, I did buy for Jack when we were together. One year I got him a beautiful, cashmere sweater from Banana Republic, and a great smelling aftershave that still makes me get a low-down tickle when I think of the way it smelled, but even then, it was more for me than for Jack. Jack was never one to care about what he wore or how he smelled. He was a real man's man who was happiest using power tools in his scruffy jeans and a sweatshirt. He always said the best smell was the smell of saw dust and clean skin. But he wore that aftershave every day because he knew I liked it. My eyes well up at the revelation. That was definitely a moment of delicate sweetness in our relationship.

A few days later, I get a card in the mail from a P.O. box number in Tennessee. I rip it open and find a Christmas card from Sam and Ella inside, along with a newspaper clipping.

Maggie,

We just wanted to thank you for the beautiful picture. And Mutt thanks you, too. He sure does love chasing tennis balls thrown by that contraption.

Sam had written it. It was definitely a man's handwriting; besides, I know this sounds mean, but I'm not really sure if Ella knows how to write. I had sent them a framed picture from the wedding, along with the Fetch It, for Mutt. My shopping trip, the other day, had put me in a generous mood.

And even more than that, we want to thank you for getting our family back together. The cat's out of the bag, Maggie McDonald! I knew you were no photographer when you forgot to bring your camera with you half the time, or took pictures with the lens cap still on! But judging from the picture you sent us, and the ones that ran in the paper, I must say that you've developed into a mighty fine one. Anyway, it seems as though Huey was runnin' low on buyers for his homegrown herbal specialty (I laugh. I know exactly what he's talking about). *He overheard you one night talkin' to some shady character you were conversin' with in the shadows.*

A light bulb goes off in my head. I remember that night. Sal/Hal had thrown rocks at the window of the trailer to get my attention. We had met outside in the bushes to settle the photograph debt, so to speak.

Anyway, money talks, and Huey thought nothin' about sellin' you out (or my dad) to the local news reporter and hence, you are now officially known as the professional wedding toaster and Huey is quite a bit richer, as a result. But it's all good. It got me and my dad reconciled. I figure anyone who goes to that much trouble for his son's wedding is worth forgiving. He is actually going to come and spend Christmas with us. My dad sleeping on a pullout couch in a trailer...now that's somethin' worth seein!' Hopefully he'll fare as well as you did. Anyway, here's the newspaper clipping. Thought you might be interested in seein' it. Keep in mind, though, that it's only a local paper...I don't think the rest of the country is aware of your newfound celebrity status, but don't tell Ella that. She's convinced that you'll be movin' out to Hollywood and that they'll make a movie out of this whole thing. Anyway, just wanted to say Merry Christmas, Maggie, and thanks for everything. Come down and see us soon. You are always welcome here.

Regards,
Sam Cartwright

I am officially outed. I am now known as a professional wedding toaster (at least to the greater Knoxville area of Tennessee). I unfold the newspaper clipping. I am curious to see what the greater Knoxville area thinks of me.

Wedding Toaster Smash Hit at Cartwright Wedding

(Well, I certainly like the headline).

November 7th—Sam Cartwright and Ella Calhoun were married on Saturday at Shady Creek Trailer Park in a modest ceremony in front of friends, family and invited guests. One in particular guest, Maggie McDonald of Boston, was hired by Cruise Cartwright of Charleston, tobacco tycoon and father of the groom, as a wedding gift for the couple. McDonald, 28, is a professional wedding toaster who first met Cartwright at a Florida wedding in Sarasota this September where she had been commissioned to give a toast. The elder Cartwright hired McDonald for his son's wedding although he wished for his participation in the matter to remain unknown.

McDonald was hired under the pretense of being a photographer for the Tennessee Tribune but records confirm that she does not now, nor has she ever, worked for The Tribune.

(No shit).

Sources say that McDonald was paid $5,000, plus expenses, to give her custom toast and all evidence indicates that she is worth every penny. Guests raved about the toast, and the newlywed couple confirms that they were "truly touched" by the words McDonald spoke.

"She truly captured the essence of their relationship," Earl Calhoun, father of the bride, says. The secret to McDonald's success is keen observation of the interactions between the couple. She reportedly stayed with Cartwright and Calhoun the week before the wedding, something she insists on with all her clients, in order to help her compose her customized toast.

Turn to page 12 to read the toast McDonald gave.

A million thoughts race through my head after I finish reading the article, the first one being; how did they get a copy of my actual toast since I don't even write my toasts down. I suddenly remember seeing Huey at the wedding, carrying a tape recorder. I have to hand it to him; he is a shrewd little man, even when he is stoned. Still, it is a pretty complimentary article. No harm seems to come of it, it even got Sam and Cruise reunited. Greater Knoxville seems to approve of me. I keep my perspective, though. It's just a local article. I don't expect anything to come of it.

My first order of business the next day is clearing things up with Ed. He calls me into his office and I enter with a little swing in my hips and practice a few hair flips on the way. I think I am getting my Christmas bonus. As much as a moron Ed can be at times, he always gives us a generous Christmas bonus. The least I can do is to let him enjoy giving it to me.

I enter his office and immediately realize that Ed has other pressing matters to settle with me, other than a superfluous cash flow.

He sits at his desk, his brow furrowed and his face red. "Mind telling me what the hell this is?" he holds up the *Tennessee Tribune*.

I let out a little girlish giggle. "A paper," I say sheepishly. Ed is having none of it.

"Cut the crap, Maggie," and he throws the paper down on his desk. "I'm not playing your games." I have never seen Ed so angry. I am certain hair flips will not work in this predicament.

"Got a friend down at *The Tribune*," Ed says as he gets up from his desk and starts pacing.

Oops.

"You shoulda known better, Maggie. Everyone's connected in this business."

The handkerchief comes out at this point and Ed starts to mop his brow fervently. Needless to say, things are not faring well for me.

"Moonlighting as a professional wedding toaster," Ed goes on. "And on company time, too."

"C'mon, Ed. It was just a fluke. It sort of just fell into my lap, honestly. It's not like I jet around the country toasting weddings on a regular basis."

"Well, maybe it can be your new career. It seems like you get paid a pretty penny for it. You're fired, Maggie."

I stand there with my mouth open.

"You heard me, Maggie," his tone is a little softer. "I'm done giving you second chances." He holds up the paper and looks at me. "I won't have you making a mockery of me, or my publication. I mean you coulda at least let

The Hub run the story." I turn to leave. It is clearly evident that I will not be getting my Christmas bonus.

By the time my mother gets home I am on my third glass of wine. I have Harry Connick, Jr.'s Christmas CD on and am singing along with him to *Silver Bells*.

"Uh-oh," she says, and she sits down next to me on the couch. "This is not a good sign. What happened?"

"Got fired today." I still can't believe the words even though they come from my mouth.

My mother can't hide the surprise from her voice. "Why?"

I hand her the article. I don't have the energy to talk. I had explained the whole thing to Carrie and Kate via a conference call earlier. I don't feel like going through the whole thing again.

My mother reads the article. She's a smart lady. She doesn't need me to explain. She pats my knee sympathetically and I am thankful for her reserve of judgment. "Well, honey, it's an opportunity for you to do something new. To tell you the truth, I never like you getting enmeshed in the details of dead people. It's morbid. You have so much living to do." She tops off my glass of wine and pours herself one. "Here's to new beginnings in the new year." We clink our glasses and get drunk together while Harry Connick Jr. sings Christmas carols in the background. My mom is the best.

Chapter Thirteen

I get up at my usual time the next morning, but then remember I no longer have a job to go to, and I roll back over and put my head under the covers. At least I can enjoy sleeping in. But then I remember it's Christmas Eve and that, in actuality, I don't have to go to work today anyway. This takes a little of the fun of sleeping in away.

I have just dozed off into a comfortable half-sleep state, warm and cozy under the covers, when I hear the doorbell ring incessantly downstairs. I wait a minute, hoping my mom will go down and answer it but it keeps on ringing after the one-minute wait time. My mom probably has a hangover. Come to think of it, I have a hangover; I'm just not awake enough to realize it yet. We had drunk a lot of wine. And anyway, who the hell rings the doorbell incessantly at 7:00 am on Christmas Eve?

"Jesus Christ," I mutter as I throw the covers off of me and thrust my feet into my slippers next to my bed.

"I'm coming," I yell as I scurry down the stairs. "Hold your horses."

I open the door; prepared to give whoever is standing there an earful. My jaw drops when I see who it is. Standing in front of me, with sunburned noses and smiles on their faces are Uncle Hor and Dolly.

"Maggie Mae," Uncle Hor says as he wraps his arms around me. "We got hitched!"

Despite being fired, it turns out to be a pretty good Christmas. My gut instincts had been correct. Uncle Hor did venture down to Nashville (by way of Gettysburg, Harrisburg, colonial Williamsburg and a few other "burgs" but I forget which ones. Uncle Hor is a bit of a history buff) and things turn out swimmingly.

As Dolly tells it, she opened the door on December the third and saw Uncle Hor standing there with a bouquet of soggy flowers. Evidently the deluge of rain that had cursed Boston for a month had made its way to

102

Tennessee. Anyway, Dolly stood there and stamped her foot and said, "Well, it's about time Horatio. I've been waiting almost twenty years for this moment, what on God's green Earth took you so long?"

And that was that. They got married at the Nashville Town Hall the very next day and Uncle Hor swore he would never let her go again and Dolly said that if he did, she might not be as forgiving this time. I smile just thinking about it. Uncle Hor seems like a new man. He walks a little taller and his skin seems to glow and he has a star struck gleam in his eye that makes you want to know what his secret is. "I'll tell you my secret, Maggie Mae," he says to me one morning over pancakes, and he points to Dolly who walks into the kitchen in her pajamas and ratty bathrobe. It warms my heart to see Uncle Hor so happy; he deserves it. "I never knew how truly miserable I was before," he says while sitting at the kitchen table, holding Dolly's hand. I hadn't known either. I guess there is something to this thing called love. I don't mean for me, but for other people.

Their honeymoon had consisted of their drive back to Boston, with stops in Little Rock, the Great Smokey Mountains of the Carolinas and, of all places, Clearwater Retirement Home, in Sarasota, Florida. "I was so enraptured with your stories when you came back from there, Maggie," Uncle Hor tells me. "I had to see such a place for myself."

They had met the whole gang. Morty and Addy and Fern and Boris and Stella and Ida and Eugene and Clarence and Alma. In fact, Uncle Hor and Dolly had liked it so much that they had bought a unit there (seems as though Dolly had had one hit in the nineties down in Nashville that had done quite well). They were heading down right after New Year's. The thought of Uncle Hor not living with us anymore makes me sad but I know it's what's best for him. He's doing what makes him happy. After sixty-three years on God's green Earth, Uncle Hor deserved to be happy. He's even going to start up a band with Eugene and Clarence. Eugene is going to play the tambourine and Clarence is going to play the fiddle. Of course, Uncle Hor would still play his harmonica.

"Oh, I forgot," Uncle Hor says to me as he reaches into his pocket, "this is for you."

I take the envelope he hands to me and find a letter from Addy inside.

Merry Christmas Maggie!

How much has happened in the last few months (all good things!) and it is all because of you! We are thrilled that Hor and Dolly will be moving down here and the best part is we know that you will be a regular visitor (with honorary residential status!)

We will take good care of them down here but they are going to fit in just fine!

Maggie, I wanted to thank you for all you did for us. You'll be happy to know that my sons are speaking with me again and are even coming down to spend Christmas with us. I am just thrilled to see my grandsons again! After so many years of pain and heart ache, I never knew I'd be able to be so happy! But you worked your magic and somehow, I know everything is okay. In fact, things are more than okay; things are perfect! Thank you for writing those letters to my sons, Maggie. You had the courage to do what I could not.

This is a little memento from me and Morty. I hope you wear it often and think of us, and know that you are truly a special woman. You truly are out lucky charm. Merry Christmas, Maggie. Give our best to Dolly and Hor and tell them we are anxiously awaiting their arrival! And you come down soon and see us!

Love,
Addy

I shake the envelop around and a beautiful gold chain with a four-leaf clover charm on it falls delicately into my hand. I start crying despite myself. I don't know what my problem is lately; I never cry, but lately it seems as though I am a damn waterworks machine. At least they're happy tears.

Even my mom seems to be happy for Uncle Hor, but sometimes, under her laughter, I can hear a hint of sadness. I think Uncle Hor picks up on it too because he would squeeze her hand at times when we were all sitting around, talking, or he would rub her shoulders while she stood at the sink washing the dishes. Uncle Hor has been my mom's rock ever since my dad died. Not having him around is going to be hard for her.

The phone call comes the day after Christmas. "Maggie McDonald?" a feminine, sultry voice asks when I pick up the phone.

"Yes?"

"My name's Daisy Walker and I'm calling in regards to the newspaper article I saw run in *The Tennessee Tribune*."

"Yes?" I say again. I don't get why she is calling me yet. I am even more confused because she doesn't have a southern accent and I don't understand how anyone outside of Tennessee would've seen that article. Although she does sound like she has some type of accent. A western twang, perhaps. I am curious to see where this is going.

"That toast you gave was just beautiful," she says. "Brought tears to my eyes just reading it."

"Thank you," I say, still a little foggy as to the point of the phone call. "Is there something I can help you with?"

"I was wondering if you had any availability in your schedule? For February?"

"Huh?" I say. Now I am thoroughly confused.

"To toast a wedding. My wedding, as a matter of fact."

"I'm sorry, who is this again?" I ask.

"Daisy Walker. From Jackson Hole, Wyoming. I want to hire you to toast my wedding."

"Have we met?" I feel like we are speaking two different languages. I haven't the faintest clue what she is talking about.

"No," Daisy Walker says, sounding just as confused as I am. "But this is what you do, isn't it? I mean you are a professional wedding toaster."

I almost spit the coffee I'm drinking right out of my mouth. "Can I ask where you saw that article?"

"In *The Tennessee Tribune*."

"But, aren't you in Wyoming?"

Daisy laughs an easy laugh and it makes me feel better. "Oh, I see why you're confused. My fiancé was at the Cartwright wedding. I think you met him. Randy Rhodes?"

My mind races back to when I saw Dolly at the wedding. She had been with her friend, Randy. A sad, solemn-looking fellow who Dolly said was heartbroken. Well, Randy's situation seems to have improved dramatically.

"Anyway," Daisy goes on. "Randy saved the article and gave it to me. I apologize for the short notice; I know you must be booked solid. Daddy is willing to pay $10,000 if you consent to doing our wedding."

Ten thousand? How can I say no. Besides, it's not like I have a job to go to anymore. I am quite sure I will be able to fit Daisy and Randy's upcoming nuptials into my calendar.

Chapter Fourteen

A little over a month later, I am on my way to Jackson Hole, Wyoming, on a private jet, no less. Turns out, Daisy's father was Assistant Secretary of State under the last administration and a cattle rancher worth millions. Daisy didn't tell me that but Dolly did. Evidently Dolly knew quite a bit about Daisy, due to the long car ride she spent with Randy from Nashville to Knoxville. Anyway, I am just happy to be flying on a private jet. I have the whole cabin to myself well, except for the small army of security that is accompanying me. Evidently, Bruce Walker is a pretty prominent political figure. I have never heard of him but that's not saying much; I'm not very political. Anyway, it's nice to have ample leg room and not worry about some bratty kid kicking the back of my seat.

I stretch out and peek out the window at the view below me. I can't believe how easy it's been this time. No aliases or undercover work or pretending to be someone I wasn't. No more having to remember minute details that belonged to a fictional life, like which breed of dog is easiest to groom or exactly what relation you were supposed to be to people you never heard of or how to use a digital camera (although now I'm quite good at it). All I have to do for this wedding is show up. I can actually be Maggie McDonald, professional wedding toaster. It's quite liberating really, although I must admit, the undercover work was sort of fun.

The plane touches ground and careens down the runway. We come to a full stop and I think it's safe to uncross my fingers. I think one of the security guards sees me because he starts chuckling to himself. I can't help be a little resentful of this observation. I mean, really...it is a small aircraft, and we are in the middle of the mountains.

I unbuckle my seatbelt and walk down the platform to the runway. The guy who was chuckling carries my suitcase for me. I think he feels bad for laughing at me. I look at my surroundings from the ground and all I see around me are mountains. miles and miles of sleeping, white mountains. This is my first venture out west and I have never seen anything like it. It's so beautiful it almost takes my breath away. For some reason, I think of Jack. This is a place he would love.

A limousine drives right onto the runway, followed by a small fleet of SUVs with tinted windows. Although I am not yet used to flying in private jets, I am getting quite accustomed to getting picked up at airports by limousine. In fact, I am beginning to feel like a bona fide celebrity, and I like it. The chauffer gets out and opens the door for me. He is a sturdy man, probably in his mid-fifties, with peppered hair and a clean-shaven face. I slide inside and am thankful that the security guys are riding in the various SUVs. It's sort of uncomfortable to ride in a limo with people you don't know.

"Name's Tony, ma'am," the chauffer says. I wonder if maybe chauffer is not the right term because he is wearing a cowboy hat instead of the typical driver's hat, and cowboy boots. "Welcome to Jackson Hole."

I look out the window as the scenery rushes by us. Everywhere I look, I can see mountains. Flat plains also come into view at times, with what appears to be big, brown lumps, scattered among the trees. "Keep your eyes open for moose. There are often sightings in this clearing, coming up on the right."

"So that's what those brown clumps are!"

Tony just laughs a hearty laugh. "Yup," he says, still chuckling, "it's pretty clear you aint from these parts!"

"Are you from these parts?" I'm pretty sure I already know the answer. Tony just has a western air about him. The security guys do too. Besides the tell-tale signs of wearing cowboy hats and cowboy boots, and big gold belt buckles that glisten when the light catches them just right, these men possess an air of ruggedness. They're distinctly handsome, with calloused hands and weathered faces from years of working off the land, and there's a slight swagger in their walk, as if their accomplishments in mastering the land gives them a confidence in any situation. I had heard all the legends and stereotypes about the quintessential cowboy, but I realize now that they are all true. Even more astonishing than that, I realize now that cowboys actually exist. I feel like I have discovered a whole subculture that still thrives in America.

"Born and reared," Tony replies. "The farthest east I've been is South Dakota."

"Have you worked for the Walkers long?" I ask curiously. I have done my homework on the Walkers. Bruce Walker had served as Assistant Secretary of State in the last cabinet for eight years, which tells me he is a smart man, but what I also came to find out was that he is a very rich man. He's a lawyer by occupation, which is what led to his career in the political arena, but what made him rich was his cattle business. Evidently, Bruce Walker has, what could be considered, a monopoly on the Black Angus cow population in western Wyoming, and most of Idaho, too.

"I've been with the Walkers for almost thirty years. Started as a ranch-hand when I was a young stag myself. Eventually worked my way up to head cattle driver. Used to drive the herd all the way to the Rio Grande country. Took quite a fall in a rodeo 'bout fifteen years ago. Got thrown from a stallion and tore up my rotator cuff pretty good. My shoulder aint never been the same since. Sorry to say, that was the last rodeo I ever made an appearance in—sure do miss them days."

"So, is that when you became Mr. Walker's chauffer?"

Tony just laughs his hearty laugh. "We don't see too many chauffeurs in these parts, but if you mean his driver, then that would be correct. Most people would just toss you out on your ass and say 'have a nice life' once you aint no good to them anymore, but Bruce Walker kept me on. He said to me, 'now Tony, you've always done a real good job for me, always worked hard, and I reckon we can find some capacity for you to work on this funny farm I got here.' I've been his driver ever since."

"Have all of the Walkers employees been with them that long?" I ask.

"Hell, no! The Walkers have quite a high turnover rate, as a matter of speakin'."

"Why?"

"Because of Daisy. She's had quite a few indiscretions, so to speak, with various members of the staff, who are no longer members of the staff, for that precise reason. She's a little spitfire that Daisy is. Bruce even has a filly named Spitfire after Daisy. Has the same temperament too—Daisy and that horse are one in the same—hard to tame."

"So, they quit?"

"Some quit. The one's Mr. Walker didn't know about quit; the one's he did know about were fired."

"Why did the ones that quit, quit then?" I'm totally enthralled at this point. This is like a western soap opera.

"Because of Daisy. That girl just has somethin' about her. Would make the poor, ranch-hands fall in love with her and then wouldn't as so much give them the time of day. Reckon their heart was broken. Couldn't stand bein' around her if they couldn't have her. Like I said, that girl is hard to tame."

"So how did she end up with Randy?" I think of the gentle, soft-spoken man I had met at Sam and Ella's wedding. He sure didn't seem like the type that a spitfire like Daisy Walker would go for.

"Randy's had it bad for Daisy ever since they started dancin' together a year and a half ago. That's why he moved to Jackson. Moved here a year ago, from Idaho Falls. He said it was because he wanted to pursue his dancin' dreams, and that may have been part of it, but everyone knows it was because he was so smitten with Daisy. Randy always says that you gotta follow your heart. He followed his straight to The Cowboy Bar, every weekend. Would drive ninety miles every weekend just to dance with Daisy. Finally decided to move here to teach dance lessons. Left a good job too, in Idaho Falls. And that's in Idaho, by the way. Was the manager of a Walmart."

This is better than any movie I have seen recently. And I don't think there is any movie studio that could think up better stuff. I mean, who has ever heard of a cowboy that teaches dance lessons?

"Anyway," Tony continues, "Daisy had her heart broken real bad. She was mixed up with Luke Cassidy, the best rodeo rider you ever saw, but just as big a bullshitter as the bull he used to ride. They say he's a descendent of Butch Cassidy, and I'll tell ya somethin' too, I believe it. He's a mean and connivin' sonofabitch. It's in his blood. Got caught throwin' rides."

"Throwing rides?" I ask. Apparently, there is a whole western lingo I am not fluent in.

"Took bets against himself in rodeos. Would get bucked on purpose and then make twice the winnings in bets on the side. Rumor has it he also was carryin' on with one of the barrel racers in the rodeo. Pretty little thing, but dumb as a doorknob. Luke figured he could get away with it."

"And Daisy found out about it?"

"Oh, she found out about it. It didn't much matter to her though. You know what they say about love, Ms. McDonald: Can make you blind. No, it was Mr. Walker that had somethin' to say about it. He told Luke Cassidy that if he ever came within fifty feet of his daughter again, he wouldn't hesitate to chase him across county lines, with a shotgun in hand. Bruce would do it too. No one messes with Daisy."

"But Randy passes the test? Mr. Walker approves of him?"

"Oh, sure. Not at first, though. I'm not sure there's any man who is good enough for Daisy in Bruce Walker's eyes—that's his little girl. But Bruce had him checked out by his sources. Background checks and so forth. Randy Rhodes doesn't have so much as a speeding ticket on his record. He asked me what I thought of Randy and I told him I didn't know of a more upstanding guy in all of the Tetons."

Tony continues on, after taking a quick breath (he is talking quite a bit). "Never married myself, always considered myself married to the land, but the Walkers are like family to me. Daisy is like my daughter. I sure am happy how everything turned out for her and Randy. Randy's a nice guy; I was rootin' for him all along, but you know what love is like, Ms. McDonald, sometimes you gotta come to your own senses, without other people tellin' you what you should and shouldn't do. I'm just glad Daisy came to her's."

"When did they decide to get married?" I ask. At the Cartwright wedding in November, Randy had been heartbroken. It was only February now—things seem to have happened quickly.

"Right around New Year's," Tony answers. "Things had just come to a head with Luke. Randy and Daisy were dancin' at the Cowboy Bar one night—to see them dance is downright electrifying—people have always said it, but it was my first particular time at any rate. Anyway, they'd always had this chemistry when they danced. I think Randy had always felt it, always known, come to think of it. I think Daisy did too, but she wasn't quite ready to give up her ways. She's got the spirit of the west in her, that one, probably always will, but their chemistry on the dance floor is undeniable."

At this point, I am beginning to realize that Tony went off topic a lot—we actually have a lot in common—but I am anxious to cut to the chase.

"So, he proposed that night?"

"*She* proposed," Tony corrects.

"What!"

"Witnessed it myself. They were right in the middle of a two-step, had that hungry look in their eye, caught up in the moment, and Daisy says to Randy, right in the middle of a turn, 'Randy Rhodes, don't you think it's about time you and I got hitched?' Randy just stopped dead in his tracks and said, 'Well, yes ma'am, I think it is.' The whole place started whoopin' and yellin' and screamin' and the rest, as they say, is history. As matter of fact, I think Daisy called you the very next day."

"Wow," I say, "that's quite a story." I have never heard a story like it before, but I guess that's the thing about love stories; everyone has their own. It's what I try to celebrate in my toasts, but I'm beginning to have my doubts about Daisy Walker. To say that she's impulsive is the understatement of the year, and I haven't even met her yet. I decide to avoid making any hasty judgments until I have witnessed the two of them together—that's what I do after all—I celebrate people's stories—and Randy and Daisy certainly had a humdinger of one. At least I know I have good material for my toast. I am the wedding toaster after all; not the marriage therapist, although something told me that Randy and Daisy might need one down the road.

"What does Mrs. Walker think of all of this?" Tony had told me Bruce Walker's position on the matter, but he hadn't said anything about Daisy's mother.

"There is no Mrs. Walker. Kitty Walker died in childbirth. That was a terrible day," Tony adds with a shudder. "Poor Bruce—he said that he didn't know it was possible to feel so much joy and so much sorrow at the same time. He named Daisy; you know. Kitty died holding her. Told Bruce to pick out a special name, and then she took her last breath. Bruce named her Daisy on account of that was Kitty's favorite flower. She was one helluva woman. Daisy looks just like her, too."

"Is Daisy like her?" I ask.

"Just in looks. Couldn't be more opposite in their ways. Kitty was a gentle soul. Domestic, tamed. She loved bein' on the homestead—took care of everyone. Daisy's more like her daddy—stubborn, impetuous—she's a true force of nature, Daisy is. But I like to think that somewhere deep inside her, a little piece of her mom is buried. Maybe that's why she's gettin' married now and settlin' down. Maybe the piece that's her mom is comin' alive."

I think of my dad, and I know exactly what Tony means. I often wonder if that is why I toast weddings; if it is really my dad speaking silently to me, and trying to awaken the part of me that is him. I'm quiet for the rest of the ride. I still need to process all of the information Tony had shared with me. More than anything, one thought keeps replaying in my head; Daisy and me are a lot alike. It scares me a little bit, to tell you the truth—Daisy sounds downright unstable to me—but one thing is for sure; I'm very anxious to meet her.

Chapter Fifteen

We pull up to the biggest log house I have ever seen. Acres and acres of land stretch out in the back, and everywhere you look, all you can see are mountains. I can't help but think how much nicer it will be to stay here than in a trailer. Tony opens the door for me and retrieves my bags from the trunk. "Welcome to the homestead," he says with a smile. He knows that I'm impressed.

We enter the foyer and I just stand there; both, because I am a little bit intimidated by my surroundings, and also because I'm not quite sure what I'm supposed to do. The security entourage has arrived and men in cowboy hats and boots are bustling by, talking into handheld devices and checking rooms for what I assume to be any unwanted visitors. I know it's just standard protocol, but it still freaks me out a little.

I stay in the foyer and wait. The security guys have disappeared into various wings of the house and it's quieter now, but it's still intimidating. Various heads of various animals mounted on walls surround me, and I can't help but wonder if Bruce or Daisy Walker is responsible for their present state of demise. I don't know if you've ever had this experience, but it's sort of disconcerting to have a moose head stare at you for a prolonged period of time. It feels like hours that I am standing in the foyer alone, surrounded by the heads of dead animals, but finally Tony comes back down the stairs with a man whom I have no doubt is Bruce Walker. He sticks his hand out to me while he puffs away on a fat cigar and offers me a firm, confident handshake.

"Howdy, ma'am. Bruce Walker. Welcome to the funny farm."

"Maggie McDonald. It's nice to meet you." I try to pry my hand from his grasp. He's crushing my fingers.

Bruce Walker has a commanding presence. He seems a lot taller than he actually is and I realize it's because of the way he carries himself. He has that same western air about him that the other men have—a rugged sort of bravado—but Bruce Walker also has a striking confidence about him. His footsteps echo when he walks, as if every ounce of him demands respect, and I notice that although all the men here wear cowboy boots, Bruce Walker's have spurs on them. I wonder if that's symbolic of his occupational status or just plain egocentric. At any rate, when you're in Bruce Walker's presence, you can't help but quake a little in your own boots. He just has that stature.

"Well, I sure am lookin' forward to your toast at Daisy's weddin', Ms. McDonald. After all, at ten thousand bucks a pop, it dang well better be good!"

Bruce Walker laughs a hearty laugh, which I am thoroughly grateful for because it masks the audible gulp that I let escape upon hearing his expectations of me. I take a quick glance around at the animal heads surrounding me, and wonder if my head might be up there too, if my toast isn't up to par.

"No, seriously, Ms. McDonald, we're all happy to have you come stay with us here at the homestead. I read your toast in *The Tribune* and it was a mighty fine tribute. I'm just glad you were able to fit my Daisy into your schedule."

"Thank you. I'm happy to be here," although, at this point, I'm not so sure I am.

Bruce Walker turns to Tony then. "Why don't you take Ms. McDonald into town and drop her at The Cowboy Bar? Randy's gonna meet her there after his three o'clock and take her over to meet Daisy."

"Right away, boss," Tony says, and he escorts me back to the limo.

"See you at dinner, Ms. McDonald," Bruce Walker calls out after me.

I can hardly wait.

The Cowboy Bar certainly lives up to its name. I have no trouble finding it, as a neon marquee with a bucking bronco and a cowboy hat mark the entrance. Inside it was dark and smoky, and bar stools designed as saddles lined the bar. There are some pool tables in the center, and a dance floor up front, with a really bad country song playing from the jukebox. There are a few cowboys present, shooting pool and smoking cigarettes, but overall, it's pretty vacant. It's only 4:00 on a Tuesday.

I plop down on a saddle at the bar and order a rum and coke. Usually, I'd just stick to a beer or a glass of wine, but I feel like I need something a little stronger today. I think I'm still on edge from all of those dead animal heads. I don't know why, but I'm also a little nervous about meeting Daisy. I mean I've never met the girl, and she had sounded perfectly lovely when I spoke to her on the phone, but let's face it, Tony had made her sound like a psycho. Couple that with Bruce Walker's not-so-subtle expectations of my toast, and the multiple animal heads, (and I'm still not sure how they end up that way, exactly) and you have a recipe for disaster. I quickly gulp down my rum and coke and order another one. I am contemplating ordering a third when Randy arrives. It's a good thing too; I am starting to feel a little tipsy.

"Maggie!" he says with a big smile. He leans over and gives me a welcoming hug. I can't believe it's the same man I had met in Tennessee just a few months earlier.

I hug him back. "And congratulations! Seems like things have improved drastically for you since the last time I saw you."

"Indeed, they have, Maggie. Indeed, they have!"

Randy can't keep the grin off his face. I must admit it's sort of weird standing there, hugging him in the middle of The Cowboy Bar. I mean, I have only met Randy briefly at the wedding, and our conversation did not extend pass, 'Hi, how are you, it's nice to meet you,' and now here we are, acting like long-lost best friends. No matter I guess; I am just happy to be toasting his wedding and getting paid $10,000 bucks. I can afford to give a little love myself for that price. "Daisy is just dyin' to meet you. I told her we would go over to the studio and see her."

"The dance studio?"

"Daisy's art studio. She has a small studio in town. A lot of the galleries in town carry her work. She's real good." The truth is I'm still a little nervous about meeting Daisy, but I am glad to be leaving the bar; I'm really getting sick of the music. The rum and cokes have loosened me up a little, at least.

The studio is just a few streets over. We walk up the stairs and Randy knocks on the door. "Come in," a sultry, female voice calls from the other side. Randy opens the door and inside is Daisy Walker sitting, in front of an easel and concentrating intently on the painting on it. She's an attractive woman in her mid-thirties, with brownish gold hair, cut in a bob style. She has big brown eyes and the longest eyelashes I have ever seen. She's a casual gal, wearing jeans and a basic, white button-down shirt. My eyes look down to inspect the footwear, and yup, she's wearing cowboy boots. sans the spurs, however. At any rate, Daisy Walker is quite a dish. I can see how descendants of famous outlaws would want to do her.

"Hey, Sassy." Randy goes over and plants a kiss on the top of Daisy's head.

"Hey." She continues to brush strokes across the canvas, without so much as looking up. Randy either doesn't mind or he doesn't notice. He just rubs her back for a minute and looks at her like she is the only thing in the world. In fact, I think he even forgets that I'm here.

"Hi," I say, after an awkward silence. "I'm Maggie McDonald. It's nice to finally meet you."

Daisy looks up. "Oh, where are my manners." She stands up and extends her hand to me. "Daisy Walker. I'm sorry, I just get so caught up in my painting sometimes, it's like I just zone out and don't notice a thing that's goin' on around me."

"I know the feeling," I say, and actually I do. Sometimes, when I'm caught up in writing an obit or preparing my toasts, it's like I become entranced. One time, the fire alarm went off at work when I was in the middle of writing an obit and I didn't even hear it. It took Ed yelling at me with a megaphone, through an open window, to shake me out of my reverie and get me out of the building. There actually had been a fire, a small one, but still. I guess painting has the effect on Daisy that words have on me.

"Looks great, baby," Randy says, as he studies the half-finished painting and continues rubbing Daisy's back.

"Oh, hush. It is not. You'll have to excuse Randy." Daisy turns her attention towards me. "He don't know a thing about art."

"Well, I know that you're the best masterpiece that was ever created," Randy says, and he plants another kiss on top of her head.

"Randy!" Daisy tries to squirm out of his hold. "You're embarrassing me!"

I'm beginning to feel a little embarrassed myself, I mean, not for myself, but you know that terrible feeling when you actually feel embarrassed for someone else? I'm beginning to feel that way for Randy. He's totally making a fool of himself, fawning all over Daisy, and she's having none of it. The worst part is, I don't even think Randy notices. Still, I am getting good research for my toast. All of my observations of my couples, both together and separate, tell me the story of their relationship, and I have a feeling, that this moment happening right now, was giving me a key insight into Daisy and Randy's.

I try to divert my focus by looking around at Daisy's paintings. They are lined up all over the room, leaning against the wall in various sizes and colors. They certainly all have a western motif running through them, and yet, they are all distinctly different. There are scenes of mountains and horses, ranch-hands and Indians, wolves and buffaloes, but what I notice most about Daisy's paintings is the intensity of the expressions in her work. You can see the fear and fierceness in the wolves' eyes, the loyalty in the expression of the horse, the exhaustion in the lines of the ranch-hand and the spirit of grief in the eyes of the Indian chief. Daisy poured her passion into her paintings. My guess is, based on what I've heard and seen of her so far, is that this is the one area of her life she takes seriously.

"Your paintings are beautiful," I tell her.

"Well, I do aim to please."

"We better get goin', Sass," Randy says, as he continues to rub her back. "Your daddy is expectin' us all for dinner."

"Oh, alright." Daisy starts putting her paints and easel away, and I swear I hear the slightest trace of disappointment in her voice when she concedes that it's time to go.

We make our way downstairs where Tony is already waiting with the limo outside.

"So, how exactly do you go about this, Maggie?" Daisy asks me once we are all settled in the limo. "How do you know what to say in your toast about me and Randy?"

"Well, I just spend time with you and Randy. See how you interact with each other, and make observations about you as a couple."

Daisy makes a face. "Gee, it doesn't sound that romantic, when you put it that way." I have to agree. It really doesn't.

"Well, all I know is that your finished product never disappoints," Randy adds. "People can't stop talkin' about that toast you gave in Tennessee."

"Well, we all have our talents, I guess," I say. I really don't know what else to say.

"You'll see, Sass, she's gonna give us a mighty fine toast," and he squeezes Daisy's knee. He really can't keep his hands off of her. I swear, in the time I have spent with them so far, Randy hasn't gone longer than five

118

minutes without making some form of bodily contact with her. I do have to admit though; it's kind of sweet. Randy really does adore her. I just hope Daisy feels the same way.

"Oh, I have no doubt," Daisy says. "Do you have any questions for us now?"

"Questions?" I don't know what Daisy means. Actually, I have about a million questions, starting with why she had proposed to Randy when she acted like she didn't even really like him, but somehow, I think that would be inappropriate, so I bite my tongue.

"You know, any questions you might have for Randy and/or me—concerning our relationship." Daisy leans back and put her hands behind her head. "You can ask us anything. Our love is an open book, so to speak."

She catches me a little bit off guard. Daisy certainly is astute. It disarms me to have her ask me, point blank, if I had questions. Well, of course I have questions! I wouldn't be able to compose a proper toast without asking questions and, more importantly, receiving answers. But my methods are somewhat different. I always get my answers—I just don't always get them by asking straightforwardly for them—and that's precisely what Daisy is challenging me to do. She is proving to be a formidable foe.

Still, the bait was left; I might as well take it. "Why does Randy call you Sassy?" I had heard him use this particular term of endearment a couple of times, not as an adjective but as a name.

"You know, I'm not really sure. I think both of us should be askin' Randy this particular question."

"It was the hair," Randy says with a dreamy effect in his voice.

"Huh?"

"You know, the day you got them streaks in your hair and got your hair cut short like that. It swings when you dance now—your hair, I mean—and when the light dances off your hair just right—it's like a river of spun gold."

Daisy just looks at Randy, like she's discovering something about him for the first time.

"Anyway, I thought to myself how both sexy and classy you are. You're both, at the exact same time, even though they're almost like opposites. So, I started callin' you Sassy because you're a perfect half of each. And wouldn't you know, I went home that night and looked up 'sassy' in Webster's Dictionary and there was the definition, right there in print; *sassy*—adjective meaning sexy and classy. And I thought I had made the word up! It was like a sign. Anyway, it was two nights later that you proposed to me."

"I never knew that," Daisy says, and then she reaches over and squeezes Randy's knee. It's the first moment of mutual tenderness I have seen them share.

We pull up to the homestead where one of the security guys is waiting outside. He walks up to meet us when the limo stops and wastes no time in opening the door and ushering us out. "Dinner's been pushed up," he tells us, "on account of Mr. Walker having an appointment later this evening." Randy and Daisy give each other knowing glances upon hearing this and Tony quietly smiles to himself. I have no idea what's going on; I'm just glad dinner has been pushed up. I'm starving.

I follow Daisy and Randy into the main foyer and down a long hallway off to the left. After a series of lefts and rights, we finally arrive at the dining room. I'm glad I'm with them because I don't think I could've found it on my own. The room is cozy and inviting. Glass paneled French doors open up to a patio at the back of the house with the most spectacular vista you've ever seen. Above the doors, there's a balcony and huge arch windows through which you can see the mountaintops peeking through. A large western scene painting decorates the log-paneled wall and I wonder if it's one of Daisy's. I'm relieved to see that there are no animal heads in here, although there is a gigantic chandelier made entirely out of elk horns and elk horn light fixtures on the wall. The elk horns don't bother me as much as the animal heads though. Actually, I sort of like them. A long wooden table sits directly in the room's center where Bruce Walker is sitting at the head.

"C'mon in," he says, and beckons us to sit down. "Sorry about the change in schedule but my ten o'clock had to bump up to nine o'clock," Bruce Walker pauses for a second. "At least now she has less of a chance of runnin' into my eleven o'clock! Ha, Ha, Ha!" Daisy and Randy give each other that knowing glance again and smile slyly. Finally, I get it. Bruce Walker is a gigolo. I wonder how I'd feel if my mother had "appointments" coming to call on her at all hours during the night.

"Maggie," Bruce says to me, pointing to the seat at the opposite end of the table. "It's okay that I call you Maggie, isn't it? Oh, of course it is," he says before I can answer. I would've said yes...but still. I sit down, thankful that I'm at the farthest point from Bruce Walker. Not only am I still slightly intimidated by him but I'm also beginning to find him somewhat obnoxious.

A member of the wait staff comes in with the breadbasket and fills our wineglasses, which I'm incredibly thankful for. "So, what'd you kids do today?" Bruce asks as he takes a large gulp of his wine. "You almost done with your new painting, Daisy?"

"Yes, Daddy. It's close to finished."

"Well, good! I'm gettin' sick of starin' at this one!" Bruce points to the painting on the wall. "Ha, Ha, Ha!"

Daisy playfully hits Bruce with her napkin. "Daddy! That's not very nice!"

"Just kiddin', sugar. You know I love your paintings."

"So now, Maggie," Bruce says, directing his attention to me. "How do you like Jackson Hole so far?"

"It's beautiful," I say, and I mean it. "You have a gorgeous spot here, sir."

"Well, thank you, Maggie. Lived here my whole life. Born and raised. Well, except for my eight-year stint in Washington, but this is where I love to be." Bruce closes his eyes and inhales deeply. "Just breathe in that mountain air. It's like a drug or somethin." Bruce takes another exaggerated breath in. "Mm, Mm. Just can't get enough of it."

The only thing I can't get enough of at the moment is food. I'm starving, and the breadbasket is now empty. I don't want to be rude but I have half a mind to ask a member of the wait staff to refill it. I mean they do in restaurants. One thing I have had enough of, however, is Bruce Walker. On top of finding him slightly intimidating and boorishly obnoxious, I'm also coming to realize that Bruce Walker is long-winded. And he's showing no sign of coming up for air.

"Yup, it sure is a special spot here," Bruce goes on. "Our own little piece of heaven and I'll tell you somethin', Maggie McDonald, you're lucky that you're not visiting as a tourist."

"Amen to that," Daisy chimes in.

"All those Californians and easterners, comin' here to use our land. For 'recreational purposes,' they claim, but the next thing you know they're forming action groups for gun control and to save the wolves. I mean can you imagine livin' on this land and not ownin' a gun? Too many damn wolves around. They think they know somethin', those hotshot tourists. And they're here in droves now, it's bein' ski season and all. Look around town next time you're in…aint half of 'em true westerners. Don't you think, Randy?"

"Well, sir, actually our economy benefits quite a great—"

"Oh, who asked you anyway? Aint no one gonna listen to some pansy-ass dancin' cowboy."

"Daddy! That's not very nice!"

"Ha, Ha! I'm just kiddin', Randy. You know I love you like a son…even if you do-si-do instead of ropin' broncos."

"Oh, I've done my share of ropin' broncos, sir. It's just I'd rather dance, I guess."

"I know you have, son. I'm just joshin' you is all."

Bruce Walker pauses to take another gulp of his wine and looks around at his company with both satisfaction and amusement twinkling in his eyes. He's enjoying this. As for me, well, it's certainly proving to be an entertaining evening, and we haven't even had the first course yet. I just don't quite know what to make of everything yet. I feel like I'm watching a sitcom on some quirky cable station, simply because there isn't anything better on.

"Speakin' of tourists," Daisy continues, "did you read about those two schoolteachers from Boston who got lost on top of Targhee?"

"I did see that," Randy answers. "They were at the top of Crazy Horse and a squall blew in. Got disoriented—couldn't tell which way was down—got lost for five hours."

"Ha!" Bruce says. "That's what I'm talkin' about. Dang tourists. Don't even research a place before they go and play on it. They don't call it Grand Foggy for nothin.' Besides, what's a little snowfall when you're skiin'? Any self-respectin' westerner knows how to handle this land and if you don't, or if you're some nitwit easterner, then you have no business bein' on the top of mountains out here."

"Hallelujah, Daddy," Daisy raises her glass, as if to toast all dimwit easterners.

"Say, Maggie," Bruce says all of a sudden. "Where did you say you were from?"

"Uh, Boston," I say meekly.

Bruce pauses for a second. "Well, at least you weren't on top of that mountain, then. Ha!"

Another member of the wait staff comes in, ready to serve the main course. I really do feel like I'm in a restaurant. "Mm, Mm," Bruce says, when the waiter puts his plate down in front of him. "Smells delicious, Garcon. If you weren't already on my payroll, I'd give you a big, fat tip right now. Ha!" The waiter looks at him, slightly annoyed. He either doesn't like being called Garcon, or just thinks that Bruce Walker is an asshole. Anyway, I'm just glad to have a plate of food in front of me. "Dig in," Bruce says, and I'm only too happy to oblige.

We all sit in silence for a minute, as we concentrate on cutting our meat. I, for one, can't wait to get a piece of it in my mouth. Finally, my steak is cut and diced. I take the first bite and almost moan out loud, it's so good. And then the silence is broken.

"Say, Daddy," Daisy says coyly, as she finishes cutting her meat, "who've you got on your plate?"

Bruce gives a knowing smile. "Seems like I got ol' Bessie here. Ha! What about you, sugar?"

Daisy smiles. "Got myself some Clover, on here!"

Daisy and Bruce brake into gales of laughter while I look at my plate, utterly horrified. It occurs to me then that I am eating a recent occupant of the ranch.

"It's just a game they play," Randy says to me, after noticing the look of utter shock on my face. "Every time they have steak for dinner, they pretend like it's one of their cows, but it aint."

"You have nothin' to worry about, Maggie," Bruce says to me, seriously. "This steak doesn't come from my ranch here."

I let out a breath of relief. "Good," I say, satisfied. Now I can enjoy my dinner.

"It comes from my ranch in Idaho! Ha!" Bruce and Daisy burst into a fresh gale of laughter, and I try not to gag on the piece of meat I'm chewing.

Randy looks around at the absurdity surrounding him, as if it's as normal as asking someone to pass the salt. "Welcome to the funny farm," he says matter-of-factly. I'm beginning to see why they call it that.

"Oh, Maggie," Bruce says between bites, "I almost forgot. I got a little somethin' for you." I'm afraid to see what it is, but Bruce leans over and opens a shopping bag that's next to his chair. "Picked this up for you in town today." And before I know what hits me, Bruce Walker retrieves a chocolate brown cowboy hat (with fringe) from the bag and throws it to me across the table, as if it's a Frisbee. Somehow, I manage to catch it, although I wish I hadn't. I mean, really; it has fringe.

"Gee, thanks, Mr. Walker," I say. I don't want to be rude.

"That'll keep you separated from the tourists. It's the mark of a true westerner. Although these..." Bruce Walker pauses for emphasis, and proceeds to put his feet up on the table. "Now these you gotta earn." He points to his brown cowboy boots, with the spurs on them, as if they're a trophy. I laugh politely. I don't know how else to react. I'm not thrilled about the cowboy hat; and I certainly don't want a pair of boots—especially boots with spurs on them. Still, I appreciate the gesture. "Yessirree," Bruce says as he continues to eat his steak, "do somethin' that really impresses me and you just might find yourself leavin' with a pair of these beauties."

I can hardly wait.

I sit in my private Jacuzzi after dinner, contemplating the events of the day. Daisy and Randy certainly have an interesting story, but I still can't put my finger on the pulse of their relationship. There had been that one moment in the car, but other than that, it almost seems like Daisy doesn't even know Randy exists. I mean, she had hardly paid any attention to him at all at the studio and during dinner, the only person Daisy had paid attention to was her father. And it's quite obvious that Randy is absolutely smitten. He just gazes at her with that starry look on his face, as though just being in her presence is enough. It is mind-boggling, to say the least, and a little disconcerting. Randy's a good guy; I don't like seeing him treated this way. Anyway, it certainly looks like I have my work cut out for me here.

Dinner had been an interesting affair. I still wasn't sure if the steak we had eaten had been a former occupant of the ranch, but it was delicious. Anyway, I may not have seen much of a dynamic between Randy and Daisy at dinner, but I certainly saw one between Daisy and her father. The apple doesn't fall very far from the tree, so to speak. It's obvious that they adore each other; Daisy is the apple of Bruce's eye and Bruce would always be the most important man to Daisy. I guess it's not unlike the relationship between me and my mom. When you suffer a loss like me and Daisy and our parents had, you hang on to whoever is left behind. And you put up walls. I can understand that, but still, I'm not completely sure that Daisy and Randy should be getting married. Randy deserves to be number one in someone's life. But what does it matter to me really? I'm just the wedding toaster.

I get out of the Jacuzzi and slip into the white bathrobe that has been left in my room for me. I really do feel like I'm staying in a luxury hotel. It sure beats sleeping on a lumpy couch in a trailer, at any rate. Down the hallway, I hear the faint float of laughter behind a closed door. Bruce Walker's ten o'clock "appointment" no doubt.

I walk into the bedroom, pick up my cell phone and dial my mom's number. She's been on my mind a lot today, partly because of the commonality between she and Bruce Walker, but mostly because I don't like thinking of her alone. This is the first time since Uncle Hor and Dolly left that my mother is alone. I know that she can take care of herself, and she probably welcomes the alone time, but my mom had a hard time when Uncle Hor left. I can still picture her clutching onto him in the driveway the morning that he left, crying softly into his jacket. It was the only time I had ever seen my mom cry and at that moment I realized how lonely she really is. I just don't like thinking of her alone in that big house now. It makes me sad.

"Hi, Mom," I say when she picks up after the second ring.

"Maggie! How's it going out there?"

"It's amazing, Mom. You should see the ranch I'm staying at. I have my own Jacuzzi and everything."

"Sounds heavenly. You deserve to have a little vacation while you're out there. How are the clients?"

"Weird, Mom. Very, very weird. I don't mean weird like they're weirdos or anything; it's just that I don't really get the dynamic between them. The bride-to-be seems to be crazier about her father than her own fiancé. I don't mean that in a perverted way, it's just that it's clear that she's her daddy's princess. I don't get why she's getting married. She just doesn't seem into it."

My mother chuckles. It's a light, upbeat little chuckle and it immediately makes me feel better because it tells me that my mom is okay.

"Well, Maggie," she says after a moment, "just remember that love is different for everyone. Not everyone has the same story. You're out there to discover what their story is and it might take a few days to figure it out."

"Yeah, I guess you're right."

We chat for a few more minutes, about the weather and what the news is from home and I hang up feeling relieved. Not only is my mother okay, but the usual apathetic tone she usually used when asking me about the weddings or my clients was absent. In fact, if I didn't know any better, I would say that my mother had sounded like a romantic. It makes me wonder if maybe she does have "appointments" that came to call on her while I'm away. I turn off the elk horn lamp on the nightstand. It's only ten o'clock but I'm tired and tomorrow is going to be a busy day. Besides, I figure out that if I'm going to find out Randy's and Daisy's story, I'm going to need as much sleep as I can get. Yup, I think as I doze off to sleep, I have my work cut out for me here.

Chapter Sixteen

I meet Randy the next morning at his dance studio, which turns out to be nothing more than The Cowboy Bar during its off hours.

"I don't actually have my own studio—yet," Randy says sheepishly. "A lot of places in town just let me use their space when it's not busy or crowded."

"Do you have to pay a user's fee?"

"No. The people here are real generous that way—I mean, if you're a local. They'll try to take advantage of the tourists if they can but if you make your livelihood here, everyone is more than willing to cut you a break. Plus, they figure it boosts business for them. The more people who know how to dance, the more people who will come out and dance."

"And order drinks."

"Exactly!" Randy continues to shuffle through his CDs, looking for the right music. "It's a good arrangement. The only problem is that people don't know where their lessons are from one night to the next because it's always changing. Now they just come to town and pop into different saloons lookin' for me. They know they'll find me sooner or later."

Finally, after three hours of listening to country music and watching couples step on each other's toes, the lessons are finished. I breathe a sigh of relief and ready myself for a trip to the bar where I plan on indulging in another rum and coke (or two). I had listened to more country music than I could stand.

"Thanks, Randy, that was great," I say off-handedly as I start to saunter over to a saddle seat at the bar.

"Where are you goin'?" Randy asks, a little surprised. "What about your lesson?"

"Huh?" I don't realize that I had agreed to take one.

"C'mon," Randy says, flashing his good-natured grin. "Don't you wanna learn the two-step?"

"Is that a trick question?"

Randy just laughs and pulls me onto the dance floor. "I'll buy you a drink after. I promise. Just indulge me for a few minutes."

I sigh begrudgingly but accept my fate of having to listen to yet more country music. Randy seems to be getting a kick out of all this. "Oh, come on now, Maggie, don't knock it 'til you try it." Randy stands facing me in the center of the floor. He raises his left-hand shoulder high and takes my right hand in his. "Put your left hand on my shoulder," he instructs as he places his right hand on my waist. "See, this is the basic position. We're already making progress."

"Well we haven't started moving yet. That's the part I'm afraid of."

Randy laughs. "Well, we're about to. I'm going to step forward with my left foot. I want you to step backward with your right foot."

I do as Randy instructs without getting my toe stomped on and am quietly pleased with myself. "Good. Now I'm going to step forward with my left foot and bring it over next to my right. What should you do?"

I think about what the opposite of Randy's step would be, or what would sequentially follow the last step I took. "Step back with my left foot and bring it over next to my right."

"Good! Now let's execute." I do exactly what I said I should do and am pleasantly surprised to find that I have executed a perfect 2-step sequence. "Left-Right-Left-touch. Right-Left-Right-touch," Randy repeats as we get the rhythm down. I laugh in spite of myself. "Wanna try it to music now?"

The dreaded moment has arrived. I rather liked doing it without music but I guess music is a necessary component when dancing, even to country music.

"Sure," I say unenthusiastically.

Randy goes over to the boom box and pops something in. I'm afraid to hear what. "Listen to the music," Randy says as he takes my hand and puts his other hand on my waist. I actually don't mind this song. It's *Sweet Home Alabama* and I find I know exactly when and where to move my feet. It's pretty fun, actually. Who'd a thought I'd enjoy 2-stepping to country music? I guess I never thought of Lynnard Skynnard as "country" before.

"That's it, Maggie," Randy says encouragingly. "You're a quick learner."

"Well, I have a great teacher," I reply and Randy blushes. I decide to use this opportunity to conduct some more research. "So, this is how you and Daisy met?"

"This is it. She came in here one day to take a lesson and we've been dancin' together ever since."

"You and Daisy have always been partners?"

"Since the first lesson. Somethin' just clicked for us. In a manner of dancin' anyway. She was with Luke then but she and I would always dance together. It was an unwritten rule."

"You mean in class?"

"In class and in competitions. Even out socially. It was always Daisy and me on the dance floor."

"You mean you do this in competitions?" I'm surprised. I mean, it's fun and all but it seems pretty basic. I had it down in about 1 minute. There isn't much variation to the step.

Randy laughs. "Well, this is the basic step but we put a spin on things— like this." Randy proceeds to spin me around in some complicated figure and then spins me around in the opposite direction. Before the room stops spinning, Randy throws another trick in. "Or like this," he says excitedly and he picks me up and snakes me around his body in some contorted position before putting me back on my feet.

"Woah," I say, after I'm sure I'm going to throw up.

Randy smiles. "Sorry, Maggie. I tend to get carried away when I dance." He leads me over to a saddle seat. "I'll buy you a drink. I'd say you earned it."

"What'll it be?"

"A coke please," I say, rubbing my temples. I still feel a little dizzy. Under the circumstances, I think it's best to leave the rum out.

"Make that two, Jerry. Thanks." Randy pulls something out of his pocket and puts it on the bar in front of me. "This is for you." It's a little Hershey's kiss. I must say I do love chocolate. "It's my thing. I always give a 'kiss' to a lady after I dance with her. Daisy likes to say I stole her heart with a kiss." He leans over to me and whispers, "Just don't tell anyone that this is the type of kiss she means."

I laugh as I pop the little chocolate into my mouth. Randy really is a sweet guy. "Don't worry, it'll be our little secret." Our cokes arrive and I stir the ice cubes around with my straw for a few seconds. I'm getting back into research mode. "So, Tony told me you moved here just to dance," I say cautiously, "and for Daisy."

"That's right. You gotta follow your heart, Maggie. Life's too short." I nod in agreement, but I still need some more answers.

"So, you just teach dance lessons?" I don't mean to sound rude but it doesn't seem like a financially lucrative business.

"I guide rafting trips in the summer and I work over at the airport in baggage claim, but my passion is dancing. I've been dancing since I was twelve. It's all I ever wanted to do."

"Do you do any other types? Any ballroom?"

Randy smiles. "This is the West, Maggie. Two-step and line dancin' is a way of life out here. It's as much a part of our culture as rodeos."

Now it's my turn to blush. "Sorry. I have a bad habit of forgetting where I am geographically at times." Randy laughs his easy laugh. He really is such a nice guy, and I don't want to see him get hurt by Daisy. I don't want Daisy to do to Randy what I had done to Jack.

"To tell you the truth," Randy says. "I wouldn't mind learning the waltz. Now that's a beautiful dance. The way it looks like you're floatin' over the floor," he picks up his drink and stares off beyond me for a minute, "man, I would love to do the waltz with Daisy."

"Why don't you ask her? You could dance the waltz at the wedding."

Randy shakes his head. "I brought it up once but Daisy wouldn't hear of it. She said she'd feel like a traitor if she did anything besides country dancin'. She's got the spirit of the West in her, Daisy does," Randy pauses to take another swig of his coke. "100 percent western. It's in her blood."

It occurs to me then that Randy knows Daisy's different. He knows she's an independent spirit. As smitten as Randy is with her, he can still see below the surface. This makes me more curious than ever as to why he loves her so much. She would never be able to give back to him what he would give to her. There's no beating around the bush anymore. I am going to come right out and ask him about it. Besides, I still need to know bits of information in order to compose my toast. I think I am well within my rights. "What is it about Daisy that you love so much?"

He gets that starry expression on his face again, just at the mention of her name. "I love the way her hair bounces all around her face when we dance. I love the way she looks at me when we're on the dance floor, like she's hungry for heat. I love the way she doesn't care what she looks like, which just makes her all the more sexier. I love the way she pours her heart and soul into her paintings and doesn't notice when she gets a spot on the tip of her nose. I love that laugh of hers, when she hears somethin' absurd or is doin' somethin' absurd or when you tickle the inside of her elbow. Like wild, carefree abandon." I nod. I think of that laugh of my mother's that I would give anything to hear again. I understand the addiction of laughter, I'm just not sure it's enough to build a marriage on. Randy pauses for a minute. "I love that she wants to be with me."

I ask the question before I even realize it. I know it's not my place to ask such a question, but I'm beginning to worry that Randy is in love with some glorified image of Daisy instead of Daisy herself. "Are you sure this is what you want, Randy?"

He looks at me, not like he's surprised to hear such a question, but like he's surprised that I don't understand. "More than anything. You gotta follow your heart, Maggie. In life, you gotta follow your heart." I just smile. I don't tell Randy that sometimes following your heart can lead to nothing but heartache.

"I love the waltz, too," I tell him, because I don't know what else I can tell him. Sometimes the illusion of love is more beautiful than it actually is.

He smiles. "I've been practicin' the steps after my lessons."

"I hate to break this to you, Randy, but the waltz requires a partner."

Randy smiles again. "Well, I always have hope, Maggie. Maybe one day I will."

Maybe one day, but I'm not banking on it.

The next few days go by in a blur. They're filled with a lot of country-line dancing, painting pictures and eating lots of steak. Truth be told, I was having a blast. I really did take an immediate liking to Jackson Hole; the snow-covered mountains, the expanse of wide-open spaces, the frontier town with great shopping; I was finding that I even was developing an affinity for country music (don't tell anyone that, though). I even wore my cowboy hat out one night, but I still haven't developed an affinity for cowboy hats. I just wanted to be polite. But I still have no idea what I'm going to say in my toast.

Usually, at this point, I have a feel for the relationship between the bride and groom and I'm able to pepper my toast with the observances I make of them; like Morty and Addy, reading to each other in bed or Sam and Ella, holding hands constantly like it was the most natural thing in the world. But with Randy and Daisy, I haven't seen any of these things.

I did see them dance at The Cowboy Bar and Tony was right; the chemistry between them on the dance floor was undeniable. They twirled and turned and two-stepped all over the dance floor like they were the only ones in the room. I saw the heat in Daisy's eyes that Randy had talked about and Randy, so gentle-spirited most of the time, seemed to come to life when he danced with Daisy. There was a sureness in his eyes and a quick confidence in his steps. But a dance only lasted about three minutes. I'm more interested in knowing what would sustain them off of the dance floor, in real life. That's what I need to capture in my toast.

I wake up with a splitting headache for, I assume, three reasons. A: The wedding is tomorrow and I still have no idea what I'm going to say; B: I had gotten drunk last night at The Cowboy Bar; and C: I'm going horseback riding with Daisy today, which scares the hell out of me. I put the pillow over my face and pretend I can't hear the alarm beeping.

I hadn't had a chance to spend some quality one-on-one time with Daisy since I've been here. Most of my time had been spent with Randy, watching his dance lessons (although I would sneak out quite often to go shopping. Jackson has some great stores). I had spent one afternoon with Daisy at her studio but she had gotten so lost in her painting that she didn't even notice when I snuck out (to go shopping). I didn't really mind; it gets pretty boring watching paint dry. Anyway, I welcome this time with Daisy; I'm in much need of information and I'm anxious to hear her perspective on things. I just wish it wasn't going to be on a horse.

Bruce had asked me at dinner last night. "Have you ever ridden a horse?"

"Just on the merry-go-round," I answered feebly.

"Ha! That's no answer! Tomorrow we'll get you ridin' on a proper horse."

"I'll take Maggie ridin'," Daisy volunteered. "I gotta take Spitfire out for a ride to stretch her legs, anyway."

"Great!" I said enthusiastically, although I didn't mean it. I didn't fancy getting on the back of anything that had the power to inflect serious bodily harm on me. And I wasn't a westerner either. I felt no need to defend my position on riding horses. And I didn't. Like a schmuck, I trudge down to the barn to meet Daisy.

"You ready, Maggie?" Daisy asks excitedly as she tries in vain to saddle up a very spirited horse who is having none of it.

"That's not my horse, is it?" I ask in a panic. The horse is standing on its hind legs now and snorting out of its nose.

"Whoa, girl," Daisy says to the horse, and then she laughs at me.

"No! This here is Spitfire. She's my girl, aren't ya, Spitfire?" She rubs her muzzle and miraculously the horse seems to settle down. "She's just a little testy. She hasn't been out on a good run in a while."

"Run?" I ask, again in a panic. I have resigned myself to ride a horse that is walking very slowly, but there would be no running, of any kind, involved. Not even trotting.

Daisy just laughs again. "Don't worry, Maggie. I aint gonna kill you or anything. I'll run Spitfire when we finish our trail ride and you're safe off of Cherokee." She gives me a sly smile. "Don't you trust me?"

I was still unsure about the Daisy factor but now I know what Tony and Randy had meant when they described Daisy. Daisy is a force of nature. She breathes life into every room she walks into and I don't mean to sound like a lesbian (not that there is anything wrong with that) but I can see how anyone, man or woman, would be attracted to her. Daisy is, in a word, magnetic. She's a hoot to go out with. I loved the way she could down three beers in a row and just laugh that laugh Randy loves so much when she lets out a big belch and stands up and sings along at the top of her lungs to whatever song the band happens to be playing (of course it's a country song). Yes, I can see why Randy loves her now. The only question remaining is, does Daisy love him.

I hear the rhythmic clink of horseshoes behind me, and turn to see Tony leading out a chestnut horse with big, brown eyes and a silky black mane. I have to admit, it is a magnificent looking creature. I presume it's Cherokee, the horse Daisy said I would be riding. At least he seems calm. "All saddled up," Tony says as he and the horse walk up to me. "Cherokee's all ready to go." Cherokee might be a beautiful horse but I'm still nervous about riding him. Tony seems to read my mind. "This is our gentlest horse, Maggie. He'll take it real slow with you."

"Well, I'm glad to hear that. Can you just remind him that I've never been on one of his kind before? At least not the live kind."

Tony just laughs. "You'll be fine, Maggie. You'll be just fine. Ol' Cherokee here will take good care of you." He leads Cherokee up to me and takes my hand and guides it to his neck. "Just let him get to know you, is all. Let him know you're his friend." He takes his hand off of mine and I continue to stroke Cherokee's neck. He seems to like it. He let out a soft snort and then moves his muzzle to my shoulder. It feels velvety. It's a very pleasant sensation, actually. "He's gettin' your scent," Tony says. "You know, it's a strong bond between a man and his horse."

"Well, I'm a woman," I say. But I know what Tony means.

Daisy rides up on Spitfire and stops when she nears us. She looks absolutely regal. "You ready to get goin', Maggie?"

"As ready as I'll ever be." Tony helps to hoist me up into the saddle. I sit up, tall and proud to be in this land. I am even wearing my cowboy hat. You know what they say. when in Rome…well, when in Jackson, wear a cowboy hat and ride a horse.

Daisy looks at me with approval and then gives a quick tug of the reins to Spitfire. "Lead the way, Spitfire, lead the way."

We roam over the grounds of the ranch and make our way up a mountain trail. True to Tony's word, Cherokee travels slowly and is perfectly behaved the whole time. It's quite enjoyable, actually. The February sun casts a gorgeous light off of the Tetons and the rhythmic up and down of the saddle is oddly comforting. Turns out, I am a cowgirl after all. Fringe and all. We pull over to a lookout area at the top of the trail. The horses get a chance to rest and we get a chance to talk.

"So, you ready for the big day tomorrow?" I ask.

"Yup. Ready as I'll ever be. The wedding planner is taking care of all the details. All I have to do is show up." Daisy gives me a sly smile. "We got ourselves a wedding toaster and a wedding planner. I figured I'd let other people worry about the weddin' stuff. I'll just be there to get married. I don't care much for the other stuff—except for you, I mean," Daisy says quickly. "All I cared about was havin' the wedding toaster there. That was the only part I had any say in plannin'. I couldn't even tell you what the menu is or what the centerpieces are. But I had to have Maggie McDonald give the toast at my weddin'." I don't think it's in Daisy's nature to pay attention to minute

134

details, but I am surprised that she's been so adamant about having me there. I mean, as far as I can tell, Daisy is marrying Randy simply because she's bored. I'm still not so sure that this union should be taking place—and I have a lack of a toast to prove it—but then again, I'm just the wedding toaster. It's not my place to question my client's motives, and besides—I wouldn't get paid for services rendered if I didn't actually perform my service at some sort of wedding celebration. But Randy and Daisy, as with all my clients, have become my friends. I don't want to see them plunge into something that they would regret later. "Why?" I ask.

Daisy looks at me. "Because you're a lucky charm. Seems right that a marriage should start out with you toastin' it. And I bet you've been told that before."

I put my hand to my neck and finger the necklace Addy had sent me. I hadn't taken it off since. "Yes, I suppose I have."

"Well, there you have it," Daisy says, but I'm still not convinced. Either Daisy wanted me there for luck that her marriage would survive or because she's not so sure herself that it will. The wedding is tomorrow and I still have no toast. Something drastic needs to be done.

"Daisy," I start cautiously, "are you so sure you want to marry Randy? You know, it's not too late if you don't want to go through with it."

She looks at me like she thinks I'm as crazy as everyone thinks she is. "Why on earth would I not get married tomorrow?"

I hesitate. This is one of those moments when you definitely do not want to put your foot in your mouth (which I've been known to do on occasion). I need time to formulate a subtle, yet sensitive, response. "Well, you and Randy don't seem to be on the same wave length all the time. That's all I mean."

Daisy snorts (or it might have been the horse). "I see," she says defensively. "Everyone is an expert on my love life except for me. Everyone thinks they know how it should be with me and Randy."

"No, that's not what I meant!" I think of my own wedding disaster three years ago. And while it certainly was a disaster, a bigger disaster had been averted in the long run. I just want to let Daisy know that I understand. And that it's okay not to go through with it. "I understand," I offer finally. "I understand what it's like when everyone expects you to do something that you really don't want to do."

Daisy looks at me, hard. "No, you don't understand, Maggie. You don't understand at all." She pulls gently on Spitfire's reins. "C'mon girl, let's go," and she starts riding away.

"Daisy!" I panic at this point, not only because I want to clear things up with Daisy but also because I'm scared to death to be left alone on a horse, even if it's a gentle horse. Cherokee, however, seems to know what to do. He turns slowly and saunters up to Spitfire. "Let me explain," I say once Cherokee and I have caught up.

"No, let me explain," Daisy says with conviction. "I know what people say about me bein' with Randy." She's quiet for a minute. "And, more importantly, I know how it looks—us bein' together. Randy would give me the moon if I asked him for it," she hesitates. "And I don't always notice that he's around." I don't say anything. It's true, after all, but what strikes me in this moment is that Daisy looks sad. "I don't mean to, Maggie, I mean I don't do it on purpose or nothin'. It's just that I'm not accustomed to havin' to account for anyone. Do you know what I mean?"

I just shake my head. Boy, do I ever. Daisy and I are actually a lot alike. And it scares me.

"I'm just a wild thing, Maggie. I like to do what I please." Daisy is quiet again but she's smiling now, at the memory of something, I think. "One time, I just jumped on Spitfire one morning and rode clear to the Rio Grande. Was gone 4 days. I had heard about these beautiful wildflowers that grow there and I wanted to pick some."

I smile. I think about the time I had climbed out my bedroom window and took off for Australia for two months. Yup, Daisy and I are definitely a lot alike.

"Anyway, the point is, Maggie, I'm likely to do that again. Whenever I feel like it. And," she continues somewhat nervously, "if Luke Cassidy ever happens to pass through town again, chances are I'll pay a visit to his sleepin' quarters."

I look at her, speechless. I had expected to hear a lot of things from Daisy Walker but I had not expected to hear this. "Well, it's true," she says with a mixture of remorse and confidence. "But the point is I'd always come back to Randy. I'd always come back," she adds with certainty.

"Daisy," I say gently, "is that really fair to Randy, though? He adores you. You should see the way he looks at you. I really think he thinks his reason for being is to make you happy."

She looks at me then, with such a fierce conviction that I'm taken aback. "I know Randy loves me, more than anything in the world. And I know that what I feel for him now is not the same as what he feels for me. But I appreciate Randy, Maggie. I appreciate him more than I've ever appreciated anyone or anything. And I want to be a good girl for him. I can't promise that I'll always be but I sure am gonna try. Randy knows me. He understands me. He understands that I'm a wild thing, and he still wants me. And, even though I know I won't change completely, I want to be my best for him. Now, aint that love, Maggie? Aint that love?"

I look at Daisy then and I see myself; an independent, free spirit who wants to do what she wants to when she wants to do it. A woman who had had the love of a decent man, but was still beckoned by ghosts in the closet and things left unexplored. But there is one difference between me and Daisy; she is willing to reciprocate in the way she knows how, even if it's not perfect. Daisy is choosing to stay and try where I chose to run away. And, in this moment, I get that love isn't always perfect, but it's still love.

I look at her with new eyes then. Of all my clients, Daisy has ended up teaching me the most. "Yes, Daisy, I suppose it is," I say. "I suppose it is."

After we get back to the barn and unsaddle the horses, I immediately run to my room under the guise of having a migraine. The truth is, I'm suddenly overcome with emotion and I need a good cry. I run up the stairs, close the door and sink down onto the floor, my back leaning against the bed, and I let it all out.

There are different degrees of missing someone. You can miss your girlfriend, when she has to work late one night and isn't there to take your phone call immediately when you find yourself in the middle of some silly crisis. You can miss your dad, who died too early in life but it's just something you've learned to live with. Or you can miss the outline of your lover, lying next to you in bed and caressing the trace of your palm like it's the most natural thing in the world. And in this moment, I miss Jack. I miss him so intensely and so acutely that it actually hurts to breathe. I know exactly where it's coming from. For the first time since my "non-wedding," I weep for Jack. And it's not because of what I had done, but it's because I miss him. I finally understand what I had let go.

It's Daisy who makes me realize it. Daisy is wise enough to understand that the love she feels for Randy is different, at least now, than the love he feels for her, but she still loves him, in her own way, and she wants to give him all that she can. Jack deserved that. Like Randy, he's a good, good man, and for the first time, I wish that I was the one who had been able to give it to him.

I finish crying and start hiccupping instead. I get up, wash my face and sit down to compose my toast. I know now exactly what I'm going to say. I had discovered Randy and Daisy's love story, and I'm going to honor it. The thoughts and words spill out of me like liquid and when I'm sure I have captured exactly what it is that I want to say, I put my notes and cards away, put on my cowboy hat with fringe and go to the rehearsal dinner. There is going to be a wedding tomorrow after all; it's time to celebrate.

Chapter Seventeen

The wedding is gorgeous. It's held right at the homestead, in the formal ballroom. It's a circular room surrounded entirely by glass windows, which affords a view of the Tetons at sunset while Randy and Daisy exchange their vows. The band motions to me and I know that I am on. I know exactly what I am going to say, and I mean every word of it. I swagger over to the mic, confident in the knowledge that I am good at what I do.

It is my extreme privilege and honor to be here with you all today—to celebrate the marriage of Randy and Daisy—a marriage that I think all of us are so happy to see take place. And while I've toasted my share of weddings and have witnessed the unique love stories of many couples, none have affected me more, or taught me more, than Daisy's and Randy's story.

I know most of you here, at one point or another, have been lucky enough to see Daisy and Randy. Anyone who has seen them dance can witness the undeniable chemistry between them, but what I have been so lucky to witness is the quiet moments of devotion that Randy and Daisy have shared off of the dance floor.

In any relationship, these moments can be hard to detect. It's not always an obvious show of affection, but I've seen it in the look in Randy's eyes when he talks about Daisy, or Sassy—as he affectionately calls her, and smiles at the sound of her laugh. I've seen it in Daisy when she has told me that, even though she has been known to jump on a horse and ride for days on a whim, she would always come back to Randy. Always come back. I've seen it when she's told me that she might not always be her best for anyone, but for Randy she wants to try. And it's in the trying that matters.

And I feel richer for being given this experience, because Randy and Daisy have taught me a thing or two about love. And what I've learned is that there is no clear definition of love. There is no formula to follow or book of instruction. Love means different things to different people and every relationship, every marriage, is different. The secret is finding what works for you and your partner and accepting each other as you are, without doubt or expectation. It is that love that we celebrate today—love free of expectation and judgment. We celebrate in Randy and Daisy a purely unconditional love.

When I first met Randy and Daisy, I thought I couldn't have met two more opposite people, but through my time spent with them, I have discovered that there is not two more suited people for each other because they get each other. They understand each other. And they celebrate each other.

So, if you'll please join me in raising your glasses—to Randy and Daisy—may your lives be filled with much love, laughter and happiness. And may you continue to celebrate each other—every day of your lives.

The toast was a hit, as I knew it would be. I don't mean that in a conceited sort of way, I just mean that it reflected exactly what I had intended it to. Daisy and Randy's own unique love story. But the toast was not the highlight for me. For me, the best part of the evening was when Daisy coyly walked up to Randy and led him onto the dance floor. We had all been ready to witness another electrifying exhibit of their two-step, but Daisy had other plans in mind. She nodded to the band and a slow sort of love song played.

"May I have this waltz, Mr. Rhodes?" Daisy asked as she sunk into him and he pulled her close. It was her wedding gift to him and I struggle to remain tear-free. I told you a beautiful waltz can make me cry.

There are lots of big wigs at the wedding. Bruce Walker is such an eccentric, colorful character that I forgot that he had once been a big political figure in Washington. All night I was introduced to senators and congressman and other important officials. I think I was supposed to know who they all were but I didn't, even though I pretended I did. I think I told you; I'm not very political. But the vice president was there and I did, at least, know who he was, even though I hadn't voted for him.

"Beautiful toast, young lady, well done," he says to me after Bruce Walker makes the introductions.

"Thank you, sir."

"My son is getting married in early May. I don't suppose you have any availability?"

I smile to myself. "I think we might be able to work something out." I write my number on a napkin for him and make a mental note to myself that I need to have business cards printed up when I get home. It's sort of embarrassing giving your cell phone number to the Vice President of the United States on a napkin.

I finish my glass of wine and take a second, like I do at all my weddings, to take in my surroundings. The party shows no evidence of slowing down even though it's getting late. The dance floor is jammed and the loud, raucous laughter of drunk cowboys fill the room. I smile to myself, satisfied. It's been a great night. My only regret is that Dolly and Uncle Hor had not been able to make it. They had been invited but had to decline due to Uncle Hor's mysterious appearance of a "quite unsightly rash" as Dolly had put it. "He's not used to all this sun down here, you know," she had offered as a feeble explanation. I think they didn't come because, although he won't admit it, Uncle Hor doesn't like to fly.

I put my empty wine glass down and take one last glance around. I have an early flight in the morning and still need to pack. I am just about at the exit when Bruce Walker approaches me, holding a big, rectangular box in his hand.

"Maggie, you're not thinking of leaving so soon, are you? The party's just heatin' up." I smile. Bruce Walker couldn't help but grow on you with his western twang and his strut full of bravado.

"It's time for this pony to turn into the barn for the night," I say cheekily.

Bruce smiles. "You're pickin' up the lingo!"

"Well, you westerners have a way of growing on people," I reply teasingly. But I mean it. "I have an early flight tomorrow so I want to turn in. But thank you, Mr. Walker, for everything. I have truly enjoyed my time here." I extend my hand and he takes it.

"Tony'll give you the check when he drops you at the airport tomorrow. Come back anytime. You're always welcome here, wedding toaster."

I smile and turn to leave.

"Maggie," he says with a touch of urgency in his voice. I turn around and he throws the box he has been carrying to me. "This is for you." I catch the box, surprised, and he pauses for a second. "I'd say you earned 'em." He looks at me, half-smiling, with acknowledgement in his eyes. It's the first time I've seen Bruce Walker semi-serious.

Bruce walks away and I open the box to find a pair of white leather cowboy boots inside.

And yes, they have spurs.

Chapter Eighteen

The next few months are an absolute whirlwind. The wedding in Jackson had gotten lots of media coverage, due to Bruce Walker being a prominent political figure and all, and my career as *The Wedding Toaster* officially took off. I did end up doing the vice president's son's wedding, at the White House no less, and lots of other weddings in between. Just for clarification, I did not get to meet *the* president however; he was at some summit talk in China. Anyway, it was pretty cool.

People magazine ended up doing a profile on me after all the press on Daisy and Randy's wedding and that really boosted business. I also got a shout-out on Perez Hilton's website. Seeing myself mixed in with the likes of the Hollywood set was really a hoot. I hoped this would land me some celebrity weddings but I haven't broken into the Hollywood scene yet. Maybe celebrities think having a wedding toaster at their weddings isn't practical; the marriages among celebrities usually don't last very long.

I average three weddings a month; jetting off to a different destination every week only to come home, five days later, exhausted, and having to jet off somewhere else. My price is fixed now; $10,000, plus expenses, unless it's a last-minute scheduling—that boosts it up to $15,000. Once there was even a bidding war started over me at the governor of Minnesota's niece's wedding; the Mexican ambassador and the Italian consulate both wanted me for the same date in April. They started arguing right there at the reception, each trying to outdo the other and win my business. It was sort of a hoot, actually. I had never had two people fight so hard for my attention before, especially important political billionaires. Anyway, I ended up doing the ambassador's wedding for the low price of $20,000. And I got a vacation in Cancun to boot.

Anyway, life is pretty crazy for me. I jet of to such exotic locales as Hawaii, Bermuda and Aspen, and of course, Cancun and the White House. I also jet off to not such exotic locales such as Minnesota, Arkansas, Nebraska, West Virginia and Vermont. Don't get me wrong—Vermont is nice, it's just not that exotic to me since I only live three hours away. I have yet to go international, except if you count Cancun, which I don't. I mean, they are on the same continent as us, but I figure I'll break into that market eventually.

My clients are mostly political figures or billionaire entrepreneurs. I did toast a wedding in Seattle that Bill Gates was at. He wasn't the client, but it was still cool to meet him. And I did toast Douglas Duran's daughter's wedding. Douglas used to be on my Favorite soap opera, *Dawn of a New Day,* but then he got killed off and I haven't watched it since. It was a bit of a disappointment to tell you the truth; he wasn't as suave or debonair as he is on TV.

Most of this is done flying by the seat of my pants, so to speak. It occurs to me that I need to get organized. Problem is, I'm never home long enough to set things up properly. I did get business cards printed up at least, and we made the guest bedroom my "office"—for now. I also have a separate phone line because I was finding it extremely annoying when my cell phone would ring non-stop and it was never even any one I knew. But then I realized that my cell phone number was the number on the business card so I had to get a whole other batch printed up. The operation is definitely a work in progress, but I'm finding my way.

Carrie comes over and helps out too. She quit her job in sales because she's pregnant but found that she was bored staying at home all day. She answers the phone and does my scheduling and airline booking. "Office of Maggie McDonald, the wedding toaster," she says when she answers the phone, which always makes me sort of laugh because we aren't in an office at all; we're in an old bedroom with peeling wall paper on the walls and a ratty old comforter on the bed. Carrie even comes when I'm away at weddings. I gave her a key to the house and she just lets herself in and out. When I get home from a wedding, she lets me know where I'm going next and for whom I'll be working. My mom brought home one of those big white boards on wheels from school and Carrie keeps my whole schedule up there, filling in where I'm going and when, and then erases a wedding I had toasted when I get back, only to replace it with another one. At any rate, I wouldn't be able to do any of this without Carrie, but even the pressure gets to her sometimes.

"Maggie, we gotta do something about business operations," she says to me, exhausted, as I blow in from a wedding I had just toasted in San Diego. "I mean, it's not even officially wedding season yet. Just think of what June will be like."

"I know. I'm just never home long enough to make any plans."

"You guys need to streamline," Kate says as she enters the room, hearing the tail end of our conversation. Kate comes over a lot—not to work, mind you—but because I think she gets caught up in the fantasy of it. She comes over too to keep Carrie company when I'm at a wedding. It's escapism for her. She likes to hear of where I'm jetting off to next and for which prominent client I'll next be working for. Kate's heard of most of the clients I'm hired by; she's very political. Sometimes she helps me choose which client to accept if there's an overbooking. This is either done by geographical location or the pyramid of political prominence. "Are you crazy? Do the wedding in Miami," she would say or, "Do the Evanston wedding. He has a shot at getting Speaker of the House."

"You should definitely look for a space to lease," Kate says now, plumping down on the bed next to me and Carrie. "Hell, Maggie, you could probably afford to buy a space somewhere. But this..." she looks around as though she's seeing the "office" for the first time. "This simply will not do anymore."

"I'm going to have to second that," Carrie says, raising her hand.

"I totally agree, I just don't know how I'm gonna find the time to do it now. I mean, everything is happening so fast. It's like, yesterday I was writing obits and today I'm being profiled in *People*."

"Which is the coolest thing *ever*," Kate says. I smile. I have to agree; it is pretty cool.

"You should get a website going, too. That will really help with bookings, plus give business a big, old shot in the ass."

I look at Kate admiringly. "Why don't you come work with us?" I say, only half-kidding. Kate's pretty savvy. Plus, I need the manpower. I don't know how much longer Carrie can last at this pace, especially being pregnant.

"Nah," Kate says as she slaps my knee. "I prefer to live vicariously through you."

"Seriously, Maggie," Carrie says. "We need to start thinking about this."

I sigh. "Well, what does the schedule look like? Do I have any available time?" I glance at the white board. We are heading into summer and I know there won't be anything, and I'm right. June, July and the first two weeks of August are already booked solid.

"There haven't been any bookings for the last two weeks in August yet, but I'm sure there will be." Carrie looks at the board and then double-checks the appointment book, just to be sure. Carrie is very thorough.

"Well, let's block off one of those weeks and we'll concentrate on improving business operations. We'll lease an office space, get a website up and running, the works."

"Okay." Carrie gets up from the bed, marker in hand, ready to block off the schedule. "Which week?"

"Hmm," I rest my chin on my hand, weighing my options. "How about the last one?"

"Great." Carrie draws a big X in the August 23—30 slot. "It's as good as done."

It's satisfying actually, looking at a big old *X* running through my schedule. I'm getting tired of airports. I'm getting tired, period. It would be nice to stay put for a week. I look at the board, trying to figure out where I'm going next. I don't know half the time, to tell you the truth. The board is all knowing. It tells me everything I need to know about my life these days.

"So, Monday, I leave for Santa Fe?"

"Check," Carrie says, giving the board a once-over. "And you leave for Nantucket the next week."

"Nantucket?" Kate says a bit disappointed. "Talk about a lack of exotic factor. Who's getting married on Nantucket?"

"Nantucket is a top choice for destination weddings," Carrie says defensively. "It's just that it happens to be close to us so we don't think of it that way." Kate shrugs her shoulders. "And besides," Carrie goes on, "our clients have to get married in Massachusetts."

"Why?" Kate is intrigued by the possibilities. "Is it a Kennedy or something?"

"No. It's James White and Wendell Johnson. Two very prominent business entrepreneurs from New Jersey."

"Well, I'll be damned!" Kate says, impressed. "You're breaking barriers all over the place, Maggie!"

146

"Yes, we are a nondiscriminatory office that supports gay rights." I am rather looking forward to my first same-sex wedding. And I do love gay men; they're a hoot and a half.

"Oh, shit!" Carrie says all of a sudden. She starts erasing furiously and curses again.

"What's the matter?"

"Oh, nothing," she says a little more calmly. "We had a cancellation today and I just forgot to wipe it off the board."

"Who?" I don't like to think of people canceling on me. Did I get a bad recommendation? Was a former client not happy with my service? Bad scenarios flood my head like alphabet soup.

"Dilbert. On June 16. Don't worry—it was only in Cleveland."

"At least you didn't lose an exotic locale," Kate adds cheerfully. This is true; I could do without a visit to Cleveland.

"What happened?"

"The groom found his bride-to-be in bed with his sister."

"His sister?" Me and Kate both say at the same time, surprised.

Carrie smiles at our reaction. "Evidently it's causing quite the scandal. She's the mayor's daughter." I feel a little stupid for overreacting. I guess I can forgive a lesbian affair for taking business away from me. "Oh, we'll fill the slot, no problem," Carrie says confidently. "There were two calls today requesting that date."

"Who?"

Carrie picks up the record of phone calls. She really is organized. She puts me to shame, actually. I never would be able to keep my own schedule straight. "Here it is. A Marvin Gladwater from Atlanta and a Samantha Chase from San Francisco." Carrie closes the book and looks up at me. "So, you wanna make someone's day?"

"I say we let geography decide," Kate pipes in. "Where's it gonna be, Mags? Atlanta or San Francisco?"

"Hmm." I scratch my chin. "I think San Francisco is a more desirable locale."

"Amen to that," Kate chimes in. "It's hot as hell in Atlanta this time of year."

"San Francisco it is." Carrie writes the name Chase in the slot. "We'll call her tomorrow."

I go downstairs for a cup of tea before I go to bed. I want to steal at least one quiet and uninterrupted moment in the madness of my life as of late. Not that I'm complaining (okay…maybe I am), things are going great, but it's nice to be home, although it's never for very long. I want to savor the moment. And there is just something oddly calming about a nice cup of tea. I walk into the kitchen. My mom sitting at the kitchen table with her own cup of tea. "Hey stranger," my mom says.

"Hi, Mom." I fill the kettle and get a mug out for myself. "Mind if I join you?"

She perks up at the suggestion. "Please do. It will give us a chance to have a visit."

"So, how was school today?" I ask her as I sit down.

She looks at me with a grin. "It's Saturday."

"Is it really? I can't even keep the days of the week straight anymore. I never know what city I'm going to be in on any given day."

My mother laughs lightly. "You're in Boston, dear. Just wanted to remind you." She takes a sip of her tea and I notice that my mother looks different. Not bad, but definitely different. I can't put my finger on it exactly, but there seems to be a contentment about her, a calmness. Anyway, whatever the reason for my mother's new found Dharma, I'm glad. The truth is I worry about my mom. Uncle Hor moving was hard for her and I'm never home for more than 48 hours at a time now. It always makes me sad to think about my mom being alone.

"Where are you off to next?"

I have to think for a second. Like I said, Carrie does a better job of keeping track of my schedule than I do. "Santa Fe. Leave Monday morning." The kettle starts whistling and I get up to fix my mug. "What did you do today?"

"I went out to lunch with Denise and then I went to visit Daddy."

I look up quickly and manage to overflow my teacup with scalding water in the process. "Oh, shit." I feel a burn on my hand and reach for a towel to mop up the mess I have just made on the counter.

My mother smiles. "You went to visit Dad?" I can't keep the surprise out of my voice. My mother *never* visits my father's grave, except on Father's Day, their wedding anniversary and the anniversary of his death. My parents were married in July and my dad died in March. Father's Day is in June, and

148

I'm pretty certain, although my time tracking skills have not been up to par as of late, that it's only May (although the exact date I could not tell you). This is definitely out of character.

"I miss him," my mother says, matter-of-factly.

"Are you okay, Mom?" I scurry back to the table, holding my cup.

"Maggie, I'm fine! I just wanted a visit with him, is all."

"But that's not like you!" My thoughts start pouring out of me then. "Mom, I know I'm not home a lot now, and I know it must be a pain in the ass…with that stupid office set up here…I've already blocked out a week in August when I'm gonna find an office space to rent and I'll only do two weddings a month…"

My mother abruptly puts her hand up to stop me. "Maggie," she says calmly, "relax. I'm fine. You have a good thing going now and I'm not about to let you change it because you're worried about me."

I look at my mom closely, trying to look for signs that her mind has perhaps been invaded by some sort of foreign matter and is now putting foreign thoughts in side of her head. This does not sound like her at all. My mother gives a little laugh, like she's getting a kick out of me. "Maggie! I'm fine! Really!"

"Are you sure, Mom? I don't like to think of you alone all the time. Although…" I squint my eyes now and raise my eyebrows as I study her even further, "you do seem…lighter or something. Should I take that as a hint that you like having the house to yourself? Should I be offended?"

My mother bursts out in a full force gale now. "Well, I do get to watch whatever I want on TV now and walk around the house in my underwear!"

I open my mouth in protest but my mother just takes my hand. "There's been a lot of changes around here in the last few months, I won't argue that," she says gently. "And when Uncle Hor left…that was difficult. But I see how happy he is now, Maggie, and I realize that it was selfish of me to want him to stay here. To always assume that he would be here with us." She pauses for a second and holds my hand tighter. "You did the right thing, Maggie. You did the right thing by telling him." I smile. It means a lot to me to hear my mom say that.

"You know, Maggie," my mom goes on slowly, "I have few regrets in my life. But my biggest regret, I can see now, is making you be as cynical and jaded about love as I've been." And for the first time in my life, I see my

149

mother cry. "People are meant to fall in love," she wipes away a tear. "There is nothing like falling in love. And I want that for you. And that's why I'm so glad you're toasting weddings. I want you to see that. Love is a gift, Maggie, and I was blessed enough to be given it with your father. That's why I go see him now. I want to remember the gift he gave me instead of shutting myself off from it." My mother pauses for another a minute to dab her eyes. "You know, he'd be very proud of you."

Now I'm crying, but it's a good cry. "And you know what," my mom says after we both stop sniffling, "I even posted my profile on a dating website for over fifties."

"Mom!" I can't believe my mother is resorting to such tactics, but I'm happy for her. Everyone deserves not to be alone; and besides, my mom is pretty hot. "Any hits yet?" I ask.

"A few," my mother says coyly. "But I'm taking my time."

We sit in the kitchen, finishing our tea and deciding if she should give Stan, the dry cleaner from Cambridge, a chance and meet him for a cup of coffee (we decide no. I mean, he's fifty-six and has never been married. You have to wonder why). I'm happy, as I sit at the kitchen table with my mom. I feel like things have come full circle. After twenty years of waiting, Uncle Hor has finally ended up with Dolly, my mom is happy and, of all things, cyber-dating, and I am, of all things, toasting weddings…professionally. Yup, my dad would be proud. I take the last sip of my tea, content in the knowledge that things are how they are supposed to be. Serendipitous, as Morty would say. Nothing would surprise me now.

Chapter Nineteen

The Chase wedding was a lucky break (for them—not for me). The lesbian daughter of the mayor of Cleveland had put the ceremonious ka-bosh on her own June 16th wedding and so, I called the Chases, because they had called earlier requesting that date, and because they live in San Francisco, and offered my services.

Immediately, I wished I hadn't. Immediately I wished I had gone to Atlanta instead. Samantha Chase, the bridezilla to be, has to be the most obnoxious, annoying person I've ever dealt with. "Well, of course you're doing my wedding," she had said to me when I called her back. "It's going to be the event of the season and I do not take no for an answer." She had said it in that syrupy sweet voice that immediately signals that you are definitely dealing with a diva, at best. She called me constantly to bore me about the details of her day and even scolded me once for not taking her call right away (because I was in the middle of toasting another wedding). Who did she think she was anyway? I didn't care that her wedding was in Napa, or that her father owned a world-renowned vineyard or that there is going to be a Cristal fountain at the wedding. I've been to a wedding at the White House, I felt like telling her, so fuck you.

There's also a somewhat annoying detail about this wedding. It would seem, that I was, yet again, hired as a "gift" for someone, which would mean that my true identity would have to be concealed, at least, at first. But I'll tell you; my days as posing as a dog groomer and attending secret, clandestine meetings in the bushes are over. And I do charge $1000 more if there is any undercover work involved. Samantha hasn't filled me in on the specifics so I'm not going to worry about it. She said she'd let me know when I arrive, which appears to be very soon. The wheels touch down on the runway and I ready myself to meet Samantha Chase, and as far as I can tell, the devil incarnate.

I know who she is the moment I see her as I walk through baggage. Not because I have ever seen her before but because she looks every bit the part of a blonde, bridezilla bitch. She's tall, blonde and leggy, of course, wearing some sort of short black summery dress and four-inch-tall stilettos and talking on her cell phone like she doesn't care who hears her conversation or in what tone she seems to be speaking.

"No, that case was supposed to have gone out on Friday. To Paris. Well, maybe if you paid attention once in a while, we wouldn't be in this predicament. The buyer explicitly stated sauvignon blanc, not chardonnay. Well, you better get creative and find a way to fix it or you won't have a job come Monday." Click.

I stand a few feet away, averting eye contact and trying to look everywhere except at Samantha Chase. It's awkward having overheard her speaking on the phone in such a manner, but it didn't seem to bother Samantha Chase in the slightest.

"You must be Maggie," she says in an overly sweet voice as she extends a perfectly manicured hand to me. "I recognize you from *People*. And Perez Hilton's website, of course."

I smile lamely. I had just debuted on Perez Hilton's website a few weeks ago and now I was looked at as sort of the "in" trend at the moment. You know; the "thing" that every girl has to have at her wedding. That's me; Maggie McDonald—absolute necessity for all things wedding—at least for girls like Samantha Chase.

"It's nice to meet you," I finally squeak out but I'm lying. It really isn't nice meeting Samantha Chase at all.

"Well, of course it is," she adds in her sugary sweet tone followed by a sugary sweet little laugh. It's one of those remarks, which is precariously given under the pretense of kidding even though you know the speaker really is not (kidding, I mean).

"Do you have your bags?"

"Yes, I'm all set," I reply.

"Good. The car's out front."

Samantha starts speed walking towards the exit and I vaguely wonder how she is able to walk so fast in such high heels; I'm struggling to keep up with her in sneakers. "It's my driver's day off," she calls back to me (I was a little way behind). "It's a good thing you don't have too many bags since I have the MG today."

We exit the terminal and a little red MG convertible is sitting right out front, in a handicap spot no less. There's a ticket on the windshield, which Samantha tears up and throws on the ground without even glancing at it. "I know someone," she says to me with a sly smile. I think it's her attempt at being funny but it's nothing more than blatantly obnoxious. My stomach begins to churn as the reality sets in that I am going to be stuck with her for the next five days. In exactly the four minutes I have spent with her I have come to the conclusion that Samantha Chase is downright deplorable. I only hope that her fiancé is more bearable.

I throw my suitcase in the backseat and climb into the passenger seat. Samantha pulls out (without looking) and promptly gives the finger to the car she almost sideswipes as the driver leans on his horn. "God! Some people!" I gingerly reach for my seatbelt.

"So, anyway," she begins, "we're going to head to our apartment in San Francisco to pick up my fiancée before we head out to Napa."

"I thought he didn't know about me," I say, surprised.

"He doesn't yet." Samantha runs a red light and a symphony of horns honking follow. I'm not sure but I think I hear a screech of brakes and a crash behind us but I'm too afraid to turn around and check. "But I decided to let him in on the plan. Otherwise it would be too hard to coordinate."

Reluctantly, I agree. It will be easier to not have to deal with covers and excuses and secret skulking around. I just want to do my thing and get the hell out of here with as few complications as possible, although I suppose I will have to refund her the extra $1000 fee since no undercover services would be rendered. I'm just a bit piss-y that there is something that I actually agree with this woman on. The less I have in common with Samantha Chase, the better.

"We'll all stay at the vineyard for the week. Since that's where the wedding is, I figured it would just be easier to stay at operation headquarters, so to speak. You'll have the whole guest house to yourself."

I nod. At least I'll have some distance from Samantha in my down time. And I have to admit; having my own guesthouse at a vineyard isn't too shabby. I do like wine.

"So," Samantha approaches another red light, and miraculously stops this time, "what's been the best wedding you've done?"

"Um," I say, stalling. I know what she means. Which wedding had been the most exquisite, or in other words, expensive. I don't dare tell her that my favorites had been at a retirement home in Florida; a ranch in Wyoming in the dead of winter; or, God forbid, a trailer park in Tennessee. "It's hard to say," I finally say. "They've all been pretty swank."

"Well," she says, copping a bit of an attitude, "I'll just have to make sure mine outdoes them all."

We turn left, up one of San Francisco's many hills and park in front of a pale pink Victorian condo. It's one of those quintessential condos that you associate with San Francisco and I fall in love with it immediately. I have to admit, although begrudgingly, Samantha Chase does seem to have good taste.

"Great place," I say as I grab my suitcase from the back seat.

Samantha rolls her eyes. "Uh. If it were up to me, it would be on the market tomorrow. Inner Mission is such a passé neighborhood. And we actually have to share the yard with the unit downstairs. And let me tell you one thing about me, Maggie; I don't share." I am disliking Samantha Chase more and more by the second. I just wish she'd shut up and stop talking already but she continues on.

"Everyone knows that the Marina is the place to live, but my fiancé bought the place before I was in the picture and restored the whole unit himself. That's what he does—he restores old houses. Frankly, I don't see the draw. I'd much rather buy something new and contemporary. Anyway, it's the one point that he puts his foot down on and I figure I'll let him have his way—for now. You know how men love their little toys."

We reach the second floor and Samantha turns the key in the door. "Darling, I'm home. And I have a surprise for you!"

"I'll be right there," I hear a deep voice that sounds vaguely familiar call out from a room down the hall.

Samantha gives me a sly smile as though meeting her fiancée is the biggest event since the invention of sliced bread. I smile back, just to be polite, but I feel like telling Samantha Chase that I have met grooms-to-be dozens of times and, contrary to her opinion, it's not that big of a thrill for me.

I continue to admire the condo while we wait. The rooms are spacious and open and I can tell that the hard wood floors have been refinished and the moldings replaced. There's a fireplace and big bay windows that lets in plenty of sunlight and the kitchen is modern, with stainless steel appliances and a center island, but with touches of antique throughout. There are stairs off of the kitchen that lead down to a private patio that offers a spectacular view of the city. In a word, the condo is gorgeous and I feel the slightest bit jealous of Samantha Chase that she gets to live in such nice digs when she doesn't even appreciate it.

Samantha likes the fact that I admire her home. "You should have seen it before it was redone. I've only seen the pictures, but what a difference. I have to admit—Jack did a great job fixing it up. I guess it's in his blood."

I startle at the name before I see him. On some level, I think I knew it would be him before he walks into the room. It all makes sense; the vaguely familiar voice, the do-it-yourself restoration...and then I see him. He walks right into the room and right back into my life. Standing not two feet away from me is Jack. My Jack. Or, at least he used to be my Jack. Now he's Samantha Chase's Jack. The shock of it nearly knocks the wind out of me.

I don't know how long we stand there for before speaking or who even speaks first. Jack and I just stare at each other, mouths open and skin literally flushed. It's undoubtedly an uncomfortable moment for all present. Samantha says it best when she says, after a long and awkward silence, "Is this supposed to be a weird moment?"

Jack breaks his gaze from me and looks at her as if he is remembering who she is. As if he is being transported back to the present.

"Darling, this is Maggie McDonald, the wedding toaster. I hired her to toast our wedding. As a surprise for you," Samantha says it slowly, like she's trying to figure out what is unfolding in front of her. She clearly has no idea what's going on; hell, I hardly know myself. Then her eyes bug as she begins to realize the scope of the situation. "Do you two know each other?"

Jack hesitates slightly before he answers. "We worked together when I lived in Boston."

I remain silent. I don't know how much of Jack's past Samantha knows and I'm not about to volunteer any information that would make this clearly awkward situation any more awkward. I follow Jack's lead. But there's one thing I know for sure; there's no way I'm going to toast this wedding.

"Oh!" Sam gives a little giggle of relief. Clearly, she doesn't know just how I figure into Jack's past. "Well, what a coincidence! This is just going to make everything so much better! Well, we better hurry. We're meeting Mummy and Daddy at the vineyard for lunch," Samantha pauses and takes a second look at Jack. "Are you wearing that shirt?"

Jack looks down at what he's wearing; a navy-blue polo with a pair of khakis. I think he looks fine, in fact, I think he looks downright hot—I had forgotten how handsome he is—but obviously, Samantha has issues with a navy blue Izod. "I was planning on it."

Samantha walks over to him and plants a slow kiss on his lips. "Wear something different," she says.

Whether Jack is truly hen-pecked or whether he just doesn't feel like making an issue over a shirt, I don't know, but at any rate, he does change his shirt to a plaid-button down. He still looks hot, though.

Chapter Twenty

We drive to Napa in virtual silence. At least, me and Jack do. Samantha continues to yammer on and on about insignificant details like what type of flowers she will be carrying and the color of the bridesmaid dresses, but me and Jack remain silent. We have been in each other's company for approximately one hour at this point and we still have not uttered one word to one another. Oddly enough, I find myself profoundly glad for the presence of Samantha Chase, even though I still detest her. Samantha's too self-absorbed to observe anything other than what specifically pertains to her and at this point in time, it's her wedding. She has no idea of the tension that connects me and Jack.

I still don't know how I end up in the car. I have no intention of sticking around for the wedding. I have already thought through what I'll do; I'll leave a note for Samantha in the morning, along with a full refund, explaining that I had gotten a phone call in the middle of the night from my mother. There's a terrible emergency at home that I need to be present for and, with my deepest regret, I will not be able to toast her wedding. I would call for a flight as soon as we get to Napa and book myself on the first available one, even if I have to fly coach.

I busy myself by staring out the window at the scenery rushing by and willing myself not to look at Jack. I am still in shock from seeing him and my body feels the effects in strange ways. My stomach feels like it has dropped to my knees and my throat is so dry, I can hardly swallow. My emotions, on the other hand, are somewhat harder to read. I don't know if I'm happy to see Jack or not. I don't know if it's relief or fear or regret that is causing my body to react this way and I wonder if there' s still a part of me that loves him. I wonder if there was ever a part of me that did.

I allow myself a quick glance at him from the back seat. His hands are gripping the steering wheel so tight that his knuckles are white. I can see his face in the rear-view window, and, probably because he can feel the presence of someone staring at him, he meets my gaze in the mirror. I quickly look away, embarrassed to have been caught in such a moment.

After exhausting every possible topic on the occasion of her wedding, Samantha finds it necessary to find a new topic to explore; namely me and Jack and the circumstances that once connected us.

"So, you wrote for *The Hub*, too, Maggie?"

"Yes."

"What did you write?"

"Obituaries."

I catch a glimpse of Jack's face in the mirror. My answer surprises him. The last he had known I wrote an animal advice column, but then again, the last I had known he had been about to marry me. Life really can turn on the blink of an eye sometimes.

"Do you still work there?" Samantha asks.

I shake my head. "Toasting weddings is pretty much a full-time gig now." I leave out the part about being fired. There's no need for extraneous details.

The car slows and we pull up in front of Canyon Cove vineyard. I have to admit, the setting is quite beautiful. A large tutor style home sits amid a large spread of rolling acres and hills and a perfectly manicured courtyard contains a small, alfresco patio with wrought iron tables and chairs. I've seen some beautiful spreads in my line of work (catering to the rich and somewhat famous has its perks), but there's something bucolic about this place. I fall in love with it immediately and find yet another reason to be jealous of Samantha Chase. Of course, it could all be related to my penchant for wine.

An attractive middle-aged couple come out to the car to greet us and I immediately know that it's Mr. and Mrs. Chase; proprietors of this fine wine establishment and parents of the bride, not to mention Jack's future in-laws. I quietly smooth down my pants with my hands and subtly try to apply some more lip-gloss.

"Welcome, welcome," Mr. Chase, a tall and distinguished looking gentleman with silver-gray hair, calls to all of us, as Mrs. Chase trails slightly behind, waving and looking pretty.

"Hi, Daddy," Samantha greets her father by kissing him on both cheeks and then greets her mother the same way.

"Hello, sir." Jack extends his hand to Mr. Chase.

"Jack," Mr. Chase says in a somewhat formal tone as he offers a firm and solid handshake.

"How are you, Mrs. Chase?" Jack asks his future mother-in-law after he offers her a polite peck on the cheek.

"Fine, just fine, Jack. Thank you."

The whole scene strikes me as odd. It's just so formal. When Jack and I had been together, he called my mother Lila and Uncle Hor, he called Uncle Hor. He used to greet my mother with a hearty laugh and a great, big smile and would twirl her around before embracing her in a big bear hug. He would slap Uncle Hor on the back and say, "How's it goin', pal?" There was none of this practice of formal etiquette and certainly none of these French greeting rituals. It's weird to see Jack acting this way now, but I remind myself that this is his new family. There is no room for the past.

"Daddy, Mummy," Samantha says as she directs her parents' attention to me, "this is the wedding toaster. Maggie McDonald."

I flinch a little bit at the intro. Usually I'm introduced by my clients as Maggie McDonald first, and then they share the fact that I am, in fact, the wedding toaster. I mean I do have a name. I am a person and not simply "the wedding toaster." Toasting weddings is what I do, it's not who I am and frankly, I think it's quite rude that Samantha introduces me this way, but at the end of the day, she's still the one paying me, so I bite my lip, smile my most gracious smile, and offer my hand.

"How do you do? It's so nice to meet you both!"

"Likewise, wedding toaster," Mr. Chase says. I couldn't tell if it's his attempt at trying to be funny or if he really thinks it's acceptable etiquette to simply call me wedding toaster. "I trust that you are going to give my Sammy one helluva toast."

"That's my job, sir," I say, smiling fake-ly. Little does he know that I have no intention of giving any toast at all.

We sit down at one of the café tables in the courtyard while a few of the staffers come and carry our bags inside. I have an impulse to tell them not to bother with mine, that I won't be here long enough for it to be worth the effort, but somehow, my mouth won't open and my feet won't move and I find myself sitting down to a glorious late afternoon lunch with my ex-fiancée and his new fiancée, along with his soon-to-be inherited in-laws. I guess you can call it a textbook example of Murphy's Law. Besides, I am looking forward to a glass or two (or three) of wine. I decide it's best to stick to my original plan, which is to steal stealthily away in the quiet of the night, and enjoy the day as much as I can. If anything, it's certainly turning out to be interesting. Besides, I still have some things I need to say to Jack and the opportunity still hasn't presented itself yet. I need to wait around. I guess you could say I'm looking for closure. Or forgiveness.

We're served lunch on the patio. The late afternoon sun casts a beautiful light on the grounds and feels warm and seductive on my shoulders. And then there is the wine. Lots and lots of wine. We end up having our own little wine tasting event as Mr. Chase kept beckoning the help to retrieve a different bottle from the wine cellar. I think he was trying to show off but I don't care. I don't care one bit. I'm getting glasses and glasses of free wine. And these are expensive bottles; not your run-of-the-mill packy store variety.

"This is our award-winning chardonnay," Mr. Chase would say to me, as he would fill my glass. Or, "This is our full-bodied cabernet. Not too dry with just a hint of a fruity after taste."

He teaches me how to swirl my glass in order to release the full aroma and body of the wine and how to tilt my glass and look at the legs (of the wine, I mean, not the glass. Or maybe it is the other way around…I never heard of a glass, or wine, having legs…oh, never mind—I think I'm getting drunk).

I find this exercise in wine tasting is two-fold. First, it offers a way to sample a variety of expensive and exquisite wines for free and second, it serves to ease the awkwardness that envelopes Jack and me. Not that it makes the situation itself any less awkward, but rather that you just don't feel the effects so much after delighting in several of these glasses of free wine. I think Jack feels the same way because he seems to be indulging in multiple glasses himself. Anyway, I am relaxed. Relaxed enough to finally speak to Jack when the opportunity arises, which it inevitably will.

We are just finishing up our desert and coffee when Mrs. Chase daintily dabs at her mouth with her napkin and ever so slightly clears her throat. "Samantha, darling, there is one small matter to attend to concerning the wedding."

Samantha pauses, holding her coffee cup in mid-air, halfway to her mouth. She looks at her mother, dead and center, and lowers her voice to sound as menacing as possible.

"What?"

Mrs. Chase pauses for a millisecond and I wonder if her own daughter perhaps intimidates her. She clears her throat again and gently lays her napkin on the table.

"The florist called. She's short on dendrobium orchids and another shipment isn't expected in until next Wednesday."

"The wedding is Saturday," Samantha says through clenched teeth.

"Yes, I know, dear but the orchids do come from Singapore. It's not like we can just call up another florist who will have them in stock," Mrs. Chase pauses again for half a second. "Freesia would be a doable substitute."

"I don't want freesia!" Samantha slams her fist down and the table shakes. "Daddy! Do something!" Samantha's face shrivels up and a sort of snorting/wailing sound starts to escape from her throat.

"Alright, alright, Sammy. Everything will be okay." Mr. Chase jumps up from his chair and runs over to console his only daughter over the absence of a certain type of flower from her bouquet. "I have a buyer in Singapore. We'll call him straight away and see what can be done. There is no way you will have to settle for freesia on your wedding day."

I steal a glance at Jack during this debacle. He has a look of absolute disgust on his face, which, oddly enough, makes me feel better. I know Jack's not the type of guy to give any credence to what type of flower you carried in a bouquet. And he certainly didn't give any sympathy for throwing a temper tantrum over it. In this moment, I feel like I still know Jack—like something deeper connected us—but I still, for the life of me, cannot figure out what he is doing with Samantha Chase.

Mr. Chase eases his daughter out of her seat, and beckons for his wife to follow. "Ellen," he says as he nods his head toward the house, motioning her to come along. "Let's go see what we can do about this." Mrs. Chase immediately jumps out of her seat and, although I'm not sure, I think I may have seen her roll her eyes. Evidently, she is accustomed to her daughter's flair for drama. The three of them head into the house and I am left alone with Jack.

The suddenness of it is a little daunting. Here I am, after three years, and quite by accident, sitting alone with the man I almost married. I shift uncomfortably in my seat and try to get a read on Jack. He's wearing sunglasses so I can't tell what his eyes are saying but his jaw is tight and his knuckles are clenched as he gives two wraps on the table. I remember that he used to do that at the office when he was stuck on a piece and was afraid he wouldn't make deadline. At least I know that I still have the power to make him nervous.

"So," I say. "Talk about surprises…surprise!"

"Yeah," Jack says indifferently, "if this is the cosmos' idea of a joke, it's not very fuckin' funny." Jack is pissed. I guess he has a right to be. But I'm a big girl and I would take what I have coming to me.

"Jack, I swear…I had no idea. I was just as surprised to see you when I walked through that door. Samantha told me she hired me as a surprise for her fiancé."

Jack snorts. "Yeah, well it's one hell of a fuckin' surprise, isn't it?" I'm making no progress in my attempt to smooth things over.

"Does Samantha know about the, uh, history…between us?"

Jack takes off his sunglasses and looks at me hard. "No, Maggie, she doesn't. Forgive me if I don't like publicizing how I was publicly humiliated and abandoned on my own wedding day."

I wince at the intensity with which he says it. "Jack," I say, swallowing hard, "for what it's worth, I am sorry."

He looks at me for a minute, letting all the anger and hate he feels towards me soak through to my skin. "Well, your word doesn't mean much, now does it?"

I have no response to this but I can feel myself start to well up. Jack reaches for his sunglasses and gets up from the table. "I'm goin' for a walk," he mutters and then, with giant strides, disappears into the vineyards.

I take sharp, quick breaths to try to keep from unfolding. The Chases will be back any minute and the last thing I need is to explain to them why I am presently in an emotional turmoil. I rub my eyes, blink back my tears and reach in my bag for both my inhaler and my sunglasses. Despite my best efforts, the shock of seeing Jack again and the following events are getting to me and I can feel my eyes burning.

I hear a mixture of voices and footsteps approaching and I pray to God that the orchid crisis has been resolved. I cannot take Samantha Chase's incessant whining and shrill voice on top of everything else. Hell, I can't even take it under normal circumstances.

"Problem solved," Ellen Chase says as they approach me. "A shipment will be here on Friday."

"Where's Jack?" Samantha asks upon noticing his absence.

"He went for a walk. He said he wouldn't be long. And actually," I start, "I was wondering if you all wouldn't mind if I go and lie down for a bit."

"Of course, of course," Ellen says. "You must be tired from the flight. Fritz will show you to the guesthouse. And please let him know if you need anything."

"Thank you," I say. I actually like Ellen Chase. She's more pleasant than her husband and daughter and she seems remotely normal. She also seems to realize that her daughter is sort of a bitch.

The butler leads me to the guesthouse and I'm grateful to finally be alone. I take out my cell and call Carrie. I curse when I get her voicemail but leave her an urgent message. "There is no way I'm doing this wedding. Jack is the groom. It's going terribly. Book me on the first flight out—even if it's coach. Call me."

I pace the room, waiting fervently for Carrie to call but after ten minutes, I curse Carrie and decide it's time to take matters into my own hands. I call the airport and then curse the woman I'm talking to because the earliest flight out is Wednesday morning. It's Monday afternoon. I decide to leave Napa anyway, the next morning, and just bide my time at a hotel in San Francisco for the day. Problem solved. I am getting the hell out of Dodge.

Carrie calls me back a few minutes later. *"Oh my God! Oh my God!"* is all she keeps saying.

"I know, I know. I can't believe it."

"Was it weird?"

I think for a moment. "It was. It was just such a shock, you know? But then it's like it wasn't weird. Like, I saw familiar habits in him that haven't changed," I'm quiet again for a second. "It's weird seeing him with someone else."

"How is she?" Carrie asks, meaning the new me. Jack's new bride; the one who would actually go through with the wedding.

"Carrie, she's terrible. She's mean and bitchy and self-centered. I really don't see what Jack sees in her, I mean, she's not his type at all."

Now Carrie is quiet for a minute, and I don't know why. It's as if she has to pick her words carefully. "Well, a lot has happened between you and Jack, Maggie, and a lot of time has passed. Things change."

"Yeah, I guess," is all I say. "I booked a flight home for Wednesday morning so you don't have to get me one."

"What are you going to tell the client?"

"I'll leave a note giving some lame excuse and I'll leave a check for a full refund."

"I'm sorry it worked out this way, Maggie."

"Don't be," I say. "It happened and, you know Carrie, at least now I know that Jack's okay. I wondered about that a lot the last few years. It's closure."

"Yeah, I guess you're right."

I say goodbye to Carrie and think about calling my mom, but she had gone to visit Uncle Hor and Dolly in Sarasota and I don't want to put a damper on her visit with my melodrama.

And then it comes over me. It is a wave of emotion of crying and slobbering onto my pillow. I lie down on my bed and expel every last bit of grief and regret and shock in me for about an hour straight. And then I'm done. I get up, take a shower and retrieve my sweats from my suitcase. Mrs. Chase had come by to check on me earlier and asked if I wanted to join them for dinner but I told her I wasn't feeling great. I'm not up for a repeat performance of lunch. The less I see of Jack, the better. Now I'm just looking forward to my exit.

I sit down at the desk and pen a brief but eloquent note to Samantha, expressing my deepest regret and apologies. I explain that I had gotten a phone call that my mother was ill and I need to leave right away. I tuck the note in an envelope along with the check, seal it, and leave it on the desk. I'll slide it under the front door of the main residence in the morning.

I turn my attention to my suitcase and think how ironic it is that I have to repack just to pack. It gives me something to do, at any rate. I empty the contents on the bed and start folding my clothes all over again, just to have them go back in the suitcase. You'd think by now that I would have gotten the art of packing down, but I never have.

Chapter Twenty-One

I'm in the middle of separating my hosiery from my sleepwear when there's a knock on my door. I open it and standing right in front of me is Jack, holding a dinner tray. The moment takes me by surprise and I hesitate before saying anything.

"Hi," he offers feebly. "Mrs. Chase thought you might be hungry so she had this sent up." I nod a thanks and take the tray from him.

"So, do you make it a hobby to wait on the guests or am I just a favorite?" I ask lamely. Really, I don't know what else to say.

Jack comes into the room, closing the door behind him. "I volunteered to take it to you." I turn to look at him, surprised. "Look, Maggie, the truth is I want to apologize to you about today. It was just the shock of seeing you, and especially under these circumstances. But I acted like a jackass and I do apologize for that."

I look at him fondly. It can't be easy for Jack to come here and apologize to me, of all people, but he had always been a gentleman. Some things never change.

"It's okay," I say. "I guess I deserve it."

Jack gives that half-grin, which I always found to be so sexy, and extends his hand.

"Truce?"

"Truce." I extend my own and our hands clasp together. His hands feel exactly how I remember them: Rough and calloused and strong and warm. It's as familiar a feeling as coming home. I had always loved his hands. It's funny how you can still know intimate details about someone when they are no longer a part of your life.

I think the familiarity startles Jack, too. His breath catches, ever so slightly, when he touches my hand and after a second or two of lingering, he pulls it away quickly. He turns and runs his hand over his head, and then he notices my suitcase.

"You goin' somewhere?"

There is no point in lying to him. "Look, Jack, I think it's the best thing for everyone if I just leave." Jack looks at me in this moment, as if I've just left him at the altar again. I don't quite get it.

"Maggie, I understand it's an awkward situation, but you just can't leave."

"Oh, I left a note," I say, reaching for the white envelope and offering it up as proof. "And a full refund. It's all here." I wonder if Jack thinks that I'm trying to swindle the Chase's out of their money, which hurts my feelings a little bit. I might overcharge clients, but I would never swindle them.

Jack closes his eyes and shakes his head. "You signed on for this, Maggie. The Chases are expecting you to fulfill a service. You can't just run away from a commitment when it's too overwhelming." I know now that Jack is talking about more than skipping out on a client. He's referring to when I skipped out on him. I stay silent. I sense that Jack has more to say and I would listen. It's the least I owe him.

"Besides," he adds on a lighter note, "do you know what I'd have to put up with if you bailed? All the whining and bitching and complaining? You don't really want to put me through that, do you?"

I smile. "I guess I've already scarred you enough for life."

"Yes, you have!" Jack says, with a full-on smile. It feels good to be joking with him. It feels natural. It also feels a little sad. Jack has moved on, and I have no business judging his decisions. All I can do now is put on a happy face.

"So, you owe me this, Maggie McDonald!" Jack continues. "Consider it your penance, for past deeds committed towards me."

"You're enjoying this, aren't you!" I say it with jest, but I really don't mean it that way. I'm a good actress.

Jack laughs. "Just a little bit! Talk about poetic justice. It is weird, isn't it? I guess there is truth to the saying, 'what comes around goes around'."

"Okay, okay!" I say loudly. "I'll do it. I'll toast your freakin' wedding! Consider it my penance for past behavior. But," I say firmly, pointing my finger at him, "after this, cosmic balance has been restored. There will be no guilt, no anger and no regrets between us, understand?" I do it for him. I

166

don't really mean anything I say at this point. I'll always feel the guilt. And, I think, the regret.

Jack smiles. "Deal." We shake on it and it doesn't go unnoticed, by either of us, I think, that our fingers linger just a tad longer than usual. "Well, I better go. They'll be waiting for me to go to dinner." Jack turns to go.

"Jack," I call, last minute. He turns back to me. "How are we going to play this?"

He knows what I mean. I don't have to explain.

"Just like we said. We know each other from the paper, back in Boston. It's not lying."

"No, I guess it's not," I say, but it's not the whole truth either.

"See you tomorrow," Jack says to me, and he walks out the door.

I sit down on the bed and sigh. *What the hell am I getting myself into?* A big part of me tells me that this is not a good idea, not in the least. But another part of me is curious. I don't know why I'm curious, exactly, but I am. At any rate, Jack and I seem to be on semi-good terms now. At least I know the week will be bearable. I grab my cell and text Carrie.

Change of plans. Am toasting wedding. Call you tomorrow.

I call the airport, cancel my flight and rip up the note. Of course, I stick the check back in my wallet and, I must admit, I'm happy to not have to part with it. Finally, I crawl into bed and turn off the light. It's been a long day and fatigue suddenly washes over me like a wave. I plump up my pillow and settle in, wondering, in anticipation, what the week will bring.

I walk into the courtyard the next morning, after a much-needed good night's sleep. I know I have overslept because I hear mumbled voices around the corner.

I turn the corner and find Samantha and Jack and Mr. and Mrs. Chase, engrossed in conversation over croissants and coffee. I timidly walk up to the table and the talking immediately stops. Talk about giving a girl a complex. I look around nervously, not knowing what the proper course of action is.

"Maggie, sit down, dear," Ellen Chase says to me. I'm happy to have a task to fulfill, instead of just standing there sheepishly.

I sit down and butter myself a croissant while Fritz pours me a cup of coffee. I steal a look at Jack, who seems to look nervous, and noticeably avoids making eye contact with me. "So, Maggie," Samantha finally says after a prolonged silence, "what is it that you typically do when preparing for your toasts? How do you spend your time?"

"Oh," I say, a little taken aback, but also, relieved. From the mood and awkward silence that has been present at the table, I'm expecting some crisis, or God forbid, that Samantha has somehow found out about Jack and I's past, but this, this is easy. This is a question I can actually answer, with both professionalism and confidence. "I spend the time with the couple and make informal observations about their relationship, which enables me to make a profound, yet personal, toast." I smile at my audience, quite proud of myself. I think I gave a rather eloquent and kickass answer.

"Do you spend all of your time with the couple, or do you spend time with them separately?"

"Well, both," I say, somewhat confused. I don't know where this is going.

"Perfect!" Samantha says, in an overly perky tone. "Maggie can spend time with Jack while I go to Portland."

My mouth drops open and Jack keeps his head down, avoiding the utter look of disbelief on my face.

"Portland, Maine?" I finally manage to sputter out.

"Oregon," Mr. Chase answers. "One of the restaurants up there is threatening to go with a rival winery's sauvignon blanc. Sammy's point person on this," he adds as he comes around the table and gives his daughter an affectionate squeeze. "There's no one better at calling a bluff."

I understand now. Samantha is flying the coop, so to speak, to take care of business, four days before her wedding. I don't think she would agree to this if she knew the implications involved.

"Samantha," I say in earnest, "I have to say, as a professional, that I don't think it's a good idea to take this trip now. Isn't there any way you can wait until after the wedding?"

"I agree," Ellen Chase adds quickly.

"It'll be fine!" Samantha pours herself another cup of coffee. "Everything's in place. The flower debacle is solved, thank god! And everything else is in place. Maggie said it herself…she usually spends time with each half of the couple alone…"

"I didn't say that exactly…" I interrupt quickly.

Samantha shoots me a look. "It's fine!" she says, reassuringly. "I'll be home Thursday, and everything will be good to go."

"The wedding is in four days, Sammy," Jack says. At least now I know where Jack stands. He doesn't think it's a good idea for us to be left alone either.

"And I'll be home in two." She turns and gives Jack a slow kiss on the lips.

And that was that. Samantha Chase was leaving her fiancé alone for two days, with his ex-fiancée. Imagine the possibilities.

Chapter Twenty-Two

A few hours later, Jack and I are sitting on the patio of the local pub. All the awkwardness of a first date seems to be present, although it definitely is *not* a date. Jack's pick of location does not go unnoticed by me, either. It's a neutral, friendly setting, absent of the intimacy and coziness of some of the finer dining establishments in Napa Valley, but that's fine with me. The situation is awkward enough without throwing romantic notions and ambience into the mix.

"So," Jack says, as he fiddles with the silverware on the table.

"So," I say back, fumbling uncomfortably with the napkin on my lap.

The level of comfort and familiarity we had experienced last night when we talked is obviously absent. In its place, fourteen hours later, is a big, gaping hole, full of unanswered questions, doubt, and sheer awkwardness (I know I keep using that word a lot but, really, there is no other way to describe this situation). This is a whole new ballgame. Neither one of us thought we would be spending a concentrated amount of time alone together. So, I do the only thing any gal can do in my predicament; I order a beer. And then, I order another, and another. At least Jack and I are on the same wavelength, because he ordered quite a few too.

We make small talk over the first drink and the appetizer; how beautiful it is here, how nice the weather is, is Barry Bonds the greatest hitter of all time…you know, the usual, polite, dance-around-the-topic banter. But by the third beer and our main entrée, and one particularly pesky and rather vicious bumblebee, things reach a more desirable level of comfort. Well, at least for me, namely because I don't get stung. But poor Jack…he has a deathly allergy to bees—always has had since he was a little boy, and almost died once when he went camping with his dad and tripped right on a hive. And today, well, today is just one of those days. I see it flying around his head while I'm eating my coleslaw.

"Jack," I say steadily and slowly. "There's a bee around your head." He immediately stiffens up and the color drains slightly from his face. I'm not mocking when I say this either; it must be a frightening thing knowing an everyday commonality for most people has the power to kill you. "Don't flinch! Just keep still and calm."

Jack freezes as if he's a statue, his French fry, dripping with ketchup, dangling from his finger in mid-air. The bee continues to buzz around him, his sound droning loudly as if it's a miniature motor. I freeze too, coleslaw dripping from my fork. I don't want any sudden movements from either of us to goad the bee into doing something foolish. It continues buzzing, louder and louder, until it lands itself right on Jack's nose. His eyes turn big, as he looks down on the yellow fixture perched on the ball of his nose.

"Uhh," he says feebly. I think he knows it's inevitable.

"Do you have your epi pen with you?" I ask calmly. At this point, I know we will most likely have to use it. This little bugger just didn't quit. I figure it's better to risk getting stung but to have the epi pen within reach.

"In my front pocket," Jack whispers.

"I want you to get it out slowly and give it to me."

"But he'll sting me!"

"He'll probably sting you, anyway, it's better that we're prepared."

Jack mulls over his options and realizing that both are grim, he decides to play it smart. He slowly reaches into his front pocket and begins to retrieve the epi pen.

I put my hand out slowly. I know exactly what to do. I had to give Jack a shot once before when we were dating. We had been sitting outside Faneuil Hall on our lunch hour when one came out of nowhere and got him on the arm. I almost laugh out loud when I remember that Jack had shown me how to use it when we first started dating.

"I don't want to seem like a total dork," he had said to me, "but it's imperative that you know how to use this. I have to do this with all the girls I date, for real. It could save my life."

I did think it was dorky at the time but I also found it endearing. Anyway, thanks to my prior training I am primed to act under the present circumstances.

Our hands are just about to meet across the table with the epi pen ready to be transferred. The bee is still sitting there, humming loudly, like it's laughing at the present state of things. I stand up slowly and grab the pen.

"Ow!" Jack screams. It's too late. Jack's nose begins to grow monumentally at an alarming rate. A red line starts to appear and I know I have to act fast. I practically dive across the table with dishes and food and silverware falling to the floor in a loud crash and people all around us looking on in perplexed wonderment. I raise the epi pen into the air and jab it into his thigh. The red line disappears immediately and, to all those present, I appear to be the hero of the day.

People begin applauding and one Chinese couple, who are undoubtedly tourists and think it's a much larger crisis than it actually is, shake my hand and start bowing to me fervently. It's quite a scene, actually, and I do take a moment to bask.

"How's your nose feeling?" I ask when we get outside.

"It hurts like hell. And it feels like the size of the Sears Tower."

"Let me see." I move his hand away from his nose. "Well, not the Sears," I say cheekily, "but definitely Empire State Building size."

"Shut up!" Jack pushes my hand away and I rib him in the shoulder, just so he knows I'm kidding. It's a nice moment, actually. It's like a barrier is knocked down and we are now able to be ourselves with each other again. I guess I have the bee to thank.

"Why is it that I'm always humiliated in front of you?" Jack says, only half-kidding.

I shake my head, slightly blushing. "Not at all." There is a slightly prolonged silence. We both know what is left unsaid. "So, did you give Samantha 'the training'?" I ask, both because I'm curious but also because I want to change the subject.

Jack laughs. He knows what I'm talking about. "Oh my God! Do you remember that? I can't believe what a dork I was! It worked though, didn't it?"

"It worked," I say coyly. "But that was your plan all along, I bet."

Jack laughs again. "Well, it's a good thing I trained you up, after today! I mean you can see the pressing necessity of it."

"Oh, I can," I say in my same coy manner, "although it worked out better for you than me. I mean, you didn't get coleslaw in your hair."

Jack laughs again. That same easy laugh that I remember. "But you still haven't answered my question," I press on. "Have you given Samantha 'the training'?"

"Sam isn't very good in a crisis. She's great in business matters, but when it comes to things in the more personal arena, she'd rather have the butler take care of it."

I think of the flower incident at breakfast the previous morning. Samantha almost had a nervous breakdown at the thought that she wouldn't have her precious orchid in the bouquet. I want to laugh when I think about her in the situation that had just occurred at the restaurant, but then I think of the reality that Jack would have most likely died if it had been her instead of me, and I don't think it's so funny anymore. "So, did you train the butler then?" I ask in a lighter tone.

"You bet your ass I did. There are a lot of bees in Napa."

We spend the rest of the day walking the quaint downtown and getting reacquainted. Both our circumstances have changed drastically since the last time we had been together and there are a lot of blanks to fill in. I fill Jack in on Carrie and Kate, and on my mom and Uncle Hor, and explain just how I came to be the wedding toaster.

"I still can't quite grasp it," I say to him as we sit down on a bench with an ice-cream cone in the late afternoon. "My life has changed so much in the past year. Sometimes I wake up and I can't remember where I'm flying off to or where I just came from."

"I saw your profile in *People*," Jack confesses, "but I sure as hell never would have guessed that Sam would hire you. That just about gave me the shock of my life."

"Me, too," I say. "It was certainly unexpected."

We're both quiet for a minute, concentrating on licking our cones to keep the ice cream from dripping and quietly dodging the subject that has just been broached. We haven't talked about our own wedding, except in vague terms, since the heated exchange of words we had yesterday. Finally, when the silence becomes too long, I ask another question.

"How did you and Samantha meet?" It is research, after all.

"I was doing renovation work at the vineyard. Putting in a new bathroom in the guesthouse. Sam came in and offered me a glass of their award-winning cabernet." He gets up and throws his napkin away. "The rest is history."

"How long have you been together?" I'm not sure I want to know the answer but I press on anyway. I begin to realize that I don't really want to know how Jack's life has evolved since I have been absent from it.

"A year and a half. I popped the question four months ago." We hail a cab and head back to the vineyard. Evidently, it's Fritz's day off. I don't ask any more questions; I've received enough information for today. Honestly, I don't think my insides can handle anymore.

I lie in bed, waiting for sleep to claim me, and think about the events of the day. After the initial awkwardness had worn off, it had actually been a nice day. I mean, except for the fact that Jack got stung and could have died, but other than that, I have no complaints. It felt good being with Jack again. It felt natural, like all the distance and space between us had been evaporated.

I can finally feel myself start to drift off. I snuggle into the sheets, with a slight smile on my face and, for the first time in a long time, I dream of Jack.

Chapter Twenty-Three

We leave early the next morning for San Francisco. Jack has to take care of a few things in the city and says he'll give me a sightseeing tour while we're there. I'm thankful for the time with him. Not only because I still need to conduct some research for my toast but also because I find I genuinely like spending time with Jack. The hours seem to pass like minutes when I'm with him and I'm reminded of why I fell in love with him in the first place.

"Your nose looks back to normal," I tell him as we drive down the dirt road that leads us away from the vineyard, the tires kicking up dust behind us.

"Well, it feels better, but I still don't think the swelling's down." He crinkles his nose up the way he used to when he got a whiff of something unpleasant. I smile at the memory, but then I bring myself to the present. I have a job to do. I will myself to ask about Samantha.

"Have you heard from Sam?" Aside from how they met, I still don't know the story with Jack and Samantha. What did he see in her? What did she see in him? Jack and Samantha seem as different to me as night and day, but I cannot discount the fact that I've often been hasty in my judgments of other couples (Morty and Addy, Sam and Ella, and Daisy and Randy come to mind), and in every case, I was proven wrong. But this is different. This is Jack. I know Jack better than anyone, or at least I used to, and I cannot, for the life of me, see what draws him to Samantha Chase.

I fiddle with the radio, just to give myself something to focus on, and then turn it off. I know what I am doing; I'm procrastinating—I don't want to hear about Jack and Samantha's relationship any more than I want a root canal—but I need to take advantage of this time in order to get the research I need. "What about Sam attracted you to her?" Jack is surprised. He shoots me a questioning look, not quite sure of my motives.

175

"It's for the toast," I say quickly. "It just helps if I get some of the details. You know…for composing my toast."

Jack looks out at the road and ponders the question. "Well, there was the physical attraction, initially…"

"Uh-huh," I say briskly.

"And other than that…" Jack's voice trails off. He either has nothing to offer on the subject or he's trying in vain to find something to offer on the subject. Either way, it doesn't speak so well for the couple-to-be when you don't really know why you're marrying the other person. I wonder if Samantha would be able to answer the question more easily.

"Sam knows what she wants," Jack answers finally. "There's no bullshit with her. She knows what she wants and she goes after it. There's something sexy about that." He pauses for a second and then adds, "You know what you're getting with Sam. It's not a guessing game."

There's more in that answer than the words he gives. Samantha won't leave Jack at the altar. She won't break his heart. She might tell him how to dress and where to live, but she won't leave him. I don't fully realize until this moment the scope of how badly I had hurt Jack. He would put up with the nagging and the nitpicking and the emotional meltdowns that Samantha is known for in exchange for the comfort and consistency of knowing that he was wanted. The revelation overwhelms me; Jack is marrying Samantha Chase because she is the opposite of me.

We drive on in silence for a while and I fiddle with the radio again, but this time I leave it on. The only station that has reception is country, but I'd rather have that fill the car than an awkward, glaring silence. Besides, I have rather come to like country music. I guess I can thank Jackson Hole for that.

"Uh…for the love of Christ, please change the station," Jack says after about one minute of airtime.

"What?"

"Don't tell me you like that song, Maggie. You don't like country."

"For your information, I'm quite fond of country music now."

Jack laughs. "You? I don't believe it! You used to cringe any time a country song came on the radio. I remember that time we were out to eat at Luna's on Newbury, and a country song came on. You made us leave because you couldn't stand listening to the song."

I did remember that. "Well, people change," I say indignantly. "Besides, it was more the principle of the matter. Country music has no place in a retro-chic fine dining establishment on Newbury Street. Ambience is everything."

Jack laughs out loud. "You haven't changed that much."

"Well, you don't like country music either."

"If I have the choice of what to listen to, then no, it's not on the top of my list, but I wouldn't leave a restaurant because of it."

"It was just desert," I say defensively. "We were almost done anyway."

Jack laughs again. "Whatever."

"And I have changed, by the way," I add.

"Like how?" Jack is amused now.

"Like, I like country music now. The rest is for you to find out."

He laughs again. "Is that a challenge?"

"It's a fact," I reply. "Take it any way you want."

"Well, you know I can't resist a challenge."

"Well, good. You have the whole day to figure it out."

The song ends and I turn the radio off to prevent any more "challenges" being posed. Instead I turn my attention out the window and to the scenery that's emerging. We are just crossing the Golden Gate Bridge, and the sun sparkled and danced on the bay.

"Wow," I say. It is a breathtaking sight.

"It is a pretty city," Jack says. "It is a pretty city, that's for sure."

And I must admit…it is a pretty city. We spend the day visiting all the key sights as well as little, out of the way discoveries that only a local could show you, and I fall in love immediately (with the city, I mean). Jack takes me to Ghirardelli Square and Fisherman's Wharf and to the top of Telegraph Hill. We walk through The Presidio and across the Golden Gate and through the Palace of Fine Arts. He takes me through Union Square and Nob Hill and all the quintessential San Francisco neighborhoods. We walk through Golden Gate Park and buy hotdogs from a vendor and laugh and lick mustard from our fingers in the waning, afternoon sun. I don't want the day to end.

"My dad would have loved this city." We gaze out on the city skyline from Telegraph Hill. "The architecture and the culture…all of it. It's an artist's city."

Jack looks at me, and smiles, pleased that I approve of his new hometown.

"Do you ever miss Boston?" I ask curiously.

Jack looks at me. "Some things I miss," he says, and a tingle runs down my spine. "Boston and San Francisco are similar cities in a lot of ways. The oldness and the architecture...the diversity of neighborhoods...but I must say that San Francisco has much better weather." I laugh. It is true. "This is my home now," he says. "This is my home," and I suddenly feel the distance and circumstances that separate us.

"So, what do you say?" Jack asks, changing the subject. "Are you hungry or what?"

"I could eat," I offer. It has been a few hours since the hotdog.

Jack checks his watch. "I just have one quick stop to make and then we'll grab some dinner."

We stop in front of a small, real estate office, with a sign that reads *Smith & Smith* out front. "I'll be right out," he says as he opens the car door. He returns a few minutes later and we drive up one of San Francisco's many hills, the city falling away behind us. "Listen, I need to go back to the apartment to pick up some things. What say we order some Thai take-out and eat there? You like Thai, right?"

We stop at the restaurant and pick up our orders and then stop at the liquor store to pick up some wine. "Don't tell Sam it's not Canyon Cove," Jack says as he brings two bottles of Berringer to the cashier. "This is the competition." But I know why he is buying it. Berringer had always been our favorite brand back in Boston. He still remembers, and the tenderness of it is enough to make my eyes fill up.

Chapter Twenty-Four

We sit on the couch, the fireplace going, even though it's a warm night, eating our Thai food and drinking wine. There is a sultry, smoky CD playing in the background and I have to remind myself that this is not real life. This is a lucky break; a moment from a time passed, that we are both lucky enough to recapture.

"What business did you have at a realtor's office?" I twirl some noodles around my fork. I know it's not really any of my business, but the two glasses of wine I had loosen me up a bit, and besides, I am curious.

"I'm putting the apartment on the market. It's a wedding gift for Sam."

My mouth drops open, despite my best effort to keep it closed. "Jack," I say finally, "You can't sell this place. You love it."

"How do you know that?"

I look around. "I can just tell." And I can. The apartment is filled with Jack's scent. His hands had refinished the hard wood floors, primed and painted the walls and affixed new light fixtures. This is what Jack loved to do, and he was actually doing it now, instead of writing about it in newspapers. It makes me sad to think he'd give it all up for some pouty, self-centered girl; someone who doesn't understand, or care, that this is his passion, but I think I finally recognize the size and depth of Jack's heart in this moment, and I regret that it doesn't belong to me anymore.

Jack just shrugs his shoulders. "She wants to live in The Marina, so…"

I change the subject, the warmth and safety of wine wrapped around me like a blanket. "You ready for the big day?"

"Everything's taken care of. All we need now is for both of us to show up."

He gives me a knowing stare. I don't know if it's the wine talking, or another attempt at getting one more dig in. I guess I deserve it, but it still casts an awkward silence that hovers over the room. I get up to clear my plate and pour myself another glass of wine.

Jack gets up and follows me into the kitchen. I can feel a nightmare coming on.

"Why did you do it, Maggie?" There is an edge of desperation in his voice. "I told myself I wouldn't ask, but God, I need to know."

"It wasn't you," I offer in earnest as I turn around to face him. "I freaked out…I wasn't ready…"

"And that's supposed to make me feel better?"

I pause. "It's the only answer I have to give."

We are both quiet for a minute, letting the past wash over us. Jack takes a few steps towards me and strokes my cheek. I have to inhale to keep from sighing out loud. I remember this touch, and after all this time, it still has the power to melt me.

"Do you regret it?" He almost whispers.

I hesitate before I give my answer. I want to tell Jack that I regret it every day. I want to tell him that I think I regretted it before I even knew I did. Something has happened to me during this strange journey of toasting weddings. Somewhere along the line, I fell in love with being in love. Somewhere along the line, I realized that I didn't want to be alone anymore. And at some point, over the past two days, I realized that I was still in love with Jack. Maybe I always was.

But I also know that Jack belongs to someone else now. It is someone else's cheek he should be stroking, someone else he should be drinking wine with while he listens to slow, sexy music. Someone else he should be marrying. As much as I disliked Samantha Chase, it is she who should be standing here instead of me.

So, I give the only acceptable answer that's appropriate. "It doesn't matter now."

Jack is so close to me now; I have to fight the impulse to reach over and trace the shape of his face. I could kiss him if I wanted to, and I don't think he would mind. I recognize the moment as a chance for a new beginning, and I know that I am standing at the proverbial fork in the road. If I want Jack back, I know that I can have him, but something has changed inside of me. It is because I love Jack that I have to let him go. I look him in the eyes, my own beginning to brim with tears. "I have to go."

I brush by him and run down the stairs and out onto the street. I gulp in the fresh air with huge breaths, trying to stop my insides from collapsing. I don't know where I'm going, and I don't know if Jack has followed me outside, or if he is yelling my name in vain. A part of me is afraid to look back; both because I am afraid he is there, and because I'm afraid he isn't. I just run. I run and run, trying, I think, to lose the burden of my penance.

I end up at the waterfront. I sit down on a nearby bench and let the events of the night flood over me. The last two days seem like a dream. It's so strange to see Jack with someone else, especially someone I loathe as much as Samantha Chase. Morty would call me and Jack meeting again serendipitous; an encounter predestined by the forces that be. I don't know about that; I just know I'm glad it had happened. And I'm not glad at the same time. There is nothing I want more than to go back to the apartment, kiss Jack hard on the mouth and tell him I still love him. I want to convince him that I am the girl for him after all, but then again, my credibility hasn't been great in that department. And the truth of the matter is I don't have the right to. As much as I despise Samantha Chase, she is the one who has the right to be at the altar this time waiting for Jack. I had had my chance once and I blew it. I wouldn't blow it for someone else, even if that someone is Samantha Chase.

I kick a pebble with my foot in frustration and I start to cry. Somewhere along this journey I had developed a conscience, and I don't like it. There was a time when I would not have hesitated to steal a man from another woman, especially from someone as revolting as Samantha. But during my tenure as a professional wedding toaster, something has changed. I realize how precious love is and I realize what I had done to Jack is unforgivable. Even if Jack could forgive me, I'm not sure I can forgive myself.

I take a few deep breaths, wipe my eyes and attempt to pull myself together. I know now what I will do. I hail a cab and have it take me to the nearest hotel. I call the airport and book the first flight out. Then I call Fritz and have him arrange to have my suitcase sent to the hotel. I don't give an excuse to the Chases; I would let Jack handle it the way he wanted to. I just tell Fritz when I call that something has come up and I need to leave ASAP. Of course, I tell him, the Chases will receive a full refund, including travel expenses. And I'm out. There's no way I'm toasting this wedding.

Chapter Twenty-Five

I let myself into my hotel room and collapse on the bed. I have been lucky enough to score a room at The Fairmont but I am too drained to thoroughly enjoy my surroundings. Besides, this time I had to pay for it instead of a wealthy client footing the bill, and that made it less fun.

I take out my cell and call Carrie. I still need to call for a flight but I have an overwhelming need to hear my best friend's voice.

"I can't do it, Carrie. I can't do it," I say between sobs.

"Slow down, sweetie. I can't understand what you're saying. What happened?"

Tremendous sobs rack my body as I sputter out to Carrie the events of the past two days. "I can't watch him walk down the aisle and marry her," I tell her. "I can't do it."

"I'll book you a flight," Carrie says sympathetically. "Get a good night's sleep, Mags. I'll call you in the morning." Carrie pauses for a second, "It'll be okay, Maggie. I love you."

"Love you too," and I click off my phone. I feel marginally better after talking to Carrie. She just listened, which is all I wanted and she didn't pass judgment on my neurotic state of mind. Everyone else…well, that would be a different story. I'd just have to wait and see.

The next morning, I am at the airport waiting for my flight, although it isn't a flight to Boston. The first available flight flying into Logan wasn't until 4:00 and I couldn't handle staying in such close proximity to Jack for another whole day; I have a tendency to flee my issues ASAP, as one extended trip to Australia, once upon a time, well illustrates. So, I do what any self-respecting girl in my position would do…I book a flight to Florida. My mom is visiting Uncle Hor and Dolly and I would love to see Morty and Addy again. I figure they have room for one more. Besides, I don't feel like being home alone and brooding. I need to be around people who know all of my idiosyncrasies and still love me.

It turns out Sarasota was just what I needed. The weather was beautiful, the cocktails were plentiful and I had a glorious long weekend off to enjoy all of it. The unexpected blip in my schedule, caused by my abrupt departure from the Chase wedding, had freed up a few days for me and I took full advantage of losing myself in carefree, schedule-free days.

Of course, there was some wallowing involved. I cried myself to sleep most nights and started dripping tears into my gin and tonic on more than one occasion. But on those occasions (and there were a few), I had my family to count on.

Uncle Hor put his big arms around me in one moment by the pool when I was particularly a mess and absorbed the convulsions that my shaking body produced.

"There's no shame in loving someone, Maggie Mae," he said to me as I gulped for air, "there's no shame in loving someone."

Poor Dolly had to deal with me when she came into the restroom at Lola's. We had all been out to dinner and I had to excuse myself during the appetizer because I was overcome with a wave of emotion and I went to the ladies' room and camped out in a stall, trying to muffle my cries with a paper towel. When I came out, mascara running down my face, I didn't have to say a word. She threw her arms around me and rocked me gently for a minute. "I credit you with bringing me and Hor back together, I just wish I could do something to make it better for you now."

But there was nothing she could do. There was nothing anyone could do. Jack was marrying Samantha in two days and I was three years too late. I had had my chance and I blew it. I had to swallow my medicine like a big girl now. And I would, but I thought I deserved a few moments of weakness.

Even Fern, Boris, Stella, Ida, Eugene, Clarence and Alma tried to bolster my spirits (word travels fast around Clearwater…by the end of my first day there, everyone had heard the story). They played endless games of shuffleboard with me and even let me score on occasion. I think Ida also spiked my tea with vodka one afternoon in hopes that it would ease my mind of unpleasant thoughts, although all it managed to do was make me feel queasy. Chamomile and vodka is *not* a pleasing combination. Anyway, I appreciated the sentiment.

I think my mom took the whole thing almost as hard as me. She never said anything to me overtly about it, never chided me or said 'I told you so' or reached out and squeezed my hand. But when I reached for the breadbasket over dinner, or stood up to shake my towel out at the beach, I would catch my mother's eye and she would be looking at me with such love and hurt. I think it physically *hurt* my mom to see what I was going through. She didn't have the words to comfort me but her eyes said it all.

I think my mom felt guilty, like she had somehow, through cosmic circumstance, caused this to happen. My mom had told me, over a cup of tea in the kitchen, just a few weeks ago, that love was worth it after all. I think she wished now that she could bite back those words but I'm still glad she had said them. My mom had finally been able to open herself up to the possibility of love, and that's all I've ever wanted. I didn't want my mom to be alone…she's too fabulous a woman.

It was Addy who I spent the most time with while I was in Sarasota. We would walk the beach in the early morning, just like we did when I first came down here to toast her and Morty's wedding. There was something about Addy that I just gravitated towards. She was warm and inviting and kind and she also, at least for the duration of our walks on the beach, was able to let me get out of myself. Whether it was the sound of the surf or the warm white sand between my toes or Addy's calming voice and unwavering optimistic attitude, I always felt better after my walks with Addy. "I got a second chance at love, Maggie," Addy said to me as she linked her arm through mine, "and I know one day you will too."

Out of all the support my friends and family had offered me, these simple words, spoken by Addy, offered me the most because they offered me hope. I knew Addy hadn't had the easiest time for the majority of her first marriage, but she was so grateful for what she had now and she reminded me that life can pleasantly surprise you sometimes. Still. I didn't want to have to wait twenty-five years to find love and happiness. I wanted Jack now.

184

Chapter Twenty-Six

By the time I leave Sarasota I feel slightly better. The time off has done me good and being with my family helped get my mind off of Jack (contrary to all I've just told you about my vacation, there were moments when I was actually happy and tear-free). But now I have to return to the grim and dismal reality of my life back in Boston. My schedule is booked for the rest of the summer and I still have to locate an office space to move into. Actually, I am glad I'll be busy; it will force me to focus on other things besides Jack. Still, getting off the plane in Boston, I suddenly feel very lonely. My mom is staying in Florida for another week and going home to a big, empty house suddenly seems very unappealing to me.

The cab lets me off at the end of the driveway and I stand there a minute, dreading the walk up to a dark and empty house. I even contemplate calling Carrie to ask if she'd meet me here but it's late and Carrie is seven months pregnant—I figure I have reached both the epitome of selfishness and desperation if I call and wake a pregnant lady, asking if she could come be with me because I don't feel like being alone in my own house. I think of calling Kate, but then remember that she's at The Cape for a week. I heave a sigh and trudge up the front walk, pulling my suitcase behind me.

As I approach the steps to the front porch and my eyes adjust to the darkness, I can make out the faint outline of a figure sitting on the bench swing. Oddly enough, I'm not afraid. I mean you should be afraid if you approach your house late at night, knowing full well that no one is home and there seems to be a stranger sitting on your porch, but I'm not. The figure stands up and flips on the porch light and I literally gasp when I see who it is. It's Jack. My Jack. I walk up the steps and stand before him on the porch and the world seems to melt away.

A million questions race through my mind, but I just stand there for a minute, content to be both quiet and alone with Jack. He takes my hand and smiles and I know that I am home. Not just home, standing on the porch in front of my house, but *home.*

"I take it you didn't get married," I say, smiling through the tears that are now running down my face.

Jack smiles his slow smile and runs his fingers in circles on my hand. "I've never gotten over you," he says to me, "and I don't think I ever will."

I half-laugh, half-cry. "I never got over you, either," I say. "I just didn't know it until I saw you again."

"Well, this is my last offer, Maggie Mae," Jack says as he pulls me close. "I believe in second chances, but not thirds. Don't make a fool of me again."

"You're still the only one who calls me that besides Uncle Hor," I tell him.

"Well, let's keep it that way."

Jack leans in and I lean in and we meet each other half way. And as we stand there, making out on the porch, I realize that I believe in serendipity after all.

Chapter Twenty-Seven

"Are you nervous?" Jack asks me as we stand, facing each other and holding hands, waiting for the next event to ensue.

"Not at all," I say nonchalantly, and I give him a playful wink.

"Well, I'm just glad you made it this time," and he gives my hand a squeeze.

Morty raises his hands before us. "By the power vested in me by the state of Massachusetts, I now pronounce you Mr. and Mrs. Jack MacDougal. Sir, you may kiss your bride!"

And it's official. After three years of waiting and a second wedding, with the bride actually present, Jack and I are finally married.

It actually became official last Tuesday, when Jack and I went to Beaumont City Hall and had a justice of the peace marry us "officially." We didn't want to take any chances, and I think Jack wanted to make sure we were actually married before I walked down the aisle. But today is our wedding.

Morty had taken an online course and had become certified as a wedding officiate (whatever that means) as a wedding gift to us and although it sounds shady, it turns out it's legit, but we took a trip to city hall anyway…just in case. Anyway, it does mean a lot to me to have Morty officiate over our wedding.

Jack and I decided to do things differently this time. We are getting married on a different day (not to mention in a different year), in a different month, at a different place. The only thing that is the same this time around (except for the fact that I actually showed up) is my wedding dress. I love this dress. It surprised me that my mom had kept it this whole time—I hadn't even known that. I guess she is a romantic after all. And besides, Jack has never seen me in it so it is like it's brand new.

Jack kisses me again and a rupture of applause and jubilant shouts echo throughout the warm, September afternoon. We had decided on a small, outdoor wedding this time around and we couldn't have asked for a better day. The sun-splashed lawn glimmers in green and the ocean sparkles like diamonds in the distance. The North Shore had always been a favorite spot of ours and it means so much to have our most intimate circle of family and friends here to celebrate with us, along with a few new friends I've made along the way. I look at them now, thankful for what each one has taught me.

Mom and Uncle Hor and Dolly sit right up front, of course, with Addy. Uncle Hor is blubbering like a baby the whole time but it's quite endearing, actually, and my mother sits tall and proud, and even beaming a little bit, happy I think with the way things have turned out. Addy looks at me and gives a nod. I think she always knew how things would work out in the end.

Behind them sit Carrie and Kate and Ben and Bernie, along with Carrie's three-week old daughter, whom she named Maggie. It warms my heart just to look at them. Carrie and Kate have been my anchors in life since the seventh grade. We had shared a lot of adventures along the way, and I think they had worried that I had lost my way at one point, but I had managed to scrape my way out of the predicaments I had found myself in, and now the trip seemed complete. We would always be best friends, absolutely, but now it would be a different journey. We are all married now (I still have to pinch myself to believe I'm finally married) and life will center on our own families instead of each other. Carrie and Kate don't have to worry about me anymore. Their work is done. I give them a wink when I catch their eye and they hold up their pinkies to me—our secret code since seventh grade—all for one. The gesture almost makes me cry.

I look out beyond and see all the familiar faces—the friends I have made just in the past year—and I can't believe how much my circle has grown. Sam and Ella, expecting their first child, wave and smile and Earl and Etta Calhoun are laughing their deep, jolly laugh, happy to have an occasion to celebrate. The whole Calhoun clan is here. Beau and Carleen and Beau Jr., Brady and Ellen and Brady Jr., and Cooper and Jo-Ann, Irma and Carl and Huey and Doris. And I must say, they are all on their best behavior (even Huey and Doris).

I spot Cruise Cartwright and Sal and Hal in the crowd. Sal and Hal give me a courteous nod and Cruise Cartwright tries to nonchalantly wipe the tears from his cheek with a handkerchief. I laugh out loud at this. I can't believe now that there was once a time when I had been afraid of this man.

I hear a familiar laugh, a laugh that sounds like a song, and I see Daisy and Randy. I mouth 'thank you' to Daisy and she smiles and nods. She knows what I mean. Daisy had been the one that truly taught me that love might not be perfect, but it's still love. She had taught me the selflessness of it, and I think because of that, I was able to find my way back to Jack.

Bruce Walker and Tony are also here. Bruce winks at me and I pull up my wedding dress, ever so slightly and stick my leg out to show him what I am wearing. Gracing my feet are the white cowboy boots he had given me, complete with spurs. Bruce laughs and I know that he's impressed. I would always be welcome on the Walker Homestead, which is a good thing because that's where me and Jack are going on our honeymoon.

And way in the back, making a ruckus as usual and stealing sips from little nip bottles in their purses are Fern and Boris and Stella and Ida and Eugene and Clarence and Alma. I give them a wave and they gave me an enthusiastic "oompah!" What can I say; it's not a party unless Fern, Boris, Stella, Ida, Eugene, Clarence and Alma are there.

I take a moment, like I do at all the weddings I toast, to soak it all in. I cannot believe how much not only my life changed in the past year, but how much everyone's here had. Usually I was the one in the back, tucked to the side, until I gave my toast that is, and here I am today, at my own wedding, with all of my former clients now celebrating me getting married. And I can't help but marvel at the realization that it is these very people, the people whose weddings I had toasted in the past year, who helped me to find love after all. The world does work in strange and mysterious ways sometimes.

Jack takes my hand and we walk down the path, our friends and guests showering us with white confetti as we pass by.

"So, you ready to party?" Jack asks me.

I smile. "That's what I've been waiting for."

Before we enter the tent, I pause for a second and look up at the sky. I know my dad is looking down on me and smiling. "Well, Daddy," I say softly, "I guess I am a romantic after all," and I can almost hear his laugh in the breeze.

We greet our friends as they file in and then take our own seats. It's not long before they all start banging their flatware on the table and chanting,

"Toast, toast!" Jack looks at me and raises his eyebrows. I hadn't really thought about who would give a toast at my own wedding and I hadn't asked anyone to…it's actually an odd predicament for me to be in, but as Jack says as he urges me out of my seat to take the mike, "there is only one wedding toaster."

I get up and take the mic. I don't have anything prepared, I mean, what are you supposed to say at your own wedding? But I'm not fazed. I do what I know how to do best…I speak the words that come to me. Somehow, I know just what to say.

Thank you all, so much for coming. It really means a lot to Jack and me to have all of our friends and family gathered in one place, to celebrate our wedding. I guess the second times a charm for us.

This year has been quite a journey for me, as it's been for most of you as well. A lot of love has gone around this year, a lot of weddings have taken place, and it dawned on me, as I stood at the altar, that's what we all have in common here today…weddings. Or, even more than that, love.

Although some people here today may argue that it was I, in some way or another, that helped you all to celebrate your love, it's really all of you that have helped me to find love, and to find my way to this moment and this day. And for that, I thank all of you. I can't thank you enough. You have all taught me an important lesson while I had the privilege of toasting your weddings and celebrating your own love stories…all of which are unique but all equally wonderful and inspiring.

Morty and Addy—you taught me that you or are never to old, or young, to find love. You showed me that love is fun and light-hearted, and meant to be enjoyed, but you also showed me that it can come with its share of heartaches but together, you are more likely to overcome the difficult times than you are alone.

Sam and Ella—you taught me that love is worth fighting for, no matter what other people say. You showed me that love is full of passion and understanding.

Daisy and Randy—you taught me that love is just love. It's not always perfect, but the perfection comes in accepting your partner's imperfections, accepting them at face value and not insisting that they change. You taught me that acceptance and compromise are the biggest ingredients in a successful marriage.

Uncle Hor and Dolly—You taught me about the patience of love. You showed me that love grows and love heals and you gave me the hope to believe in second chances.

And Mom—you taught me what a precious gift love is. I know Dad was taken away from you too quick and too early, but your love for him lives on when you tell me stories about him or you hang a painting he created or you bring flowers to the cemetery. You have shown me the eternal power of love.

And Jack—you have taught me the power of forgiveness, and for that I will always be grateful.

By this time, I am sobbing. I am so just overcome with emotion and gratitude and humility. Love is just such a gift, and I am so grateful that I have found it, or, rather, that it has found me.

My mother stands up then and raises her glass. "To Maggie and Jack. May your lives together be happy, healthy and full of love, today and every day." She pauses for a moment and she says, choking back a few tears, "Daddy would be proud."

The tent erupts in applause and laughter and tears and smiles (with a few "yee-haws" and "oompahs!" thrown in for good measure). I look around at the scene in front of me, a smile on my face and tears running down my cheeks. I must say it's the best wedding I have attended in a long time…because it's mine.

Epilogue

Boston may be an artist's city but San Francisco is definitely a romantic's city. The lights dance off the bay at night and tropical flowers bloom in February. It's a good thing I like it so much too because it's my home now. Jack had given me a second chance…the least I could do was let him pick the city we would live in. We live in the condo he almost sold but didn't and life could not be any sweeter.

I was able to find a small office space to lease in Union Square and I had a web site professionally created. Business is booming but I only do one wedding a month now. I like being home. And I've finally broken into the international market. Jack travels with me when he can; we just got back from Paris where I toasted the wedding of the president's niece. I guess you could say Jack and I get multiple honeymoons in romantic places now.

I also write a weekly column for the *San Francisco Globe* now, although it's not the obituaries and I don't dispense any advice on pets. It's more of a love column, actually, which is sort of funny because after the mess my romantic life had been in for years, I should be the last one giving advice on matters of the heart. But on the other hand, things had turned out rather swimmingly for me after all so I guess I do have a profound and insightful thought or two on the subject. At any rate, it's pretty popular with readers, which makes the editors very happy.

Jack's restoration business is also booming. A cable station just offered him a series in which they film him restoring old houses. Only the pilot has aired so far but it has gotten rave reviews. I'm not surprised…I knew Jack was always good with his hands.

Uncle Hor and Dolly are still having a ball with Morty and Addy and company. In fact, they all just went skydiving and evidently Fern and Boris mooned everyone on the way down to the ground. Uncle Hor offered to send me the pictures but I politely declined.

Sam and Ella asked me and Jack to be godparents to their baby. The baby is still in utero but we will go down for the christening in the spring. I've already blocked the week out on my schedule and despite the uncomfortable accommodations, I'm actually looking forward to going back to Shady Creek. No one knows quite how to throw a party like the Calhouns (except for maybe the Sarasota gang).

Daisy and Randy are doing great. Daisy hasn't even gone on any three-day horseback hiatuses since they've been married. I guess marriage agrees with Daisy more than she thought it would. They're still dancing up a storm at The Cowboy Bar and producers from *Dancing with the Stars* have even approached Randy about doing some choreography work for the show. Evidently, they really liked his two-step.

I miss Carrie and Kate tons, but we have our weekly three-way conference call. Carrie loves being a mom and loves not having to work. She and Ben just bought a house in the 'burbs and she is currently shopping for a mini-van. And Kate just shared the news with us last week that she is expecting! It was unplanned and I think Kate's freaking out a little bit but like I told her, sometimes the best things in life are unplanned.

And my mom...my mom is doing great. Although the cyber-dating thing didn't work out too well for her, she got along rather well with Tony at our wedding (remember Tony; the Walker's driver?). Anyway, they've been having a long-distance relationship since then. They switch off flying out to see each other once a month and my mom hasn't been this happy, I think, since my dad was around. I can hear it in her voice. She has her old laugh back. As Tony puts it, he's been married to the land long enough and just wants a good woman by his side now. My mom retires at the end of the year so the timing couldn't be better. We'll have to see what happens with this one...there may be another McDonald wedding to toast in the future after all.

That's it for now. Everything else is a work in progress. One thing I've learned is that you take each day as it comes, and when you least expect it, life usually surprises you. And when things don't work out the way you planned, hold on tight, have a glass of wine (preferably pinot—chilled) and enjoy the ride. You just don't know what's waiting for you around the corner. Until then…this is Maggie MacDougal, signing off and going home to my hubby.

Out.

CPSIA information can be obtained
at www.ICGtesting.com
Printed in the USA
BVHW040747060821
PP12486000001B/1